Tales of Suicide
A Selection from Luigi Pirandello's
Short Stories for a Year

Translated from the Italian
and with an Introduction
by Giovanni R. Bussino

Dante University Press, Boston

©Copyright 1988
by Dante University of America Press
ISBN 0-937832-31-6

Library of Congress Cataloging in Publication Data

Pirandello, Luigi, 1867-1936.
   Tales of suicide
   Translation of: Novelle per un anno. I. Title. PQ4835.I7A24
1988   853'.912 87-24549 ISBN 0-937832-31-6 (pbk.)

With permission from the *Amministrazione Pirandello*

Dante University of America Press
PO Box 81258 Wellesley MA 02482
www.danteuniversity.org

To my dear sisters,

Irma and Lucy

In memory
of
Louise Raia Palci
(The Foundation)

CONTENTS

Introduction
Sun and Shade
Sunrise
The Black Shawl
This Makes Two!
Into the Sketch
In Silence
The Trip
The Stuffed Bird
The Lonely Man
The Trap
The Imbecile
The Fish Trap
By Himself
The Long Dress
Candelora
While the Heart Suffered
Aunt Michelina
Nothing
An Idea
A Challenge
Chronology
About the Author and the Translator

... the motivating impulse of Pirandello's work and perhaps the key to the understanding of it, is to be found in his compassion.
—**Felicity Firth** (University of Manchester)

INTRODUCTION

Suicide, the act of killing oneself voluntarily and intentionally, is clearly one of the most important themes developed by Pirandello during his long literary career. Although he never focused on self-destruction as an end in itself, he made ample use of it to dramatize his tragic view of the human condition. Indeed, this theme recurs with astonishing frequency in his short stories, plays and novels. It even appears sporadically in his poetry.

Considering for a moment only Pirandello's dramatic works, upon which his feme has mostly rested, it is interesting to note that the first play published by the author, *The Epilogue {1898)* [later entitled *The Vise]*, ends in suicide, and that several of his better-known pieces, including *As You Desire Me, To Clothe the Naked* and *The Doctor's Duty,* are variously inspired by this same theme. Moreover, his greatest play, *Six Characters in Search of an Author,* also contains a scene of self-murder, that of the Boy.

Surprisingly, the reasons that sparked Pirandello's keen interest in suicide have never been explored and hence they merit examination. First, we should bear in mind that in the late nineteenth and early twentieth century there was great social, political and economic turmoil throughout Western Europe. As European society approached the new age, hopeful that its antiquated structures would give way to evolutionary progress, signs of instability appeared, precipitating what can only be described as a serious crisis. Individuals began to see themselves trapped in a specific time and reality whose inequitable conventions fractured the human personality and strained relations between men. In these troubled times self-destruction was rampant, and the problem, which was to reach a temporary peak only at the beginning of the third decade, did not escape the attention of responsible intellectuals. It is hardly coincidental that in 1897 the famed sociologist Emile Durkheim published his classic treatise, *Le Suicide,* or that in 1910 Sigmund Freud and other psychologists met in Vienna to discuss this alarming situation, which seems to have particularly regarded the young. This worrisome phenomenon naturally caught the eye of creative writers, as the Italian suicidologist, Enrico Altavilla *(Psicologia del suicidio,* Napoli, 1910), one of Pirandello's contemporaries, noted (not without some exaggeration):

> *given the frightening increase in voluntary deaths, art reflects the effects of this influence, and to such an extent that we can say that out of one*

hundred works of art that daily see the light, at least seventy-five portray suicide.

Since Pirandello was especially attentive to the most serious problems of his day, it stands to reason that he too would have been inspired to depict the pressing reality of voluntary death in many of his works.

The second cause for Pirandello's interest in suicide is the fact that the prospect of self-destruction springs naturally from his somber outlook on life, a vision rooted in his own grim, eclectic philosophy. In the virtually godless world he imagined, where truth is relative, reality an ever-changing nightmare and man the prey of either hypocritical society, whimsical fate or his own self-deceptions, suicide understandably looms as a tempting outlet. Let me point out, however, that although suicide is the ultimate, irrevocable escape sought by many of the author's characters, it is by no means the only one. Several of them yearn for a similar liberation in madness, a condition which they ape (as in the play *Henry IV);* others seek relief in bizarre flights of fantasy (as in the tale *Geography as a Way Out);* and still others attempt to lose themselves in a mystical union with nature or the totality of Being (as in the novel *One, No One and a Hundred Thousand).*

For the third source of this theme we should consider the fact that from early childhood Pirandello was a diligent, indefatigable reader and undoubtedly was conversant with the varied treatment of suicide in the works of many of the world's greatest writers, from the Greek and Roman stoics, to Shakespeare, Dostoevsky, Maupassant, Flaubert and others. Of course he was particularly familiar with the theme as it appears in Italian literature, where the subject has had a long and rich history. For our purposes here suffice it to recall that Dante dedicated an entire canto of his *Inferno* to suicide (Canto XIII), Ariosto often resorted to the theme in his *Orlando Furioso,* Leopardi frequently discussed the problem in his *Zibaldone* and Capuana, the author's friend and mentor, not only wrote *Un suicidio, &* short story which deals philosophically with the issue, but also other tales and even a novel similarly inspired. Such literary influences must have captured the author's imagination, prompting him to express his own unique conceptions of the theme.

Incidentally, among the many volumes which still survive in Pirandello's personal library (presently part of the Centro di Studi Pirandelliani, in Rome), a number of which being novels or collections of plays and short stories that contain portrayals of self-imposed death (e.g. Goethe's *Werther,* Boccaccio's *Decameron* and Shakespeare's *Complete Works),* we also find a heavily underlined treatise on the suicide problem of that time: Geremia Bonomelli's *Il suicidio* (Roma, 1910). This work was written by a prelate, and so Pirandello, an unbeliever, no doubt rejected some of the ideas it contains, but the numerous sentences presumably underlined or otherwise highlighted in the author's own hand suggest much more than just a casual interest in the subject.

Italian opera of the nineteen century, much of which was inspired by the theme of suicide, may also have played some role in directing the author's attention to the subject and, together with its literary counterparts, may even account for the melodramatic overtones in several of his works. We know, in feet, from a letter he wrote to his sister Rosalina, dated October 31, 1886, that he was quite fond of Ponchielli's *La Gioconda,* a musical masterpiece which contains the famous "Suicidio!" aria. Significantly, the first few words of this solo composition appear in Pirandello's short story *Nothing.* We also know that elsewhere in his writings the author shows a certain familiarity with Verdi's *// Trovatore,* Puccini's *La Tosca* and other such operas that end in suicide.

Lastly, since it is universally recognized that Pirandello's work is highly autobiographical, it may be assumed that the author's various experiences with self-imposed death had much to do with his frequent and exceptional concentration on the subject. The pertinent biographical data that I shall now review in some detail were gleaned primarily from Federico Vittore Nardelli's *Vita segreta di Pirandello* (Roma, 1962) as well as from various collections of the author's personal letters.

Pirandello's first known encounter with suicide occurred during his impressionable early years. Nardelli recounts that one day young Pirandello sneaked into an old tower in Agrigento that served as a morgue, to view the body of an unknown, forty-year old Frenchman who reportedly had died by his own hand. As the curious and frightened youngster looked at the cadaver, he also perceived in the darkness the entwined shapes of a man and a woman who, taking advantage of the privacy afforded by the secluded chamber, were making love. According to the critic Leonardo Sciascia, this traumatic experience later determined Pirandello's artistic portrayal of love—love constantly defiled by the odor of death. To this I should add that, somehow, it probably also triggered the author's lifelong obsession with the idea of suicide itself.

We learn of another of Pirandello's experiences with voluntary death from a letter he wrote to his parents on March 1,1886. In this missive he relates that his dear friend Enrico Palermi, "blinded by violent passion, attempted suicide." He also states that he assisted Palermi at his bedside and reports on his frightful condition: "His breathing is labored, almost choking. It is feared that he has punctured his left lung. He has a fractured rib but, fortunately, he has not injured his heart."

Despite the horror that this attempted suicide inspired in Pirandello, the author toyed with the idea of following his schoolmate's example the following year. It is reported that, while still a high school student,

Pirandello seemed on the verge of taking his own life when the engagement proposed to his cousin Linuccia was opposed by her parents, who argued that the young man did not have the means by which to support a wife. It is also revealed, incidentally, that another suitor, whose amorous overtures were rebuffed by Linuccia at that time, actually did attempt to kill himself.

Linuccia's parents finally consented to the engagement when Pirandello agreed to abandon his studies to work in his father's sulphur mine. But his father soon realized that his son had little aptitude for the mining business. Consequently, in an effort to gain a four-year postponement of a marriage that he too opposed, Pirandello senior sent his son back to Palermo to continue his studies. There, the troubled youth, greatly disenchanted with life yet somehow clinging to it, confided (in the above-cited letter to Rosalina):

> *I write and study to forget myself— in order to save myself from despair... But don't think that my lack of illusions and hope will ruin me. A positive and scientific concept of life makes me live like all the other worms. At certain moments of abandon I speak like a fool and feel an impetuous desire not to live, but then it all ends. There forms in my brain a black, horrible, bloodcurdling void, like the mysterious bottom of the sea populated with monstrous thoughts that flash as they pass by menacingly.*

Despite this denial, the biographer Nardelli still believes that young Pirandello, tormented by the thought of being so close to happiness and yet so far from it, would have committed suicide even during this final year in Palermo had his father not changed his decision by sending the boy to Rome to continue his education, thereby delivering him from his awkward relationship with his cousin.

But even in Rome, Pirandello, obviously still disillusioned, wrote another letter to Rosalina, dated March 9, 1888, in which he confessed that that very evening he had, for a moment, considered throwing himself off the Ponte di Ripetta, a bridge spanning the Tiber. And in still another letter to her, written approximately one year later, Pirandello, referring specifically to his deteriorating relationship with Linuccia, stated:

> *If I don't kill myself, it's for the sake of all of you, but for pity sake don't force me to carry on as if I were alive. I've got death in my heart. My last remaining illusion has collapsed—love...*

Soon thereafter Pirandello went to Bonn to complete his doctoral studies. He was a student in that ancient city for almost two years, and this was probably the happiest time in his life because he not only found a stimulating intellectual environment but also his first carefree love in the person of the beautiful and charming Jenny Schulz-Lander. Nevertheless, it is significant that the first words he penned in one of his notebooks, the so-called Taccuino di Bonn—words inspired by the state of mind he was in upon his arrival from Italy—were on the subject of death: "Death! No longer to be aware of anything. To leave this dream. And yet dying is frightful." At this point we should note that Pirandello's otherwise studious and jovial life in Bonn was punctuated on at least one occasion by a frightful reminder of suicide. It is reported that Pirandello learned from Jenny that her stepfather had killed himself some years before. This event, the unusual details of which apparently made a great impression on the young author, were later immortalized in two of his short narratives, Christmas on the Rhine and Sunrise.

Upon returning to Italy, Pirandello settled in Rome and married Antonietta Portulano, the daughter of his father's business partner. But a few years later, in 1903, Pirandello, now a married man with three children, again contemplated suicide, having found himself in extreme financial straits due to a cave-in at his father's mine, a calamity which represented not only the collapse of his parents' fortune, upon which he depended for his own financial security, but also the loss of his wife's dowry. The shock of this disaster unbalanced his wife and she was never to recover from her resulting paranoid schizophrenia.

Briefly, Pirandello believed that if he were to take his own life, that is, if he were to commit an altruistic suicide, his family's predicament would quickly be resolved since his wife's father would then have been obliged to provide for Antonietta and the children. But after some uncertainty Pirandello rejected this awesome alternative. To weather the setback, he decided instead to request payment for the works he had already sent to publishers and for those he intended at that time to write. He also began to offer private lessons in German and to do some translations. Moreover, having become a professor at the Teachers' Training College in Rome, he volunteered to be sent to the provinces in the summer as an exam commissioner, an assignment which brought additional income.

It appears that Pirandello never again contemplated suicide seriously and from this point on persistently sought refuge from his afflictions in creative writing, an activity he pursued until his natural death, which occurred in 1936 when he was at an advanced age.

In all the available biographical material there are only three further mentions of suicide in connection with Pirandello after 1903. The first is the fact that the author was again visited by the specter of self-destruction in 1918 when his beloved daughter Lietta, finding herself unjustly accused by her demented mother of having an incestuous relationship with her father, attempted to end her life by means of an antique pistol kept in their home. After the weapon misfired—the bullet dislodged in the tip of the rusty barrel—the young girl wandered about Rome in search of the Tiber, determined to hurl herself from one of its bridges. The would-be suicide fortunately got lost in the maze of streets and, after making her way out of Villa Borghese, ended up at one of the ancient gates of the city (either Porta Pinciana or Porta Pia), where she was recognized by an acquaintance who attended to her grief. Afterwards the distraught girl was sent to a local boarding school for a few months and then to Florence to live with an aunt so that she might recover from her trauma at a safe distance from her mother.

The second is a vague allusion to self-annihilation in a letter he wrote to his daughter, dated March 7,1922. Here he confesses: "The only thing that still makes me endure this torturous life is the thought of your welfare, my dear children."

The final incident is admittedly marginal. Reportedly, the brother of Pirandello's close friend and colleague, Pier Maria Rosso di San Secondo, committed suicide, an event which moved the author to pity, as can be deduced from a letter to his friend Alberto Albertini, dated February 28, 1917.

To date there exists no comprehensive or systematic study of voluntary death in Pirandello, but the few critics who have touched upon the theme (for the most part on its appearance in the author's short stories) provide us with several useful or stimulating ideas.

In his seminal monograph, *Luigi Pirandello* (Firenze, 1948), Arminio Janner, one of the first critics to address the subject, contends that Pirandello's works should be viewed as efforts on the part of the author to provide "irrefutable documentation" for his pessimism, which, this critic further contends, has poetic rather than philosophic validity. Among the works Janner cites to illustrate his thesis are several tales of self-imposed death, *In Silence, The Long Dress* and *Into the Sketch,* stories which he shows support Pirandello's conviction that "life is profoundly and inextirpably unjust." And among the short stories that exemplify Pirandello's idea that "in life people are unjust to one another," Janner discusses *This Makes Two!* He likewise analyzes *The Trip, Nothing, Candelora, Aunt Michelina* and similar tales of suicide or death that underscore the somber notion "that love is a fleeting illusion."

Franz Rauhut *(Der junge Pirandello* [Munchen, 1964]) is another major critic who comments on suicide in Pirandello's oeuvre. According to him, this recurrent theme has a biographical origin. Rauhut maintains that it is rooted in the existentialist love/hate attitude toward life, as expressed in the author's early poetry and personal letters.

Other minor but noteworthy observations are made by Zina Tillona ("La morte nelle novelle di Pirandello," *Forum Italicum,* 1967), who for the most part echoes ideas previously expressed by Janner. She points out that in Pirandello's depiction of suicide "death becomes a defensive weapon, a tragic challenge to fete." She also notes that "suicide is the ultimate recourse of the defeated, the only escape possible from a life that has become so terrible as to be more frightening than death; at once a confession of defeat and a violent reaction, the triumph of the individual." This critic further observes that "the Pirandellian woman, in suicide, remains faithful to her instinctive and affective nature," and that "the suicide of women is almost always connected with love." She also correctly states that "sometimes suicide, and especially that of the male, assumes an ideological nature in that the character arrives at suicide at the conclusion of clear reasoning."

The contribution of a more recent scholar, Franco Zangrilli *(L'arte novellistica di Pirandello* [Ravenna, 1983]), is worth mentioning at this point. Zangrilli, in his analyses of select Pirandellian tales, introduces the idea that an important motive for suicide can be found in the characters' resolve to be faithful to their innermost moral reality.

It is interesting to note that most of the critics who have dealt with the subject of suicide in Pirandello have variously sought to specify the reasons why the author's characters commit or attempt the tragic act. Their observations, even when combined to avoid repetition, form a long list which includes: to escape from an impossible situation (financial ruin etc.), to avoid disgrace, to escape mortal illness or encroaching old age, to avoid being victimized by a rigid social order, to protest against society's unjust oppression, to challenge fete or death in the hope of dominating it, to end the torture of unrequited love, to resolve the problem of isolation and, as I have just mentioned, to affirm their innermost moral reality.

What should further be observed, however, is that quite often the motivation for suicide in Pirandello, as in life, is quite complex. It frequently embraces several reasons simultaneously, its nature being both psychological and social. Moreover, in certain Pirandellian works the primary motive for suicide can be ascribed to a general *taedium vitae,* the inevitable result of a relentless series of negative experiences.

It should also be noted that, to date, critics have not sufficiently emphasized the great richness and diversity of this Pirandellian theme which, when viewed as a whole, constitutes a veritable mosaic of suicidal phenomena, particularly those prevalent at the turn of the century. Not only does the author examine various general and specific reasons for suicide but he also delves into the complex psychology of its victims, while at the same time depicting the attitudes of the society that surrounds them. He also probes the multiple means by which individuals seek to end their sad lives, the most common being firearms, blades, asphyxiation, hanging, jumping from heights, drowning and poison. He also varies the settings of the suicidal act to reflect actual reality. Sometimes he depicts it as occurring indoors; other times he represents it as taking place outside, in public places, and often enough in an idyllic environment. He portrays suicide victims in all age groups without distinction: adolescents, the middle-aged and the old. Both males and females attempt suicide in Pirandello and, despite the feet that there is no shortage of aborted attempts, these attempts are, on the whole, successful. Sometimes, too, the act is shown to be premeditated, with the victim leaving a note. At other times it is described as having been done on impulse, that is, to have been subconsciously motivated. Sometimes suicide occurs in the author's work as a result of intrapsychic debate and, therefore, its nature is more psychological. At other times it takes place as a result of unfulfilled needs and wishes pertaining to some other person or persons that surround the tragic victim, and hence it has greater sociological implications. In certain cases Pirandello portrays the suicidal character as being exceedingly resigned to his fete and even stoical, but more often than not he portrays him as still being deeply attached to life. In such cases the victim is described as seething with emotion, his hands trembling, his hair standing on end, as he confronts the frightful void.

However, besides these realistic portrayals of suicide which reflect in some measure the author's veristic experience, there is an added element that is unmistakably Pirandellian: the typical soul-torture of the characters, which consists of obsessive philosophizing about life and death, and of relentless self-analysis. In this regard, the frenzied behavior of Marta, the suicidal protagonist of the novel, *The Outcast*^ readily comes to mind. I should emphasize here that despite such frequent philosophizing, we very seldom find reflections on the suicide's destiny after the fatal act, since the author's agnosticism generally precluded religious considerations.

It must be stressed that though the majority of Pirandello's works dealing with suicide are essentially mournful, as would be expected given the very nature of the theme and the author's grim Weltanschauung, a "comical" vein runs through most of them, which helps transcend their intrinsic horror. I am alluding to the author's characteristic *umorismo,* a bittersweet humor that invites the reader or spectator both to smile knowingly at the errors and foibles of the characters and at the ironic turns of fate that affect their tortured lives, and a moment later, to feel compassion or sympathetic indulgence toward them, as the author himself does (though never overtly). In this dual esthetic technique lies much of the sensitivity, the humanity, the remarkable originality of Pirandello's art.

It should also be noted that of all the authors who have focused on the theme of suicide, both ancient and modern, Pirandello was one of the most prolific and imaginative. Moreover, in contrast to the majority of such writers, Pirandello neither morally condemns nor glorifies self-destruction but, at the same time, does not treat it with detachment or cool indifference. As I have already suggested, the benevolence and pity that the author feels toward his hapless characters subtly pervades his artistic treatment of the subject.

In conclusion, whatever the reasons were that inspired the Sicilian author to dwell on suicide, be they sociological, philosophical, cultural or personal (or a combination of any or all of the above), he undeniably brought the theme to great literary heights, giving it renewed vitality and paving the way for subsequent writers to continue a modern discourse on the subject and to explore it in novel artistic ways. I am referring here particularly to certain existentialist authors, notably Alberto Moravia among the Italians and Albert Camus among the French, all of whom, like Pirandello, focus on the absurdity of life but who more explicitly reject self-murder in their efforts to give life its value and its dignity.

***

The present volume brings together a gripping selection of Pirandello's many tales inspired by suicide. Given the fact that the author wrote over 244 *novelle*—many of which, as noted, deal with the theme in question—the twenty tales presented here constitute an abundant, though far from exhaustive, collection of such works. Other Pirandellian tales inspired by this problem include *The Watch, He Chants the Epistle, The Doctor's Duty, Puberty* and *The Day Dawns*.

Lest the reader be mislead by the title of the present work, let me say in advance that not all the tales in this collection culminate in the protagonist's voluntary death, although this is the general case. For instance, several of them conclude with the protagonist merely attempting or postponing the act, and in two of the pieces there is not only an aborted suicide attempt but what can actually be termed a happy ending.

Another clarification is in order. Since the tales selected were written over a long span in the author's life (from 1896 to 1935) and, obviously, at different moments of inspiration, the reader will notice structural and stylistic variations. Some of the works are rather long (e.g. *The Black Shawl)*, some very short (e.g. *The Challenge)*. The mood also varies considerably from one of grim tragedy to broad humor, from deep pessimism to the restorative irony of sophisticated art. It is my hope that the chronological arrangement will reveal the progressive development in the author's creative vision, from the naturalistic descriptions of the earlier stories, to the increasingly "metaphysical" or surrealistic tenor of the later works.

As for the translation itself, I have sought to render as faithfully as possible the author's characteristic ideas, language and style into standard American English equivalents. At the same time I have been careful to maintain the distinctive yet un-definable flavor of the original Italian texts. To this end, for example, I have employed quotation marks even for unspoken discourse (that is, for vivid imaginary dialogue) and I have conserved the author's own paragraph divisions. For the same reason I have also reproduced certain distinguishing features that are meant to reflect colloquial Italian speech, such as the author's "fractured" syntax and his frequent use of ellipsis and exclamation points.

G. R. Bussino
Burbank, California
January, 1988

Sun and Shade

Amid the branches of the trees that formed a sort of delicate green portico over the very long avenue encircling the walls of the old city, the moon would suddenly and unexpectedly appear. It seemed to be telling a very tall man who at this unusual hour was venturing out alone in the perilous darkness,

"Yes, but I see you."

As if he had really been discovered, the man stopped and, slapping his large hands on his chest, exclaimed,

"Me! Right! Me, Ciunna!"

Then all the leaves, endlessly rustling above his head, seemed to be whispering his name confidentially to one another: *"Ciunna... Ciunna."* It was as if, after knowing him for so many years, they knew why it was that he was walking in such great solitude along that creepy avenue at this hour. And they kept on whispering mysteriously about him and about what he had done... ssss... Ciunna! Ciunna!

He then turned to peer into the darkness of the long avenue, broken here and there by so many ghostly moonbeams, wondering if anyone... sssx .. He looked around and, ordering himself and the leaves to be silent... ssss... he continued to walk, his hands clasped behind his back.

Very quietly... two thousand seven hundred lire. He had stolen two thousand seven hundred lire from the tobacco storehouse. He was therefore guilty... ssss... of embezzlement.

Tomorrow the inspector would arrive and say,

"Ciunna, two thousand seven hundred lire are missing."

"Yes, indeed. I took them, Signor Inspector."

"You took them? How could you!..."

"With two fingers, Signor Inspector."

"Oh, is that so! Good for you, Ciunna! You took them like you would a pinch of snuff, huh? Well, on the one hand, my congratulations to you; but, on the other, if you don't mind, please come along to jail."

"Oh no, Signor Gavaliere, I beg your pardon. The fact is that I do mind, and so much so that if you would allow me—look, tomorrow I, Ciunna, will take a carriage and go down to the marina. This fellow will throw himself into the sea, with the two 1860 medals on his chest, Signor Inspector, and a fine ten kilogram weight fastened to his neck like a scapular. Death is an ugly thing. It gets you nowhere, but after sixty-two years of faultless living, Ciunna will not go to jail."

For two weeks how he had had these odd dialogued soliloquies, which were accompanied by very lively gestures. And, like that moon amid the branches, all of his friends and acquaintances who made fun of his strange and comical way of acting and speaking would briefly appear in these soliloquies.

"For you, Niccolino!" continued Ciunna, mentally addressing his son. "For you I have stolen! But don't think I have any regrets. Four children, good Lord, four children out in the street. And your wife, Niccolino, what does she do? Nothing. She laughs and gets pregnant again. Four plus one equals five. That blessed woman! Go ahead, my son, proliferate, keep on proliferating. Populate the town with little Ciunnas! Since poverty allows you no other satisfaction, propagate, my dear son! Trie fish that'll eat your papa tomorrow will then be obliged to feed you and your numerous offspring. Fishing boats of the marina, bring in a load of fish every day for my little grandchildren!"

This thought, that the fish would have that particular obligation, came to mind now. Up until a few days ago, he had exhorted himself like this:

"Poison! Poison! It's the best kind of death! A little pill and that'll be the end of it!"

And through an attendant at the Chemical Institute he had gotten a few small arsenic crystals. With these in his pocket, he had in fact gone to confession.

"It's all right to die as long as you're in a state of grace."

"But not with poison," he now added. "Too many convulsions. Man is a coward. He calls out for help. What if they save me? No, no, it's better there in the sea. The medals on my chest, the little weight around my neck and then—splash! But I've got a big belly. Gentlemen, a floating Garibaldian! A new species of whale! Come on, tell me, Ciunna, what's in the sea? Little fish, Ciunna, and they're hungry, just like your little grandchildren on land, just like the little birds in the sky."

He would arrange to have a carriage for the next day. At seven o'clock, in the coolness of the morning, he would be on his way. An hour more or less to go down to the marina and, at eight thirty—good-by, Ciunna!

Meanwhile, as he proceeded down the avenue, he composed in his mind the letter he would leave. To whom should he address it? To his wife, poor old lady, or to his son, or to some firiend? No, he would have nothing to do with his friends! Which of them had helped him? To tell the truth, he had not asked anyone for help, but that was because he knew in advance that no one would have taken pity on him. Here was the proof. For two weeks now, everyone in town had seen him going around like a chicken without a head. Yet not a single soul had stopped to ask him, "Ciunna, what's the matter?"

II

The next morning, awakened by the maid at exactly seven o'clock, he was surprised to find that he had slept soundly the entire night.

"Is the carriage here yet?"

"Yes, sir, it's downstairs, waiting for you."

"I'm ready! Hey! Rosa! My shoes! Wait, I'll open the door."

As he climbed out of bed to get his shoes, he was again surprised to see that, the night before, he had left his shoes outside the door for the maid to polish. As if it were important for him to go off to the other world with polished shoes.

He was surprised for the third time in front of the wardrobe where he had gone to get the suit he usually wore when he took a short trip, in order to save the other, his "town suit," which was a little newer or not so old.

"For whom am I saving it now?"

In brief, it was as if in the bottom of his heart he still didn't quite believe that in a short while he would kill himself. The sleep... The shoes... The suit...

Lo and behold! Now he was washing his face, and now he was stepping in front of the mirror, as usual, to knot his tie carefully.

"What? Am I just playing around?"

No, there's the letter. Where had he put it? Here in the drawer of his night stand. Here it is!

He read the inscription: "For Niccolino."

"Where shall I put it?"

He thought of putting it on the pillow of his bed, right on the spot where he had rested his head for the last time.

"Here they can find it more easily."

He knew that his wife and the maid never came in to make up the room before noon.

"By noon it'll be more than three hours..."

He didn't finish his sentence but looked around as if to say good-by to the things he was leaving forever. At the head of the bed he spotted the old ivory crucifix, yellowed with age. He took off his hat and bent his knees to kneel.

But, actually, he didn't even feel fully awake yet.

The blissful torpor of sleep was still in his nostrils and eyes.

"My God... my God," he finally said, suddenly dismayed.

And he squeezed his forehead strongly in his hand.

Then he thought about the carriage waiting downstairs and he darted out.

"Good-by, Rosa. Tell them I'll be back before nightfall."

As the carriage rattled along and crossed the town (that fool of a driver had put bells on the horses as if for a country festival), Ciunna felt, in that fresh morning air, that his comic vein, which came so natural to him, had suddenly been reawakened, and he imagined that the musicians in the municipal band, with the plumes of their small helmets fluttering in the wind, were running after him, shouting and signaling with their arms for him to stop or go slower because they wanted to play him a funeral march; and that, since they were running behind him at breakneck speed, they were unable to do so.

"Thanks a lot! Good-by, my friends! I'll gladly do without it! The rattling of the windowpanes and these cheerful bells will be enough for me."

Once they had passed the houses at the edge of town, his chest expanded at the sight of the countryside which seemed flooded in a sea of golden grain, with almond and olive trees afloat here and there.

To his right, he saw a peasant woman with three children coming out from behind a carob tree. For a second he gazed at the large dwarf tree and thought, "It's like a hen protecting her brood of chicks." He waved the tree good-by. He was in the mood to wave everything good-by for the last time, but without any feeling of sorrow. It was as if the joy he felt at that moment compensated for everything.

The carriage proceeded with difficulty down the dusty road, which was now steeper than ever. Long lines of carts were going up and down the road. He had never noticed the characteristic trappings on the mules pulling those carts. He noticed them now; it was as if those mules had adorned themselves with all those multicolored tufts, tassels and ribbons just to welcome him.

To the right and to the left there were several crippled or blind beggars who were sitting here and there on piles of rubble. These were men who came up from the seaside village to the hilltop city or went down to the former, all for a coin or a piece of bread that had been promised them for some particular day.

The sight of these men saddened him. Abruptly he thought of inviting them to climb aboard the carriage and join him. "Let's be merry! Let's be merry! Let's all go throw ourselves into the sea! A carriage full of desperate fellows! Come, come, my lads! Climb up, climb up! Life's a beautiful thing and we shouldn't trouble it with the sight of us."

He restrained himself so that he wouldn't have to reveal to the driver the reason for his trip. But he smiled again at the thought of all those beggars in the carriage with him and, as if he really had them there beside him, whenever he saw some others along the way, he would repeat the invitation in his dialogues with himself, "You come too! Climb aboard! I'll give you a free ride!"

III

In the seaside village, everybody knew Ciunna. In feet, "Good old Ciunna!" he heard someone call out as soon as he stepped down from the carriage. And he found himself in the arms of a certain Tino Imbro, his young friend, who immediately planted two noisy kisses on his cheeks and clapped him on the shoulder.

"How goes it? How goes it? What brings you here to this godforsaken town of bumpkins?"

"A little business..." answered Ciunna, with an embarrassed smile.

"Is this carriage at your disposal?"

"'Yes, I've rented it."

"Very good. Driver, go un-harness the horses! My dear Ciunna, I don't care how badly you might feel—your eyes are dim and your nose and lips are pale—I'm going to prevent you from leaving. If you have a headache, I'll make it go away. I'll cure you of *anything whatsoever* you might have!"

"Thanks, Tino, my friend," said Ciunna, touched by the festive reception given him by the jovial young man. "But look, I really have some very urgent business to attend to. And then I've got to go back up right away. Besides, I don't know for sure, but it's possible that the inspector may suddenly and unexpectedly arrive today.

"On Sunday? Without any warning? Why?"

"Ah yes!" replied Ciunna. "Do you expect such people to give you any warning? They pounce on you when you least expect it."

"I won't hear any excuses," protested the other. "Today is a holiday and we should enjoy ourselves. I'm going to keep you here. I'm a bachelor again. Did you know that? My wife, poor thing, all she did was cry day and night... 'What's the matter, my darling? What's the matter?' *'I want my mamma! I want my papa!'* 'Oh, that's why you're crying? You silly woman, go to your mamma, go to your papa. They'll give you some porridge and some very good tidbits...' Tell me, you who are my teacher, did I do well?"

Even the driver laughed from where he sat, and so Imbro shouted,

"Idiot, are you still there? Beat it! I told you Go un-harness the horses!'"

"Wait," said Ciunna at this point, as he took his wallet out of the inside pocket of his jacket. "I'll pay him in advance."

But Imbro held his arm back.

"God forbid! When it comes to paying and dying, the later the better!"

"No, I'll pay in advance," insisted Ciunna. "I've got to pay in advance. If I stay even for a short while in this town of 'fine gentlemen,' as you can understand, I'll risk having the very soles stolen off my shoes as soon as I lift a foot to move."

"That's the way to talk, my old teacher! *I can finally recognize you!* Pay, go ahead and pay, and then let's be on our way."

Ciunna shook his head slightly, as a mournful smile formed on his lips. He paid the driver and, turning to Imbro, asked,

"Where are you taking me? Mind you, only half an hour."

"You're joking. The carriage is paid for. It can wait until evening. I don't want to hear any no's. I'll plan the day's agenda. See? I've got my bag. I was going swimming. Come with me."

"Not on your life!" Ciunna energetically said. "Me, swimming? That's just what I need, my friend!"

Tino Imbro looked at him in wonder.

"Afraid of water?"

"No, listen," replied Ciunna, digging his feet in like a mule. "When I say no, it's no. I'll take my swim later, if at all."

"But now's the time!" cried out Imbro. "A good swim and then, with a healthy appetite, straightaway to the Leon d'oro, where there'll be a lot of wining and dining! Let yourself be served!"

"A real little party. But no! You make me laugh. Anyway, see, I don't have a swimsuit, I don't have a robe. I still believe in decency."

"Come on!" exclaimed Imbro, dragging Ciunna by the arm. "You'll find everything you need at the rotunda."

Ciunna yielded to the lively, affectionate tyranny of the young man.

A little later, in a dressing stall of the baths, he plopped down on a bench and leaned his drooping head against the boards of the wall, with all his limbs dangling and an expression of almost wrathful suffering marked on his face.

"A small sample of the element," he murmured.

He heard some knocking on the boards in the adjoining stall, and Imbro's voice:

"Are we ready? I've already got my swimsuit on. Tinino with his pretty legs!"

Ciunna rose to his feet.

"I'm about to undress."

He began to undress. While taking his watch out of his vest pocket to hide it prudently inside one of his shoes, he decided to look at the time. It was about nine thirty and he thought, "I've gained an hour!" He began to climb down the wet ladder, thoroughly chilled.

"Down, down into the water!" yelled Imbro, who had already dived in and threatened to splash him with a handful of water.

"No, no!" Ciunna yelled in his turn, trembling and feverish, with the sort of anguish that confuses you or holds you back before the mobile, glassy compactness of seawater. "Look, I'm getting out! I'm not joking... I can't stand it... Brrr, how cold it is!" he added, skimming the water with the tip of his contracted foot. Then, as if suddenly struck with an idea, he plunged entirely into the water.

"Very good!" Imbro shouted as soon as Ciunna was back on his feet, all dripping wet like a fountain.

"Brave, eh?" said Ciunna, running his hands over his head and face.

"Can you swim?"

"No, I just dog paddle."

"I'm going out a way."

The water in the pool was not deep. Ciunna crouched, holding onto a pole with one arm and striking the water gently with the hand of his other arm as if he were trying to say to it, "Behave! Behave!"

That swim was truly an atrocious mockery: he, in his shorts, crouching and held up by the pole, coming to terms with the water.

But a short time later, Imbro, coming back into the pool and looking around, no longer found his friend. Had he gone out already? He was about to make his way toward the ladder of the dressing room to investigate when, lo and behold, he suddenly saw Ciunna pop up out of the water before him, sputtering noisily and with a purplish face.

"Hey, now! Are you crazy? What've you done? Don't you know you can burst a vein in your neck doing that?"

"Let it burst..." said Ciunna, panting, half-drowned, his eyes bulging from their sockets.

"Did you swallow any water?"

"A little."

"Hey, now," uttered Imbro, and with his hand he made a gesture as if to question his old friend's sanity again. He looked at him for a while, then asked, "Were you trying out your wind or did you feel sick?"

"Trying out my wind," replied Ciunna glumly, again running his hands over his sopping hair.

"The boy has passed with flying colors!" exclaimed Imbro. "Come on, let's go, let's go ahead and get dressed! The water's too cold today. Besides, we've already worked up an appetite. But tell the truth, are you feeling sick?"

Ciunna had begun to belch, sounding like a turkey.

"No," he said when he had finished. "I'm feeling very well! It's all gone! Let's go, let's go ahead and get dressed!"

"Spaghetti with clam sauce, and—glug, glug, glug—a good bottle of wine! Just leave it up to me. A gift from my wife's relatives, bless her soul. I've still got a nice little barrel left. You'll see!"

IV

It was about four o'clock when they got up from the table. The driver appeared at the door of the restaurant.

"Should I harness up?" he asked.

"If you don't go away!..." threatened Imbro, his face flushed, pulling Ciunna over to him with one arm, and with the hand of his other arm, grabbing an empty flask.

Ciunna, no less flushed, let his friend pull him in. He smiled but did not reply, happy as a child because of that protective gesture.

"I told you that we're not leaving before evening!" added Imbro.

"Of course not! Of course not!" said a chorus of many voices in approval.

The dining hall had became filled with around twenty of Ciunna's and Imbro's friends. Other customers in the restaurant joined them for dinner, forming a long table that at first was merry but then became increasingly noisier. They laughed, shouted, drank toasts as a joke and, in brief, made an infernal racket.

Tino Imbro jumped onto a chair. He had a suggestion to make! They should all go board the English steamer that was anchored down at the port.

"The captain and I are *worse* than brothers! He's a young man of thirty with a fine beard and a lot of guts. He's got some bottles of gin that you wouldn't believe..."

The suggestion was received with stormy applause.

Around six o'clock, when the party broke up after the visit to the steamship, Ciunna said to Imbro,

"My dear Tinino, it's time to go! I don't know how to thank you."

"Don't think about that," cut in Imbro. "You'd better think instead about taking care of that little business you told me about this morning."

"Ah yes, you're right." said Ciunna, knitting his brows and groping with his hand for his friend's shoulder as if he were about to fall. "Yes, yes, you're right. And to think that I came down here for that very thing... In feet, I really have to go."

"But if you can forgo it...," observed Imbro.

"No, replied Ciunna grimly, and he repeated, "I have to go. I've drunk, I've eaten and now... Good-by, Tinino, I really can't forgo it."

"Would you like me to accompany you?" Imbro asked.

"No! Ah, ah, you'd like to accompany me? That would be curious. No, no thanks, my dear Tinino, no thanks. I'll go by myself. I've drunk, I've eaten and now... Good-by, eh?"

"Then I'll wait for you here with the carriage and we can say good-by later. Hurry!"

"I'll hurry! I'll hurry as fast as I can! Good-by, Tinino!"

And off he went.

Imbro made a wry face and thought, "The years! The years! It seems impossible that Ciunna... After all, what could he have drunk?"

Ciunna turned around and, lifting his finger and shaking it at the height of his eyes, which were winking slyly, said to him,

"You don't know me."

Then he made his way toward the longer branch of the port, the western branch, which still had no quay but was made up entirely of rocks piled one on top of the other, among which the sea thrust itself with hollow thuds followed by deep eddies. His legs didn't carry him well. All the same, he leaped from one rock to the other, perhaps with the vague intention of slipping and breaking a shin bone or of tumbling almost involuntarily into the sea. He panted, snorted and shook his head to get rid of a certain annoying sensation in his nose. He didn't know whether it came from his perspiration, his tears or from the spray of the waves that thrust themselves among the rocks. When he got to the top of the reef, he plopped down, took off his hat, shut his eyes and mouth and puffed out his cheeks as if preparing to throw away, with all the breath he had in his body, the anguish, desperation and rage he had accumulated inside.

"Phew! Now let's see," he finally said, opening his eyes after snorting.

The sun was setting. The sea, which was glassy and green near the shore, took on an intense golden hue over the vast and tremulous expanse that reached to the horizon. The sky was aflame, and in the bright light, the air was very limpid over those blazing, shimmering waters.

"Me, there?" said Ciunna a short time later, looking at the sea beyond the farthest shoals. "For two thousand seven hundred lire?"

It seemed to him a paltry sum; it was like taking a barrel of water from that sea.

"No one has the right to steal, I know that, but it remains to be seen whether one doesn't have the duty, by God, to do so when you've got four children crying for bread, and this filthy money in your hands, that you're counting. Society doesn't give you the right but, as a father, you have the duty to steal in such cases. And I'm much more than a father to those four innocent children over there! If I die, how will they get along? By begging in the street? Ah, no, Signor Inspector, I'll make you cry, like me. And if you, Signor Inspector, have a heart as hard as this rock here, well, go ahead and send me before the judges. I'd like to see if they'll have the heart to sentence me. I'll lose my job? I'll find another one, Signor Inspector. Don't be mistaken. I won't throw myself in there! Look at the fishing boats! I'll buy a kilogram of mullets as large as this, and I'll return home to eat them with my grandchildren!"

He got up. The fishing boats were coming in at full sail, veering. He hurried to arrive at the fish market on time.

Among the rush of people and their shouts, he bought some mullets which were still alive and wriggling. But... where should he put them? A small basket costing a few cents, some seaweed inside and—"Don't worry, Signor Ciunna, they'll arrive in town very much alive."

On the road, in front of the Leon d'Oro, he again found Imbro, who immediately made an expressive gesture with his hands.

"Are you okay now?

"What? Oh, the wine... Is that what you thought?... Nonsense!" said Ciunna. "See, I've bought some mullets. A friendly kiss, my dear Tinino, and a million thanks." "For what?"

"Some day, perhaps, I'll tell you. Oh, driver, put up the hood; I don't want to be seen."

V

As soon as they were outside the village, the road became steep.

The two horses were pulling the closed carriage, their bent heads accompanying every laborious step with a nod, while the dangling bells seemed to measure the slowness and difficulty of their effort.

From time to time the driver encouraged the poor skinny animals with a long and plaintive call.

Halfway home, it was already nighttime.

The darkness that had fallen upon the scene, the silence that almost seemed to be waiting for some slight noise in the bleak solitude of those poorly patrolled places, awakened the spirit of Ciunna, who was still a bit befuddled by the wine and dazzled by the splendor of the sunset on the sea.

Gradually, as the darkness deepened, he closed his eyes as if to delude himself in believing he could sleep. Instead he now found himself staring wide-eyed, in the darkness of the carriage, at the windowpane in front, which was continually rattling.

He felt as if inadvertently he had just been awakened from a dream. Meanwhile, he couldn't find the strength to pull himself together, to lift a finger. His limbs were leaden and his head felt dreadfully heavy. He was slouching back in a relaxed position, with his chin on his chest, his legs against the front seat and his left hand plunged down the pocket of his pants.

What! Was he actually drunk?

"Stop," he muttered with a thick tongue.

And he imagined, without losing his composure, that he was getting out of the carriage and was about to roam the fields aimlessly in the night. He heard some barking in the distance and thought that the barking was meant for him, as he wandered down there in the valley.

"Stop," he repeated a little later, almost inaudibly, again lowering his sluggish eyelids over his eyes.

No! He must quietly, ever so quietly, jump down from the carriage without stopping it, without being seen by the driver. He must wait until the carriage has gone a little way up the steep road, and then thrust himself into the countryside and run, run as far as the sea in the distance.

Meanwhile he was not moving.

"Splash," he tried to say with his torpid tongue.

Suddenly, a thought flashed in his mind, which made him start, and with his trembling right hand he swiftly began to scratch his forehead.

"The letter... the letter..."

He had left the letter destined for his son on the pillow of his bed. He could see it now. At that moment, in his house, they were weeping over his death. The entire town, at that moment, was buzzing with the news of his suicide. And the inspector? The inspector had certainly come. Ciunna thought, "They probably gave him the keys; he must have noticed that the cash register was empty. Dishonorable suspension, misery, ridicule, jail."

Meanwhile the carriage continued on its way, slowly and laboriously.

No, no. Trembling from anguish, Ciunna wanted to stop it. And then? Jump out of the carriage? He took his left hand out of his pocket, and with his thumb and index finger he grasped his lower lip as if to reflect, while with the other fingers he squeezed and crushed something. He opened that hand, extending it out the window, in the moonlight, and he looked into his palm. He was surprised. The poison. There in his pocket was the poison he had long since forgotten. He blinked and then thrust it into his mouth. He swallowed. Rapidly he again thrust his hand into his pocket, took out some other small pieces and swallowed them as well. Emptiness. Dizziness. His chest, his stomach, were being ripped open. He felt he was losing his breath, so he poked his head out the window.

"Now I'm dying."

The broad valley down below was bathed in a cool, faint moonlight. The high hills in front rose up, blackly etched against an opal sky.

At the sight of that delightful lunar tranquility, he felt a great inner calm. He leaned his hand against the door, rested his chin on his hand and waited as he looked outside.

From the bottom of the valley there arose a clear and constant chiming of crickets; it seemed like the voice of the moon's tremulous reflection on the running waters of a placid, invisible river.

He lifted his eyes to the sky, without taking his chin off his hand. Then he looked again at the black hills and again at the valley as if to see how much still remained for the others, since nothing was left for him anymore. Before long he would no longer see, no longer hear anything... Had time perhaps stopped? How come he still didn't feel even a hint of pain?

"Am I not dying?

And suddenly, as if the thought had given him the awaited sensation, he drew back and with one hand he squeezed his stomach. No, he still didn't feel anything. And yet... He ran his hand over his forehead. Ah! It was already wet with cold sweat! The fear of death, at that sensation of cold, overcame him. He trembled all over under the enormous, black, horrid, irreparable imminence of death. He twisted in the carriage, sinking his teeth into a cushion to stifle the scream that followed the first sharp pang in his entrails.

Silence. A voice. Who was singing? And that moon...

It was the driver, singing monotonously, while the weary horses struggled to pull the black carriage up the dusty road whitened by the moonlight.

Sunrise

I

In short, the little lamp on the writing desk was almost at its end. Shielded by a green shade, it sobbed desperately and every sob made the shadows of all the objects in the room jump as if it were sending them to the devil. It couldn't have been more eloquent.

It could have also seemed like something spooky because, as Bombichi walked about that room, in the profound silence of the night, and was swallowed by the darkness and immediately re-vomited to the light by the lamp's hiccups, he heard from time to time the hoarse, raspy voice of his wife, calling him from downstairs, as if from under the ground,

"Gosto! Gosto!"

But he would invariably stop and quietly respond to that voice with two bows and the words:

"Drop dead!" Drop dead!"

Meanwhile, since Bombichi, white as a ghost, was all dressed up in a tail coat with a shiny shirt front and had countless flashes of laughter in his corpselike face, which were accompanied by jerky gestures that also jumped to the ceiling, who knows what he might have been taken for? Consider also that, next to the lamp on the desk, there was a small revolver with a mother-of-pearl handle that was also flashing... Ugh, yes, and how!

"So pretty, eh?"

Because Gosto Bombichi seemed to be alone, but there are moments when one starts talking to oneself exactly as if one were someone else. That other himself, for example, who three hours ago, before he went to the club, had told him so rightly not to go. But, no sir, he had insisted on going anyway, that is, to The Club of the Good Friends. And, yes sir, what kindness! You should have seen the gracious look in their thieving faces as they pilfered his last thousand lire, being content to remain creditors for another two or three thousand he promised them; he no longer remembered precisely what the figure was.

"Within twenty-four hours."

The revolver—that was his only recourse. When time slams the door in the face of every hope and tells you that nothing can be done, it's useless to keep on knocking. It's better to turn around and go away.

Besides, he was fed up. It had left a bitter taste in his mouth! Anger? No. Not even anger. Nausea. Because he had amused himself so much in having life in the palm of his hand like a rubber ball and making it bounce with clever little blows, down and up, up and down, striking it to the ground and catching it in his hand, finding a female partner and playing catch, throwing it back and forth with certain rhythmic movements and running forward and back, blocking here, catching there, missing the catch and dashing after it. But now it had become irremediably punctured and deflated in his hands.

"Gosto! Gosto!"

"Drop dead! Drop dead!"

His greatest calamity... there it was. It had suddenly and unexpectedly befallen him six years ago while he was traveling in Germany, in the delightful region of the Rhine, in Cologne, on the last night of carnival, when the old Catholic city seemed to have gone completely mad. But this was not enough to excuse him.

He had left a cafe on Höhestrasse with the best of intentions to go back to the hotel to sleep. All of a sudden, he had felt someone tickle him with a peacock feather behind the ear. Damn that atavistic apish skill! At first he had grabbed that teasing feather and as he suddenly turned around in triumph (foolishly!) he had seen three women before him, three young ladies who were laughing and shouting as they trampled about like wild mares and waved their countless fingers with glistening rings before his eyes. To which of the three did the feather belong? None of them would say. So, instead of taking it out on all three of them, he unfortunately chose the one in the middle and had very courteously returned the feather to her on the condition, as carnival tradition mandates, that she receive either a kiss or a pat on the nose.

She chose a pat on the nose.

But, in receiving it, that blasted girl had half closed her eyes in such a manner that he felt all his blood stirring. One year later, she was his wife. Now, after six:

"Gosto!"

"Drop dead!"

No children, fortunately. On the other hand, who knows! If he had had any, perhaps he would not have... Enough! Enough! It was useless to think about it! As for her--that witch with dyed hair, she would have adapted somehow if she really and truly did not feel like dropping dead, as he was amorously suggesting to her.

Now quickly, a letter with a couple words, and that should suffice, right?

"I will not see tomorrow's dawn!"

Oh! At this point Gosto Bombichi stood there as if dazzled by an idea. Tomorrow's dawn? Why, in his forty-five years of life he couldn't remember ever having seen the sun rise. Never. Not even once! What was dawn? What was it like? He had heard so much talk about it as being an extremely beautiful sight that nature offers free of charge to whoever wakes up early.

He had also read quite a few descriptions of it by poets and prose writers and, yes, in brief, he knew more or less what it could be like but, no, he had never seen a dawn with his own eyes, word of honor.

"By God! I lack it... I lack it as an experience. Since poets have made so much of it, it's probably a worthless sight, but I lack it and I would still like to see it before I go. It'll occur within a couple of hours... What an idea! Very beautiful. To see the sun rise at least once, and then..."

He rubbed his hands together, happy because of this sudden decision. How great it would be to be free from all misery, relieved of every worry and to be there, outside, in the open countryside, like the first or last man on the face of the earth, standing erect, or better, sitting comfortably on some rock, or even better, leaning your shoulders against a tree trunk and seeing the sunrise! Why yes! Who knows what a delight it would be to see another day start for others and no longer for oneself. Another day, the usual worries, the usual business, the usual faces, the usual words and the flies, dear God, and to be able to say, "You are no longer for me."

He sat down at his desk and, between one sob and another of the little dying lamp, he wrote these words to his wife:

Dear Aennchen,

I'm leaving you. As I've told you so many times before, life has always seemed like a game of chance to me. I've lost and I'm paying the penalty. Don't cry, my dear. You would only ruin your eyes uselessly, and you know I don't want that Besides, I assure you that it's really not worth the trouble. So, good-by. Before daybreak, I'll be in a spot where one can greatly enjoy the sunrise. At this moment a very great curiosity to see this so highly praised spectacle of nature has arisen in me You know that, customarily, those who are sentenced to death are never denied the fulfillment of any reasonable last wish I want to grant myself this one.

Since I have nothing else to say to you, I'll just end by begging you to forget me.

Most affectionately yours,
Gosto

Since his wife, downstairs, was still awake and if she should suddenly come upstairs would notice the letter and then that'll be the end of everything, he decided to bring it along and throw it, without a stamp, in some mailbox in the city. "She'll pay the fine and maybe that'll be her only sorrow." "You... here," he then said to the small revolver, making room for it in a pocket of his black velvet vest, which was opened broadly on his shirt front. And exactly as he was dressed, with his top hat and tail coat, he left his home to go greet the sunrise, wishing the best to those remaining behind.

II

It had rained, and along the deserted streets, the sleepy street lamps reverberated their yellowish, quivering light on the wet pavement. But now the sky was beginning to brighten. It sparkled here and there with stars. Thank goodness it would not spoil the spectacular sight for him.

He looked at his watch. A quarter past two! How could he wait like that along the streets, three hours perhaps, perhaps more? When did the sun rise in that season? Nature, too, like any theater, put on its performances at certain fixed hours. But he was unprepared for this timetable.

Since he customarily came home very late every night, he was used to the echo of his own footsteps in the long silent streets of the city. But, the other nights, his steps had a well-known goal: every new step brought him closer to his home, to his bed. Instead now...

He stopped for a moment. Coming from afar, close to the ground, a light was moving along the sidewalk, leaving behind a staggering shadow like that of an animal with unsteady legs.

It was a *ciccaiolo* [a man who picks up (and sells) cigar and cigarette butts] with his little lantern.

There he was! To think that that man could live off of what others threw away, an ugly little thing—bitter, poisonous, repugnant.

"Gads, how repugnant and dismal life was too."

Nevertheless, he was tempted to search a bit along with that *ciccaiolo*. Why not? At this point, he could permit himself anything. It would be a diversion, another experience. By God, he lacked a lot of them, indeed he did. He called the man and gave him the cigar he had just lit.

"Oh! Are you going to smoke it?"

With an idiotic smile, the grimy, hairy man opened his toothless, stinking mouth and answered,

"First I'll reduce it to a butt, then I'll add it to the others. Thank you, young man."

Gosto Bombichi looked at him with revulsion. But the man looked at him too, with his red-rimmed eyes glazed with tears from the cold and that stale smirk on his lips as if...

In fact, winking an eye, he finally said, "If you'd like, young man, she's only a few steps away."

Gosto Bombichi turned his back on him. Ah, enough! He must get out of the city as soon as possible, out of that sewer. Away, away! By walking out in the open, he would find the best spot from which to enjoy the final spectacle, and then good-by!

He walked with a brisk pace until he had passed the last houses on that street which led to the countryside. Here he paused again and peered around in dismay. Then he looked up. Ah, the sky was spacious and free, and it glistened with stars! What countless sparkles, what continuous throbbing! He heaved a sigh of relief. He felt refreshed. What silence! What peace! How different the night was here, even though it was only a stone's throw from the city... Time, which there, for the people, was war, a tangle of sad passions and bitter, restless boredom, here was bewildering, self-forgetful peace. A few steps further, another world. And yet for some reason he felt a strange sense of reluctance, almost one of fear, to move his feet.

The trees, stripped of their leaves by the first autumn winds, rose about him like ghosts with gestures fraught with mystery. He saw them like that for the first time and he felt an indefinable sorrow for them. Again he paused, perplexed, almost overwhelmed by fearful astonishment. He again looked around in the darkness.

The glittering stars that spangled and spread across the sky did not manage to light up the earth. It seemed that the bright twinkling up there was answered far, far away, by a continuous sonorous vibration from the entire earth—the chirping of crickets. He cocked his ears to that harmony, with his entire soul suspended. He also then perceived the faint rustling of the last leaves, the indistinct swarming of the vast countryside in the night, and he felt a strange sensation of anxiety, an anguished consternation for all that indistinct unknown flourishing in the silence. Instinctively, to free himself from these minute and very subtle perceptions, he set off.

In the gully to the right of that country road, a brook flowed silently in the darkness. Here and there it was lit up for a second as if catching the reflection of some star, or perhaps it was a firefly which, now and then, in its flight, flashed its green light above it.

He walked along that gully up to the first stepping-stones and climbed up the slope, at the side of the road, to enter into the countryside. The earth was drenched with the recent rain. The undergrowth was still dripping wet. He went sloshing through the mud a few feet and stopped, discouraged. Poor black suit! Poor patent leather shoes! But finally, come on! What fun it was even to get everything dirty like that!

A dog barked a short distance away.

"Oh no... if you don't mind... To die, yes, but with healthy legs."

He tried to go back down to the road. Splash! He slid down the muddy slope. Naturally, one of his legs ended up in the water in the gully.

"A half footbath. Well, well, patience. I won't have time to catch a cold."

He shook the water off his leg and climbed up with difficulty from the other side of the road. Here the ground was firmer. The countryside was less wooded. At every step he expected to hear another bark.

Gradually his eyes became accustomed to the darkness. They perceived the trees, even the ones that were far away. No sign of any nearby habitation appeared. Completely intent on overcoming the difficulties of the road, with that sopping wet foot that felt as heavy as lead, he no longer thought about the violent decision that had thrust him that night there in the countryside. He walked a long, long time, continually going farther in, on an oblique course. The countryside sloped slightly downwards. Far, far off in the distance, on the horizon, a long range of mountains stood out, blackly etched in the starry dawn. The horizon was broadening. For quite a while now there were no longer any trees. Oh, come now, wasn't it better to stop here? Perhaps the sun would rise over those distant mountains.

He again looked at his watch and at first it seemed impossible to him that it was already about four o'clock. He struck a match. Yes, it was exactly six minutes to four. It astonished him that he had walked so much. In feet, he was tired. He sat down on the ground. Then he spotted a rock not far away and went to sit more comfortably on it. Where was he? Darkness and solitude!

"What madness!"

This exclamation came to his lips spontaneously, by itself, like a sigh from his good sense which had been stifled for a long time. But, roused from the momentary bedazzlement, his crazy spirit, which he had allowed to drag him toward so many insane adventures, immediately regained its dominion over his good sense and took possession of that exclamation. Yes, that nighttime trip, which was hardly merry, was madness. He would have done better by killing himself comfortably at home, without that footbath, without dirtying his shoes, pants and tail coat like that and without getting himself so tired. It's true that shortly he would have all the time in the world to rest. Besides, at this point, since he had gotten this far... Yes, but who knows how long he would still have to wait for that blessed dawn... Perhaps more than an hour, an eternity... And he opened his mouth with a formidable yawn.

"Oh! Oh! What if I should fall asleep... Brrr... its even cold and awfully damp."

He turned up the collar of his tail coat. He thrust his hands in his pocket and, all huddled up, he closed his eyes. He wasn't comfortable, no. Well! It was all out of love for that spectacle... He went back in his mind to the halls of the club, which were illuminated with electric lights... They were warm, splendidly furnished... He again was seeing his friends... and was already yielding to sleep when all of a sudden...

"What happened?"

He opened his eyes wide, and the black night gaped all around him with its frightful solitude. His blood tingled in all his veins. He found himself in the grip of a most vivid feeling of excitement. A rooster, a rooster had crowed in the distance, somewhere... Ah, yes, and now another, farther away, was answering it... down there where it was pitch dark.

"By God, a rooster... what a scare!"

He rose to his feet and, for a while, walked back and forth without leaving the spot where he had crouched for a moment. He saw himself like a dog that feels the need to turn around two or three times before curling up again. In fact, he again sat down, but once more on the ground, next to the rock, in order to be more uncomfortable and thus prevent himself from being overcome with sleep.

There it was, the ground: somewhat hard, somewhat hard rather than not... the old, old Earth! He still felt it! For a little while longer... He reached over with his hand to touch a bush which had taken root under the rock and he caressed it as one caresses a woman by running one's hand over her hair.

"You wait for the plough to break you open; you wait for the seed to fertilize you..."

He withdrew his hand, which had taken on the scent of wild mint.

"Good-by, my dear!" he said gratefully as if a woman had compensated him with that scent for the caress he had given her.

Sad, gloomy, he again plunged mentally into his stormy life; all its boredom, all its nausea gradually took on the appearance of his wife. He imagined her in the act of reading his letter four or five hours from then... What would she do?

"I'll be here..." he said, and saw himself dead in that spot, sprawled out in the middle of the countryside, under the sun, with flies around his lips and with his eyes closed.

A little later, the darkness behind the distant mountains began to dissipate ever so slightly with the first hint of dawn. Oh, how sad, how depressing that very first light of the sky was, while on earth it was still night, so that it seemed that the sky felt sorry to have to reawaken it to life. But gradually the entire sky over the mountains brightened with a delicate and very cool green light which became golden as it gradually increased and vibrated with its own intensity. Delicate, almost fragile, now pink in that light, the distant mountains seemed to be breathing. Finally, the flaming solar disk arose, seemingly pulsating with its triumphal fierce heat.

On the ground, Gosto Bombichi, dirty, still huddled up, his head propped against the rock, slept quite soundly, while his heaving chest, like a noisy bellows, accompanied his slumber.

The Black Shawl

"*Wait* here," Bandi said to D'Andrea. "I'll go tell her you've come. If she still refuses to see you, go in anyway."

Since they were both nearsighted, they stood there face to face, speaking very close to each other. They looked like brothers, being about the same age and having the same build: tall, thin and rigid. That rigidity belied the narrow-mindedness of the sort of person who does everything precisely and meticulously. Whenever they talked to each other like that, rarely would one of them not adjust the other's glasses on his nose, or his tie under his chin or, not finding anything to adjust, would touch the buttons of the other's jacket. What is more, they spoke very little and their sad, reticent dispositions showed clearly in their somber faces.

Raised together, they had helped each other with their studies until they went to the university, where one of them received a degree in law, the other in medicine. Even though they were now separated during the day by their different professions, they still took their daily walks together at sundown along the avenue at the edge of town.

So thoroughly did they know each other that a slight gesture, a glance, a word, was enough for one of them immediately to understand the other's thought. Hence those walks always began with a brief exchange of words and then were continued in silence as if one had given the other something to mull over for a long spell. They walked along with bowed heads like two tired horses, their hands clasped behind their backs. Neither of them ever felt tempted to glance toward the railing at the side of the road to enjoy the view of the open countryside down below, a varied scene of hills, valleys and plains, with the sea in the distance that was completely lit up under the last glimmers of dusk. It was such a beautiful sight that it seemed utterly incredible that those two could pass in front of it without even turning to look.

A few days earlier, Bandi had said to D'Andrea,

"Eleonora isn't feeling well."

Having looked into his eyes and gathering that his sister's illness was probably not serious, D'Andrea had said,

"Would you like me to come visit her?"

"She says no."

As they strolled together, their brows knitted as if they felt some deep-seated resentment, they began thinking about the woman who had acted as a mother to them and to whom they owed everything.

D'Andrea had lost his parents when he was a boy and had been taken in by an uncle who was utterly unable to give him a proper upbringing. Eleonora Bandi, orphaned at eighteen and with a brother much younger than herself, was able to manage at first by carefully and wisely economizing with the little her parents had left her. Then, by giving piano and singing lessons, she had been able to maintain her brother as well as his inseparable friend, at school.

"But in return," she used to say jokingly to the two young men, "I've taken on all the flesh that you two lack."

She was, in feet, an extremely large woman, but her facial features were very sweet and she had that same inspired air as those huge marble angels in flowing robes that one sees in church. The expression in her beautiful black eyes had a velvety softness because of her long lashes. This, together with the harmonious sound of her voice, seemed to be trying to subdue, though not without pain and effort, the impression of haughtiness that her huge body might have given at first glance. This impression only made her smile sadly.

She played the piano and sang perhaps not very correctly but with passionate feeling. If she had not been born and raised amid the prejudices of a small town and had not been burdened with the care of her little brother, she might have ventured into the life of the theater. That had once been her dream. But it was nothing more than a dream. She was now already almost forty. On the other hand, the prestige she enjoyed in town for her artistic talents compensated her, at least in part, for her failed dream. And the satisfaction of having realized another dream, that of paving a future for the two poor orphans, compensated her for the sacrifices she had made for such a long time.

Doctor D'Andrea waited for quite a while in the living room for his friend to come back and call him.

That room, full of light despite its low ceiling, filled with old-fashioned, shabby furniture, seemed to emanate an aura of other times and to be content with the unchanging reflection of its faded antiquity in the silence of the two large mirrors facing each other. The old family portraits hanging on the walls were the only true residents there. The only new thing was the baby grand, Eleonora's piano, which the people depicted in those portraits seemed to look down at with a scowl.

Finally, tired of the long wait, the doctor got up, went up to the doorway, poked his head in and, through the closed door, heard crying in the other room. He then went to tap on that door.

"Come in," said Bandi as he opened the door, "I can't imagine why she's being so stubborn."

"Because there's nothing wrong with me!" screamed Eleonora through her tears.

She was sitting in a huge leather armchair and, as usual, was dressed in black. She was large and pale but still had her usual childlike face that now, more than ever, seemed strange, and perhaps even more ambiguous than strange because of a certain hardness in her eyes, a sort of mad stare that she tried, nevertheless, to hide.

"There's nothing wrong with me, I assure you," she repeated, this time more calmly. "For goodness sake, leave me alone. Don't worry about me."

"All right!" her brother answered harshly and angrily. "Anyway, Carlo is here. He'll tell me what's wrong with you." He left the room, slamming the door behind him.

Eleonora brought her hands to her face and burst into violent sobs. D'Andrea stayed there for a while looking at her, somewhat angered and embarrassed, then asked,

"Why? What's wrong with you? Can't you even tell me?"

Since Eleonora continued sobbing, he went up to her and gently but coldly tried to push her hand away from her face.

"Come on, calm down. Tell me what's wrong. I'm here to help."

Eleonora shook her head. Then, suddenly, with both hands she grabbed his hand and, wincing as if from a sharp pain, she moaned,

"Carlo! Carlo!"

D'Andrea bent over her, his stern demeanor making him feel a little awkward.

"Tell me..."

She then rested her cheek on his hand and begged him desperately in a low voice,

"Make me... make me die, Carlo. For goodness sake, help me! I can't do it myself; I don't have the courage, the strength."

"Die?" asked the young man, smiling. "What are you saying? Why?"

"Yes, die!" she continued, choked by her sobs. "Teach me how, you're a doctor. Free me from this agony, for goodness sake! I've got to die. There's no other solution for me except death."

He stared at her, bewildered. She too raised her eyes to look at him but immediately shut them, again wincing and huddling up as if she had suddenly been assailed by a very most feeling of revulsion.

"Yes, yes," she then said resolutely. 'Yes, me, Carlo, I'm lost! Lost!"

Instinctively D'Andrea retracted his hand, which she was still holding in both her own.

"What! What are you saying?" he stammered.

Without looking at him, she placed a finger over her mouth, then pointed to the door and said,

"If he should find out! Don't tell him anything, for pity sake. Make me die first. Give me... give me something. I'll take it like medicine. I'll believe it's medicine you're giving me, as long as you do it right away!

Oh, I don't have the courage! I don't have the courage! You see, I've been struggling in this agony for two months without finding the strength, the way to end it all. What help can you give me, Carlo? How about it?"

"What help?" repeated D'Andrea, still utterly bewildered.

Eleonora stretched out her hands again to take hold of his arm and, looking at him with a supplicant's eyes, added,

"If you don't want to make me die, couldn't you... save me... in some other way?..."

Hearing this suggestion, D'Andrea stiffened ever more, knitting his brow sternly.

"I beg of you, Carlo!" she insisted. "Not for me, not for me, but so that Giorgio won't find out. If you believe that I've ever done anything for the two of you, or for you in particular, help me now, save me! Must I end up like this after having done so much, after having suffered so much? Must I end up disgraced like this at my age? Oh, what misery! What horror!"

"But how, Eleonora? You! How did it happen? Who did it?" said D'Andrea, curious and dismayed, not finding any other questions to ask her but these in the face of her great anguish.

Eleonora pointed again to the door and covered her face with her hands.

"Don't remind me of it! I can't think about it! So, won't you spare Giorgio this shame?"

"How?" asked D'Andrea. "It's a crime, you know. It would be a double crime. Instead, tell me, couldn't we find some other solution?"

"No!" she replied flatly and glumly. "Enough. I understand. Leave me now! I can't take it anymore..."

She let her head drop onto the back of the armchair and relaxed her limbs, utterly exhausted.

Carlo D'Andrea, his eyes fixed behind the large lenses he wore for nearsightedness, waited for a while without finding the right words. He still was unable to believe her revelation or to imagine how this woman, until now a paragon of virtue, of self-denial, could sink so low. Was it possible? Eleonora Bandi? In her youth she had refused so many suitors, one more desirable than the other, all for the love of her brother. Why was it that now, now that her youth was gone... Ah! Perhaps it was because of this...

He, a thin man, looked at her voluminous body, and the suspicion in his eyes suddenly assumed a lewd and ugly glint.

"Go, then," Eleonora abruptly said to him, irritated. In the silence, even without looking at him, she felt the unspoken horror of that suspicion in his eyes. "Go, go tell it to Giorgio so that he can immediately do with me as he likes. Go."

D'Andrea left the room almost without thinking. She raised her head a little to watch him go. Then, as soon as the door was shut, she fell back to her former position.

II

After two months of horrible anguish, this confession of her condition lifted her spirits unexpectedly. She felt that the worst was already over.

Having no more strength to fight, to resist the torment, she would now abandon herself to destiny, whatever it might be.

Would her brother come in before long and kill her? Fine, so much the better! She no longer had the right to any consideration or pity. Yes, she had done more than her duty for him and for that other ingrate but, in a single moment, she had lost the fruit of all her good deeds.

She blinked her eyes, again assailed by revulsion.

Yet, in the depth of her conscience, she felt somehow responsible for her wretched deed. Yes, she, she who for so many years had found the strength to resist the impulses of youth, she who had always harbored pure and noble sentiments, she who had considered self-sacrifice as a duty... Now, in a moment, she was lost! Oh misery! Misery!

The only explanation she felt she could put forward to excuse herself—what weight could it have in her brother's eyes? Could she say to him, "Look, Giorgio, maybe I fell because of you."? And yet, that, perhaps, was the truth.

She had been like a mother to that brother, right? So, as a reward for all the help gladly and lavishly given to him, as a reward for sacrificing her own life, she hadn't even been granted the pleasure of catching a smile, even a slight one of satisfaction on his lips or on those of his friend. It appeared as though both of them had hearts poisoned by silence and boredom, and weighed down by some sort of foolish distress. Once they received their degrees, they immediately threw themselves into their work like two horses and they did so with such diligence and fury that before long they succeeded in becoming self-sufficient. Now, this rush somehow to repay the obligation they owed her, as if both could hardly wait to do so, had wounded her deeply. Almost at once she found herself deprived of a purpose in life. What was there left for her to do now that her two young men no longer needed her? Moreover, she had irredeemably lost her youth.

Not even the first earnings he got from his profession brought back a smile to her brother's face. Did he perhaps still feel the weight of the sacrifice she had made for him? Did he feel that he was bound for his entire life because of this sacrifice, condemned, in turn, to sacrifice his own youth and the freedom of his feelings for the sake of his sister? She decided to speak to him openly.

"Don't worry about me, Giorgio! All I want is to see you happy and content... Understand?"

But he had immediately cut her short.

"Quiet, quiet! What are you saying? I know what I have to do. Now it's my turn."

"But how? Like this?" she would have liked to shout at him, she who, without giving it a second thought, had always sacrificed herself with a smile on her lips, and a light heart.

Knowing his closed and hard obstinacy, she had not insisted. But, meanwhile, she felt she could not continue in that stifling sadness.

From day to day he redoubled the earnings from his profession and surrounded her with comforts, even insisting that she stop giving lessons. In that disheartening forced inactivity, she had then unfortunately entertained a thought which at first had almost made her laugh:

"What if I were to find a husband!"

But she was already thirty-nine and then, with that body of hers... Oh, come now, she would have had to fabricate a husband expressly for herself! And yet that would be the only way to free herself and her brother from that crushing debt of gratitude.

Almost unconsciously she then began to take more care of her appearance, to assume a certain air of marriageability as never before.

The two or three fellows who had once asked her to marry them, by now had wives and children. This had never bothered her before but now, thinking about it, she felt irritated. She even felt envious of some of her old friends who had managed to settle down.

She alone had remained like this...

But perhaps she still had time. Who knows? Did her life, which had always been so active, have to end up like this? In this void? Did that ardent flame of her passionate spirit have to be snuffed out like this? In these shadows?

She was overcome with a feeling of deep regret. At times she was embittered by a certain restlessness that altered her spontaneous charm, the sound of her words and her laughter. She became sarcastic, almost aggressive, when she spoke with anyone. She herself was aware of this change in her disposition, and at certain times she almost hated herself, feeling revulsion for that vigorous body of hers and disgust for the unexpected desires that suddenly flared up and deeply troubled her.

Meanwhile her brother had recently purchased a form with his savings and had a nice little villa built on it.

On his insistence she first went there for a month's vacation. Then, reflecting on the thought that her brother had perhaps bought that farm to free himself from her occasionally, she had decided to settle there permanently. In that way she would leave him completely free and would no longer bother him with her company or her presence. There, gradually, she too would get that strange idea out of her head, the idea of getting married at her age.

The first days went well and she thought it would be easy to go on like that.

She had already gotten into the habit of rising every day at dawn and taking a long walk through the fields in the bewildering silence of the meadows, stopping here and there where the grass shivered in the cool air, to listen, enchanted, to the crowing of roosters that called each other from one barnyard to another. She would also pause to admire some rock streaked with green moss, or the velvety lichen on the twisted trunk of some ancient Saracen olive tree.

Yes, there, so close to the earth, she would soon renew her spirit, her way of thinking and feeling. She would become like that good wife of the sharecropper who was always very happy to keep her company and who had already taught her so many things about the country, so many things about everyday life that were simple but yet revealed a new, unexpected and deeper meaning.

The sharecropper, instead, was intolerable. He boasted of having liberal ideas. He had traveled all over the world. He had been to America, had spent eight years in *Boinosary* and did not want his only son, Gerlando, to be a lowly tiller. For this reason he had maintained the boy in school for thirteen years. He wanted to give him "a bit of lettering," as he would put it, so that he could send him to America, a great country, where undoubtedly he would make a fortune.

Gerlando was nineteen and, for all his thirteen years of study, had barely reached the third year in technical school. He was a rough fellow, big and husky. His fother's fixation was a real torment for him. From the company of his schoolmates he had acquired, despite himself, a certain city air that, unfortunately, served only to render him more awkward.

By using a lot of water every morning, he managed to control his bristling hair and to part it on one side, but once it had dried, it would rise thick and bushy here and there as if sprouting there and then from his scalp. Even his eyebrows seemed to be sprouting a bit below his low forehead, and already above his lip and chin the first hairs of his mustache and beard began to sprout in little tufts. Poor Gerlando! Being so big, so dense, so bristly, he aroused pity as he sat there with an open book in front of him. Some mornings his father sweated blood to rouse the boy from his deep, sound sleep—the sleep of a well-fed and satisfied pig—and to send him on his way, still dazed and staggering, his eyes drowsy, to the nearby city, that is, to his torture.

When Eleonora came to the country, Gerlando had his mother beg her to persuade his father to stop tormenting him with this school business, with this school business, with this school business! He couldn't stand it anymore!

And, in feet, Eleonora tried to intercede for him but—ah no, no, no, no—the sharecropper had all due respect and regard for the young woman but he requested that she not meddle. So, partly out of pity, partly to amuse herself, partly to keep busy, she began to help the poor young man as much as she could.

Every day, after lunch, she had him come up to the villa with his schoolbooks and notebooks. He would arrive feeling uneasy and embarrassed because he noticed that she found his dullness, his stupidity, amusing. But what could he do about it? This is what his father wanted. As for studying, ah yes, he was a dumbbell. He had no problem realizing that. But when it came to chopping down a tree, slaughtering an ox, by God... And Gerlando would show his muscular arms with such tender eyes and a smile which revealed his strong, white teeth...

Abruptly, Eleonora stopped the lessons. She didn't want to see him again. She had her piano brought in from the city and for several days she shut herself in the villa to play, sing and read in a frenzy. Finally, one evening, she noticed that this big fellow, suddenly deprived of her help, the company she had given him and the jokes she took the liberty of indulging in with him, was lying in wait to spy on her, to hear her sing and play. Yielding to an ill-inspired thought, she decided to surprise him. She suddenly left her piano and dashed swiftly down the stairs of the villa.

"What are you doing there?"

"I'm listening..."

"Do you like it?"

Yes, very much, Signora... I feel I'm in paradise."

Hearing this remark, she had burst out laughing, but suddenly Gerlando, as if spurred by that laugh, rushed upon her there behind the villa, in the darkness, beyond the beam of light coming from the open balcony up above.

That was how it had happened.

Overwhelmed in that manner, she had been unable to repel him. Under that brutal assault she had felt feint—she no longer knew why—and, yes, she had yielded to him, even though she had not wanted to.

The next day, she returned to the city. And now? Why wasn't Giorgio coming to shame her? Perhaps D'Andrea hadn't told him anything yet. Perhaps he was thinking of a way to save her. But how?

She buried her face in her hands as if not to see the void opening before her. But the void was within her as well. There was no way out. Only death. When? How?

The door swung open and Giorgio appeared with a haggard face. He was very pale, his hair disheveled and his eyes still red from crying. D'Andrea was holding him by an arm.

"I only want to know this," he said to his sister, with clenched teeth and a whistling voice, almost stressing each syllable. "I want to know *who it was.*"

Eleonora, her head bowed, her eyes shut, slowly shook her head and began to sob.

"You will tell me," shouted Bandi, drawing near but restrained by his friend, "and whoever it was, you'll marry him!"

"Oh no, Giorgio!" she then moaned, lowering her head more and more and wringing her hands in her lap. "No! It's impossible! Impossible!"

"Is he married?" he asked, as he drew closer to her with his fists clenched, threatening her.

"No," she hastened to reply. "But it's impossible, believe me!"

"Who is he?" continued Bandi, trembling all over and drawing even closer to her. "Who is he? His name... At once!"

Feeling her brother's rage upon her, Eleonora shrugged her shoulders, tried to raise her head slightly and moaned under his ferocious eyes,

"I can't tell you..."

"His name, or I'll kill you..." roared Bandi at this point, raising a fist over her head.

But D'Andrea intervened, pushed his friend aside and said to him sternly,

"Go away. She'll tell me. Go, go..."

Then he forced his friend out of the room.

III

Her brother was inflexible.

Before the wedding, during the few days needed for the proclamation of the banns, he persisted obstinately in stirring up the scandal. To avert the jokes that he was expecting from everyone, he decided, in a fit of rage, to broadcast his shame in the coarsest language possible. He appeared to have gone crazy, and everyone pitied him.

Nevertheless, he had quite a struggle with the sharecropper before the man consented to the marriage of his son.

Despite his liberal ideas, the old man at first seemed flabbergasted. He refused to believe that such a thing was possible. Then he said,

"Don't worry, Vossignoria, I'll stomp on him. Do you know how?

Like we crush grapes! Or rather, let's do this: I'll turn him over to you, bound hand and foot, and Vossignoria can do whatever you want with him. I'll furnish the whip for the lashings but first I'll soak it for three days so that it'll strike harder."

But when he realized that his master had not intended that, but something else, namely, marriage, he was again flabbergasted.

"What! What are you saying, *Vossignoria*? A rancy lady such as that, with the son of a miserable tiller?"

And he flatly refused.

"Excuse me, but the lady had common sense and wasn't a child. She knew right from wrong. She should never had done with my son what she did. May I speak frankly? She would bring him up into her house every day. *Vossignoria* can understand what I mean... A rough boy... At that age, you don't reason, you don't pay much attention... Now, can I lose a son just like that? God only knows how much he has cost me! The *signorina*, speaking with all due respect, is old enough to be his mother..."

Bandi had to promise that he would cede the farm as dowry and send a daily payment to his sister.

So the marriage was arranged and, when it took place, it was a real event for that small town.

It seemed that everyone took great pleasure in publicly demolishing the admiration and respect that had been shown to the woman for so many years. It was as if between the admiration or respect of which they no longer considered her worthy, and the ridicule with which they now accompanied her to this shameful wedding, there was no room for even a little pity.

The pity was all for the brother, who, naturally, refused to take part in the ceremony. Not even D'Andrea took part, finding the excuse that he had to keep poor Giorgio company on that sad day.

An old city doctor who had been an intimate friend of Eleonora's parents and who had lost the majority of his patients to D'Andrea, fresh from his studies and with all the conceit and sophistry of the latest therapeutics, offered to serve as her witness and brought along another old friend as second witness.

Eleonora rode with them in a closed carriage to the town hall, then to an out-of-the-way chapel for the religious ceremony.

The groom, sulky and gloomy, was in another carriage with his parents.

The latter, all dressed up, conceited and serious, were in good spirits because, after all, their son was marrying a real lady, the sister of an attorney, who was bringing him as dowry, a farm with a magnificent villa, and money to boot. Gerlando, to live up to his new status, was to continue his studies. His rather would look after the farm since that was his specialty. The bride was a little old? All the better! An heir was already on the way. According to the law of nature, she would die first and Gerlando would then be rich and free.

These and similar reflections were also being made in the third carriage by the groom's witnesses, peasant friends of his father, in the company of two old uncles on his mother's side. The groom's countless other relatives and friends were waiting in the villa, all in their Sunday best, the men in their blue woolen suits and the women in their garish new wraps and kerchiefs. They came this way because the sharecropper, with his liberal ideas, had prepared a first-class reception.

At the town hall, before entering the room designated for matters of civil status, Eleonora was assailed by a fit of crying. The groom, who kept to one side, was in the middle of a small group of relatives. They urged him to rush over, but the old doctor begged him not to let her see him and, for the moment, to stay away.

Not yet fully recovered from her violent crisis, Eleonora entered the room. When she saw the young man beside her, whose embarrassment and shame made him look even more bristly and awkward, she felt an impulse to rebel. She was about to shout "No! No!" and looked at him as if to urge him to do likewise. But a little later both of them said yes as if they had been sentenced to an inevitable punishment. The other ceremony was quickly performed in the solitary little church and the sad cortege headed for the villa. Eleonora did not want to part from her two old friends but she was obliged to climb aboard the carriage with the groom and her in-laws.

On the way, not a word was exchanged in the carriage.

The sharecropper and his wife seemed dismayed. From time to time they raised their eyes to catch a glimpse of their daughter-in-law. Then they exchanged looks and lowered their eyes. The groom, utterly withdrawn into himself and frowning, looked outside the window.

At the villa they were received with the resounding noise of firecrackers and with festive shouts and rounds of applause. But the appearance and demeanor of the bride chilled all the guests however much she tried at least to smile at those simple folk who tried to give her a warm welcome their own way, as is customary at weddings.

She soon asked to be excused but, finding a nuptial bed prepared in the room where she had formerly slept during her vacation there, she suddenly stopped at the doorway. "There, with him? No! Never! Never!" Now, overcome with disgust, she ran off to another room. She locked herself in and plopped down on a chair, pressing her face very, very hard with both hands.

Through the door she heard the voices and the laughter of the guests who were baiting Gerlando, congratulating him not so much on his bride as on the wealthy family he had married into and the beautiful piece of land he now owned.

Gerlando stood at the balcony, filled with shame, and the only answer he could give them was an occasional shrug of his powerful shoulders.

Yes, shame. He felt ashamed of being a husband that way, with that woman. Yes, indeed! And it was all his father's fault because of his blasted fixation with school. For that reason the signorina who had come to live there treated him like a stupid and helpless boy and had made fun of him, which hurt his feelings. Now, look what had happened. The father thought about nothing else than that beautiful piece of land. But as for himself, how could he live from then on with that woman who made him feel so uneasy and who certainly blamed him for her shame and dishonor? How would he dare raise his eyes and look into her face? And, on top of it all, his father expected him to continue going to school! Just imagine how his schoolmates would make fun of him! His wife was twenty years older than he and looked like a mountain, yes, indeed...

While Gerlando was torturing himself with these reflections, his father and mother were attending to the final preparations for the banquet. Finally both of them triumphantly entered the dining room where the table was already set. The table service had been furnished by an innkeeper in the city, who had also sent a cook and two waiters to serve.

The sharecropper went up to Gerlando, who was out on the balcony, and said to him,

"Go and tell your wife that it'll be ready in a few minutes."

"I'm not going, no sir!" grunted Gerlando, stamping his foot. "You go."

"You're supposed to go, jackass!" his father shouted. "You're the husband... Go!"

"Thanks a lot... But no sir! I'm not going!" Gerlando stubbornly repeated, fending him off.

Then the father, enraged, seized him by his jacket collar and gave him a big shove.

"You're embarrassed, jackass? First you put yourself into this mess, and now you're embarrassed? Go! She's your wife!"

The guests hastened over to make peace and to persuade Gerlando to go upstairs.

"What harm could there be? You'll just tell her to come and have a bite..."

"But I don't even know what to call her," shouted Gerlando, exasperated.

Some of the guests burst out laughing, others promptly restrained the sharecropper, who made an attempt to slap his imbecilic son for spoiling the reception prepared with such great solemnity and at such great expense.

'You'll call her by her first name," said his mother softly and persuasively. "What's her name? Eleonora, isn't it? So then, call her Eleonora. Isn't she your wife? Go, my son, go..."

With that, she sent him to the nuptial room.

Gerlando went to knock at the door. He knocked softly the first time. He waited. Silence. What was he supposed to say to her? Was he really supposed to speak familiarly with her at first? Ah, what an awful predicament!... Meanwhile, why, why was she not answering? Perhaps she hadn't heard him. He knocked again, this time louder. He waited. Silence.

Then, with great uneasiness, he tried calling in a low voice as his mother had suggested. But what came out was an *Eneolora* which sounded so ridiculous that immediately, as if to cancel it, he called out loudly and clearly,

"Eleonora!"

He finally heard her voice coming from behind the door of another room, asking,

"Who is it?"

He went up to that door, his blood stirring violently.

"Me." he said. "Me, Ger... Gerlando... It's ready."

"I can't come..." she answered. "Go ahead without me."

Gerlando returned to the dining room, relieved of a great weight.

"She's not coming! She says she's not coming! She can't come!"

"Hurrah for the jackass!" exclaimed his father, who called him nothing else. "Did you tell her it was already on the table? Why didn't you force her to come?"

Then the sharecropper's wife intervened. She gave her husband to understand that perhaps it would be best to leave the bride alone for that day. The guests agreed.

"The emotion... the discomfort... it's understandable!"

But the sharecropper, who was bent on showing his daughter-in-law that, when required, he knew how to do his duty, became grumpy and brusquely ordered that the dinner be served.

All the guests looked forward to the exquisite dishes soon to be served at the table but they were seriously dismayed by all the extras that they saw sparkling on the new tablecloth, dazzling their eyes: four glasses of different shapes, large and small forks, large and small knives, and what looked like quills wrapped in tissue paper.

Seated well back from the table, they perspired, also because of their heavy woolen Sunday clothes, and they looked at one another's hard, sunburnt faces, which were twisted from the unusual scrubbing they had received. They didn't dare lift their big hands, deformed by the labor in the fields, to pick up those silver forks (the small one or the large?) or the knives, under the eyes of the waiters who, going around serving in white cotton gloves, made them terribly uneasy.

Meanwhile, as the sharecropper ate, he looked at his son and shook his head, his face having assumed an expression of contempt.

"Look at him, look at him!" he grumbled to himself. "What does he look like, sitting there alone at the head of the table without his bride? How could the bride have any respect for a big monkey like that? She's right, she's right to feel ashamed of him. Oh, if it had been me in his shoes!"

The dinner ended in an atmosphere of general gloom and the guests, with one excuse or another, went away. It was already almost evening.

"And now?" said the sharecropper to Gerlando when the two waiters had finished clearing the table and everything in the villa was quiet again. "Now what are you going to do? You'll have to get out of it by yourself!"

He ordered his wife to follow him to the farmhouse where they lived, not far from the villa.

Left alone, Gerlando looked around, frowning and not knowing what to do.

In the silence he felt the presence of the woman who had locked herself in that other room. Perhaps at this very moment, no longer hearing any noise, she would be coming out. What was he supposed to do then?

Oh, how gladly he would have run to the farmhouse to sleep near his mother, or even outside, under a tree. If only he could!

What if, meanwhile, she was waiting for him to call her? What if she, resigned to the punishment that her brother had inflicted on her, considered herself in her husband's hands and was waiting for him to... yes, to invite her to...

He bent an ear. No, no, there was complete silence. Perhaps she had already fallen asleep. It was already dark. Moonlight was entering the dining room through the open door of the balcony.

Without thinking of lighting the lamp, Gerlando grabbed a chair and went to sit on the balcony, which, from that height, provided a sweeping view of the open countryside sloping down to the sea, in the distance.

The major stars shone brightly in the clear night and the moon cast a sheet of shimmering silver on the sea. From the vast fields of yellow stubble, there arose the tremulous chant of crickets, like the continuous chiming of numerous bells. Suddenly a horned owl nearby emitted a languid, mournful *tu whoo,* and from afar another answered it like an echo, and both of them continued for a while to sob like that in the clear night.

Resting his arm on the railing of the balcony, he instinctively concentrated on the sound of those *tu whoos* that called to each other in the enchanted silence under the moon, hoping to escape the torment of his restless uncertainty. Then, catching a glimpse of the wall below that encircled the entire form, he thought that now all this land was his and those trees were his: the olive, almond, carob, fig and mulberry trees. The vineyard, too, was his.

His father was quite right to be happy about that, because from now on he would no longer be subject to anyone.

In the final analysis, the idea of having him continue his studies was not such a crazy idea. He would be better off, better off there in school than here all day long in his wife's company. He would take care of those schoolmates who might want to laugh behind his back. He was now a gentleman and he no longer cared whether or not they threw him out of school. But this would not happen. On the contrary, he resolved to study diligently from then on, so that one day, before too long, he would be counted among the "gentlemen" of the town without feeling uneasy, and would be able to speak and deal with them as an equal. All he needed was another four years to obtain his diploma from the technical school. Then he would be a land surveyor or an accountant, and his brother-in-law, the lawyer, who seemed to have thrown his sister to the dogs, would have to take his hat off to him. Yes sir. And then he would have every right to say to him, "What have you given me? An old woman... I've studied, I've got a gentleman's profession and I could have aspired to marry a beautiful young girl as rich and wellborn as she!"

Thinking of this, he fell asleep with his forehead on his arm resting on the railing.

The *tu whoos*, one nearby, the other far away, continued their alternating voluptuous lament. The clear night appeared to make the moonlight quiver over the countryside trilled with crickets, and now the deep rumbling of the sea arrived from afar like an obscure reprimand.

Late that night, Eleonora appeared like a shadow in the doorway of the balcony.

She had not expected to find the young man asleep there. She felt at once both sorrow and fear. She stood there for a while, deliberating whether she should awaken him to tell him what she had decided to do, and to make him go away from there. But, as she was about to rouse him, to call him by his name, she felt her courage fail and she retreated ever so quietly, like a shadow, to the room that she had left.

IV

An agreement was easily reached.

The following morning Eleonora spoke to Gerlando in a motherly way. She let him be the master of everything, free to do whatever he wished, as if they were not bound to each other in the least. For herself, she only asked that she be left alone, off to the side, in that little room, together with the old house servant who had been present at her birth.

Late that night, Gerlando, all stiff from the dampness, had left the balcony and had gone to sleep on the couch in the dining room. Now, surprised that way in his sleep, he had a great desire to rub his eyes with his fists, and he opened his mouth as he tried to frown. He said yes, yes to everything by nodding his head, not so much because he wanted to show that he understood but to indicate that he was persuaded. But when his rather and mother learned of the pact, they became enraged, and Gerlando tried unsuccessfully to make them understand that it suited him fine like that and that it actually made him more than happy.

To calm his rather to some extent, he had to promise him formally that, at the beginning of October, he would return to school. But out of spite his mother insisted that he choose the best room to sleep in, the best room to study in, the best room to eat in—all the best rooms!

"And you give the orders! Crack the whip, understand? If you don't, I'll come myself and see to it that you're obeyed and respected."

In the end she swore that she would never again speak to that simpering snob who was scorning her son like that, such a fine young man who was far superior to the likes of her.

From that very day, Gerlando began to study for his make-ups, to resume the preparation he had interrupted. True, it was already late, with scarcely twenty-four days left, but who knows? Perhaps with a little effort he would finally succeed in obtaining the diploma for which he had tortured himself the past three years.

Having recovered from the painful bedazzlement of those first few days, Eleonora, on the advice of Gesa, her old servant, began to prepare a layette for the future baby.

She hadn't even thought of it, and that made her cry.

Since Eleonora was inexperienced in that work, her old servant helped and guided her. She gave her the measurements for the first little shirts, the first bonnets... Ah, destiny had reserved this consolation for her, and she had not yet thought of it. She would have a baby boy or girl to look after, to dedicate herself totally to! But God had to grant her the favor of sending her a boy. She was already old. She would soon die, and how could she leave that father a baby girl in whom she would impart her own thoughts and feelings? A boy would suffer less from the condition of life in which bad luck would soon put him.

Tormented by these thoughts and tired of her work, she would pick up one of the books that she had had her brother send her when she had first arrived there, and begin to read for diversion. Every now and then, nodding her head, she would ask the servant,

"What's he doing?"

Gesa would shrug her shoulders, purse her lips and answer,

"Hum! He's sitting with his head on a book. Is he sleeping? Thinking? Who knows!"

Gerlando was thinking. He was thinking that, all things considered, his life was not very cheerful.

Here he was. He had a form, and it was as if it wasn't his. He had a wife, and it was as if he didn't have one. He was at war with his relatives, and he was angry with himself because he could remember nothing, nothing, nothing at all of what he had studied.

Meanwhile in his restless inactivity, he felt painful desires stirring within him, among which, that of possessing his wife because she had shunned him. True, the woman was no longer desirable, but... what sort of pact was that? He was the husband and he, if anyone, was supposed to decide such things.

He would get up, leave the room and pass in front of the door of her room, but immediately, as soon as he caught sight of her, he felt all desire to have his way vanish. He would snort and, so as not to admit that he lacked courage right when he was about to act, he would tell himself that she wasn't worth it.

Then one day he returned from the city a defeated man. He had failed the examination for his diploma, failed it once more. And now he had had enough! Really enough! He didn't want to hear about it anymore! He took his schoolbooks, notebooks, drawings, squares, boxes, pencils, and brought them down in front of the villa to make a bonfire with them. His father dashed over to stop him but Gerlando, enraged, warded him off.

"Let me do what I want! I'm the boss!"

The mother appeared, and several peasants who were working in the fields also ran up. Wisps of smoke, first thin, then menacingly more dense, poured out from that pile of papers, amid the cries of the onlookers. Then came a flash as the flames crackled and rose. Hearing the cries, Eleonora and the servant went out to the balcony.

Gerlando, livid and puffed up like a turkey, shirtless and furious, was tossing into the flames the last books he held under his arm—the instruments of his long and useless torture.

At the sight of such a spectacle, Eleonora could hardly keep from laughing and she quickly withdrew from the balcony. But her mother-in-law, having noticed that, said to her son,

"The lady finds it amusing, you know. You're making her laugh."

"She'll cry!" screamed Gerlando in a threatening tone as he raised his head and looked up at the balcony.

Eleonora, understanding the threat, blanched. She realized that the sad and tired peace she had enjoyed until then was over for her. Fate had granted her nothing more than a moment of respite. But what could that brute want from her? She was already exhausted. Another blow, even a slight one, would do her in.

A little later she found Gerlando before her, gloomy and panting.

"From today on, there's going to be a change in our lives!" he announced. "I'm fed up. I'm going to become a farmer like my father, and you're going to quit playing the lady. Away, away with all this linen! The baby to be born will become a former too and he will not need so many frills and fancy clothes. Dismiss the servant. You'll prepare the meals and look after the house as my mother does. Understand?"

Eleonora got up, pale and quivering with indignation.

"Your mother is your mother," she said to him, looking him squarely in the eye. "I am myself and I can't become a peasant like you."

"You're my wife!" screamed Gerlando, accosting her violently and grabbing her by an arm. "And you'll do what as I say. I'm the boss here, understand?"

Then he turned to the old servant and pointed to the door.

"Out! Get out of here right now! I don't want servants in my house!"

"I'm coming with you, Gesa!" cried Eleonora as she tried to free her arm from his grasp.

But Gerlando would not let go. He held on to it even more tightly and forced her to sit down.

"No! Here! You'll stay here, chained to me! I've been ridiculed because of you and now I've had enough! Come on, leave that lair of yours. I don't want to be left alone to cry over my anguish anymore. Out! Out!"

He pushed her out of the room.

"What have you cried over up until now?" she said to him with tears in her eyes. "What have I ever asked of you?"

"What have you asked? Not to be disturbed, not to have any contact with me as if I were... as if I didn't deserve your affection, you old lady! You had a servant wait on me at the table, when it was your duty to wait on me to my complete satisfaction, as wives do."

"But what could you possibly want from me?" Eleonora asked him, downhearted. "I'll serve you with my own hands from now on. All right?"

In saying this, she burst out sobbing. Then she felt her legs giving way beneath her and she let herself go. Gerlando, dazed and confused, held her up with Gesa's help, and both of them set her down on a chair.

Toward evening, she was suddenly in labor.

Gerlando, repentant and frightened, ran to call his mother. A farmhand was sent to the city to fetch a midwife. Meanwhile, the sharecropper, seeing the farm in jeopardy if his daughter-in-law should have a miscarriage, treated his son roughly.

"Jackass, jackass, what have you done? What if the baby should die now? What if you don't have any more children? You'll be out in the street! What'll you do? You've left school and you don't even know how to hold a hoe in your hands. You're ruined!"

"What do I care?" shouted Gerlando. "As long as she gets nothing!"

The mother appeared, her arms in the air.

"A doctor! She needs a doctor right away! I think it's serious!"

"What's wrong with her?" asked Gerlando, shocked.

But the father pushed him out the door, shouting,

"Run! Run!"

On the way Gerlando, trembling all over, lost heart and began to cry, forcing himself, nevertheless, to run. When he was halfway there, he ran into the midwife coming with the farmhand in a carriage.

"Hurry! Hurry!" he shouted. "I'm going to get the doctor. She's dying!"

He stumbled and fell heavily to the ground. All covered with dust, he got up and again started running desperately, sucking at the hand that had been scraped.

When he returned to the villa with the doctor, Eleonora was close to death, having lost a great deal of blood.

"Murderer! Murderer!" whined Gesa as she looked after her mistress. "It was his fault! He dared lay his hands on her."

Eleonora, however, shook her head as if to deny it. She felt she was gradually slipping away along with her blood. She felt her strength waning. She was already cold... Well, she was not sorry to die. Death like this was sweet, a great relief after her atrocious torment. Looking at the ceiling, her face waxen, she waited for her eyes to shut by themselves, slowly, very slowly and forever. She already could no longer make anything out. As if in a dream she again saw the old doctor who had stood as her witness, and she smiled at him.

V

For the entire time Eleonora lay between life and death, Gerlando never left her bedside, day or night.

When she could finally be taken from her bed and placed on the armchair, she seemed like another woman. She was transparent, almost colorless. She saw Gerlando before her, looking as if he too had just gotten over a mortal illness, and all around his relatives, eager to be of help. She looked at them with those beautiful black eyes that were large and sad in her pale, thin face, and she felt that no relationship between them and her existed anymore. It was as if she had just returned, new and different, from a distant place where every bond had been broken, and not only with them but with all her former life.

She had trouble breathing. At the slightest sound, her heart jumped in her breast and beat wildly. She was exhausted.

Then, with her head resting on the back of the armchair, and her eyes shut, she regretted that she had not died. What was she doing there? Why were her eyes still condemned to see those faces around her and those things from which she already felt so, so very distant? Why this reunion with the oppressive and nauseating appearances of her past life? It was a reunion that at times seemed to become more painful, as if someone were pushing her from behind, forcing her to see and to feel the presence, the living, breathing reality of an odious life that no longer was hers.

She was firmly convinced that she would never again get up from that armchair. She believed that from one moment to the next she would die of a broken heart. But that was not to be. After several days she was able to rise to her feet and, with some help, to take a few steps around the room. Then, with time, she was also able to descend the stairs and go outside, supported by Gerlando and the servant. And finally, she got into the habit of going at sunset to the brink of the cliff that marked the southern boundary of the farm.

From there a magnificent vista opened out over the slope of the plateau, down to the sea. The first days she was accompanied, as usual, by Gerlando and Gesa; then she went only with her servant, and finally, she went alone.

Seated on a rock in the shadow of a century-old olive tree, she gazed at the coastline curving gently, its tiny inlets and bays forming a jagged line with the sea that changed with the shifting winds. She first saw the sun as a fiery disk sinking slowly amid the murky mist that covered the all-gray sea to the west. Then she saw it dip triumphantly into the flaming waves in a wondrous display of glowing clouds. She also saw Jupiter's bright light streaming calmly in the damp twilight sky, and the pale, diaphanous moon shining dimly. With her eyes, she drank in the sad sweetness of the approaching evening. She breathed deeply and blissfully, feeling the cool, silent breeze penetrating to the depths of her soul as a superhuman consolation.

Meanwhile, over there, in the farmhouse, the old sharecropper and his wife had resumed their conspiracy against her, inciting their son to look after his affairs.

"Why are you leaving her alone?" his father pointedly asked him. "Can't you see that now, after her illness, she is grateful to you for the affection you've shown her? Don't leave her for a moment. Try to enter her heart more and more. And then... and then see to it that the servant no longer sleeps in the same room with her. Now she's well and no longer needs her at night."

Irritated, Gerlando shook all over at these suggestions.

"I wouldn't dream of it! It won't even cross her mind that I might... Certainly not! She treats me as a son... You should hear the things she says to me! She feels she's already old, over the hill, and finished as far as this world is concerned."

"Old!" joined in his mother. "Naturally, she's no longer a youngster but neither is she old, and you..."

"They'll take the land away from you," pursued his father. "I've already told you, you're ruined, out in the street. If your wife should die and there are no children, the dowry will return to her family. The only result will be this: you will have sacrificed your studies and wasted all that time without any satisfaction. You'll be left empty-handed! You had better attend to this, attend to this while there's still time. You've already wasted too much of it... What are you waiting for?"

"Be gentle," continued his mother. "You've got to approach her gently and possibly tell her, 'See? What have I ever gotten from you? I've respected you as you've wished, but now think a little about me. What will happen to me? What will I do if you leave me like this?' Good lord, after all, she doesn't have to go off to war!"

"And you can add," his father pressed, "you can add, 'Do you want to please your brother, who treated you like he did, and let him throw me out of here like a dog?' It's the honest truth! You'll be thrown out like a dog. They'll kick you out, and your mother and I, we poor old folks, will be kicked out with you."

Gerlando made no attempt to answer.

Hearing his mother's words of advice, Gerlando felt some sort of relief, but an irritating one, like a tickle. His father's predictions stirred him up and enraged him. What should he do? He saw the difficulty of the undertaking but he also saw its urgency. At any rate, he had to try.

Eleonora now sat at the table with him. One evening, at supper, seeing him staring at the tablecloth, deep in thought, she asked,

"How come you're not eating? What's wrong with you?"

Although for several days he had been expecting this question brought on by the way he was behaving, he was unable to answer on the spot as he had planned, but made a vague gesture with his hand.

"What's wrong with you?" Eleonora insisted.

"Nothing," replied Gerlando uneasily. "My father, as usual..."

"Again this business about school?" she asked smiling, in an effort to induce him to talk.

"No, worse!" he said. "He raises... he raises so many doubts in my mind. He torments me with thoughts of my future because he says he's old and I'm like this, without a trade. As long as you're here, everything's fine but then... Then nothing, he says..."

"Tell your father," Eleonora replied gravely, half shutting her eyes as if not to see him blush, "tell your father not to worry about it. I've taken care of everything. Tell him to relax. As a matter of feet, since we're on this subject, listen, if I should suddenly die—we're all living on borrowed time —you'll find a yellow envelope in the second drawer of the bureau in my room. There's a paper in it for you."

"A paper?" repeated Gerlando, confused, embarrassed and not knowing what to say.

Eleonora nodded affirmatively and added,

"Don't worry about it."

The next morning, Gerlando, relieved and happy, related to his parents what Eleonora had told him. But they, and especially the father, were not at all satisfied with that.

"A paper? Tricks!"

What could that paper be? Her will, that is, the bequest of the farm to her husband. What if it were not drawn up according to the rules and regulations? Suspicions could easily arise in that it was the writing of a woman, a paper produced without the help of a notary. Wouldn't they have to deal with her brother the next day, a man of law, a swindler?

"Lawsuits, my Son? God forbid! Justice is not for poor folks. That brother now, out of anger, would be capable of making you see white for black and black for white."

Besides, that paper, was it really there in the drawer of the bureau? Or did she just tell him that so that she wouldn't be bothered?

"Have you seen it? No. Well then? But, even supposing she lets you see it, what would you be able to make out of it? What would we be able to make out it? Whereas if you had a son... that's all you'd need! Don't let her bamboozle you. Listen to us! Flesh! Flesh and blood! Not paper!"

And so one day, as she sat under the olive tree on the cliff, Eleonora suddenly found Gerlando beside her. He had come up furtively.

She was wrapped in a large black shawl. She felt cold even though it was such a mild February that it already seemed like spring. The vast slope below was all green with the new crops. The very calm sea in the distance, together with the sky, maintained a pinkish hue that was slightly faded but delightfully soft, and the shaded countryside seemed enameled.

Tired of gazing at that marvelous harmony of colors in the silence,

Eleonora had rested her head against the trunk of an olive tree. Only her face, which seemed even paler, could be seen below the shawl pulled up over her head.

"What are doing?" Gerlando asked. "You look like Our Lady of Sorrows."

"Just looking..." she answered with a sigh, half shutting her eyes.

But he added,

"If you could only see how... how fine you look in that black shawl..."

"Fine?" said Eleonora, smiling sadly. "I feel cold!"

"No, I mean how attractive you look," he explained, stammering, and he sat on the ground beside the rock.

Eleonora, with her head resting on the tree trunk, shut her eyes again and smiled to keep from crying. She was assailed by a feeling of regret for having wasted her youth so miserably. When she was eighteen, yes, she had been beautiful. Very much so!

All of a sudden, as she sat there absorbed in thought, she felt herself shaken gently.

"Give me your hand," he begged her, as he sat there on the ground and looked at her with glossy eyes.

She understood his message but pretended not to.

"My hand? Why?" she asked. "I can't pull you up; I don't have any more strength, not even for myself... It's already evening. Let's go back."

And she got up.

"I didn't mean I wanted you to pull me up." Gerlando explained, still sitting on the ground. "Let's stay here in the dark. It's so beautiful. .." As he said that, he was quick to embrace her knees, smiling nervously with parched lips.

"No!" she screamed. "Are you crazy? Let go of me!"

To keep from falling, she supported her arms on his shoulders and pushed him back. But, in so doing, the shawl came loose and, as she leaned over him kneeling there, it wrapped around him and hid him inside it.

"No! I want you! I want you!" he then said as if inebriated, clasping her ever more tightly with one arm while with the other he reached up to take hold of her waist, wrapped as he was in the scent of her body.

But with a supreme effort she managed to free herself and ran to the edge of the cliff. She turned around and cried,

"I'm going to jump!"

At that moment she saw him approaching her violently. She leaned back and plunged over the cliff.

He scarcely managed to keep from felling himself. In shock, he screamed with his hands in the air. He heard the terrible thud down below.

He looked down and saw a pile of black clothes lying on the green slope. The shawl, opening in the wind, fell softly farther away.

With his hands in his hair, he turned to look in the direction of the farmhouse, but his eyes were suddenly met by the large pale face of the moon that had just emerged from the thick olive grove up there. And he stood there gazing at it in terror as if it had seen him from the heavens and was accusing him.

This Makes Two!

After wandering for a long time through the sleeping district of Prati di Castello, hugging the walls of the barracks and instinctively shunning the light of the lamps under the trees of those extremely long avenues, Diego Bronner finally reached Lungotevere dei Mellini. Feeling tired, he climbed onto the parapet of the deserted embankment and sat down feeing the river, his legs dangling in the void.

Not a single lamp was lit in the houses on the opposite bank, over there on the Passeggiata di Ripetta, all of which were shrouded in darkness and formed black silhouettes against the vast expanse of feint light that the city beyond radiated into the night. Along the river bank, the leaves of the trees lining the avenue were motionless. In the great silence one could only hear the chirping of distant crickets and, below, the doleful rumbling of the black waters of the river, in which the street lamps from the opposite bank were reflected with a continuous serpentine quivering.

A thick band of endless small clouds, wispy, low and ash-colored, raced through the sky as if hastily summoned there, down there toward the east, to a mysterious encounter, and it seemed that the moon from up above was passing them in review.

Bronner, his face upturned, remained there for a while to contemplate the flight of clouds which animated with such mysterious vivacity the luminous silence of that moonlit night. Suddenly he heard the sound of footsteps on the nearby Ponte Margherita and turned around to look.

The sound of footsteps ceased.

Perhaps someone, like himself, had stopped to gaze at those small clouds, and at the moon passing them in review, or down at the river with those quivering reflections of light in its black, flowing waters.

He heaved a deep sigh and continued gazing at the sky, somewhat annoyed by the presence of that unknown person who was disturbing his sad pleasure of feeling alone. But he was here in the shadow of the trees, and so the stranger, he mused, would not be able to see him. As if to make sure of it, he turned around again to look.

Near a lamp attached to the parapet of the bridge, he spotted a man in the shadows. At first he could not understand what that fellow might be doing, standing there silently. He saw him place what looked like a package on the ledge at the foot of the lamp. A package? No, it was his hat. And now? What! Was it possible? Now the stranger was climbing over the parapet. Was it possible?

Instinctively Bronner cringed backward, stretching out his arm and blinking his eyes. He huddled up and then heard the dreadful splash in the river.

A suicide? Just like that?

Opening his eyes, he again stared into the darkness below. Nothing. Only black water. Not a shout. Noone. He looked around. Silence, calm. Had no one seen? Had no one heard? Meanwhile the man was drowning... And he, nailed to the spot, was not moving. Should he shout? By then it was too late. Huddled in the shadows, trembling all over, he let the man's horrible fate come to fruition; yet, all the while, he felt crushed by the complicity of his silence with the night, and from time to time he asked himself, "Is it over? Is it over?" It was as if with his eyes shut he could see the unfortunate man in his desperate struggle with the river.

Opening his eyes again as he straightened up after that moment of terrifying anguish, he felt that the profound silence of the sleeping city guarded by the lamps was a dream. But how those reflections quivered in the black water! He turned his eyes in fright to the parapet of the bridge and saw the hat left there by the stranger. The lamp shone on it with a sinister light. He was seized with a long fit of trembling in his back. His blood still tingled in his veins. He felt all his muscles shivering spasmodically. It was as if that hat could accuse him! He got down from the parapet and, seeking the shadows, quickly set out for home.

"Diego, what's wrong?"

"Nothing, Mother. Should something be wrong?" "No, I just thought... It's already late..."

"You know that I don't want you to wait up for me. I've told you that, so many times. Let me come home when it suits me."

Yes, of course. But you see, I was sewing... Do you want me to light the night lamp for you?"

"God! You ask me that every night!"

As if lashed by this reply to her superfluous question, the old mother, bent with age and slightly limping, hurried to his room to light the lamp and prepare his bed.

He followed her with his eyes, almost with rancor, but as soon as she had disappeared behind the door, he heaved a sigh of pity for her. But, immediately afterwards his impatience returned.

He stayed there waiting without knowing why, nor for what, in that dismal entrance hall with its very low ceiling covered with sooty wallpaper torn here and there and with hanging shreds where flies had gathered and slept in clusters.

The room was crammed with dingy old furniture mixed in with cheap new furniture and new objects of dressmaking. There was a sewing machine, two full-breasted wicker mannequins and a massive, smooth table for cutting cloth, upon which lay a large pair of scissors, a piece of chalk, a tape measure and several coquettish fashion magazines.

But Bronner scarcely noticed any of this.

He had carried back with him, as a scene from a theater, the spectacle of that sky overrun with those low, wispy clouds, and of the river with those reflections from the street lamps; the spectacle of those tall houses in the darkness, that stood out opposite him against the glow of the city, and that of the bridge with that hat... With all this came the frightening impression, as in a dream, of the impassiveness of all those things that were there with him, present, more present than himself. Because, since he was hidden in the shadows of the trees, it was actually as if he were not there. His horror now, his confusion stemmed precisely from this, from having remained there at that moment like those things that were present yet absent. Like the night, the silence, the river bank, the trees, the lamps. He hadn't cried out for help, *as if he had not been there.* And now here he was, dazed and distraught, as if what he had seen and heard had been a dream.

Suddenly he saw their large gray cat spring agilely on the massive table. Two green eyes, motionless and empty.

Those eyes frightened him for a moment, so he frowned, annoyed.

A few days before, the cat had managed to pull down from a wail of that room a cage with a goldfinch in it that his mother had raised with loving care. With diligent and patient ferocity, by thrusting its paws through the bars, it had pulled out the bird and had eaten it. His mother was still upset about that. He, too, still thought about the massacre of that goldfinch. But the cat—there it was, completely unaware of the harm it had done. If he had chased it rudely from the table, it wouldn't have understood at all why.

And so, yes, there were already two proof
of his guilt that night, two other proofs. This second one was suddenly springing up before him with that cat, just like suddenly the other had with that suicide from the bridge. One proof was the feet that he couldn't be like that cat, which, a moment after it completed its massacre, no longer thought about it. The other was the feet that people, when confronted with a deed, cannot remain impassive like things can, however much they might try, as he had, not only not to get involved in it but also to stand back as if absent from it.

His curse lay in remembering and in not being able to hope that others would forget. Yes, these two proofs. A curse and a feeling of hopelessness.

For some time now his eyes had acquired a new way of looking. He looked at his mother, who had just come back after having prepared his bed and lit his night lamp, and he saw her no longer as his mother but as a poor old woman like any other, as she intrinsically was, with that large wart next to the right side of her slightly pug nose, her pale flaccid cheeks streaked with small violet veins, and with those tired eyes that, in meeting his strangely merciless glance, would immediately sink behind her glasses as if from shame. Of what? Ah, he knew very well of what! He let out an ugly laugh and said,

"Good night, Mother."

Then he went to lock himself in his room.

Quietly, ever so quietly, so that he wouldn't hear her, the old woman again sat down in the small room to sew and... to think.

God! Why was her son so pale and upset that night? He couldn't have been drinking because he didn't drink, or at least she hadn't smelled anything on his breath. But could he have fallen again into the hands of those bad companions who had ruined him, or perhaps even into worse hands?

This was her greatest fear.

From time to time she bent an ear to find out what he was doing in his room. Had he gone to bed? Was he already sleeping? Meanwhile she cleaned her glasses, which clouded over each time she sighed. Before going to bed, she wanted to finish the work she had started. The small pension her husband had left her no longer sufficed now that Diego had lost his job. Besides, she nurtured a dream, even though it would have meant her death. It was to put aside enough money by working and saving to send her son far away, to America. For she knew that her son Diego would never again be able to find a job here and would be lost forever in the sad idleness that had been devouring his soul for the past several months.

To America... yes, there! After all, her son was so clever! He knew so many things! He used to write once, and his articles even appeared in the newspapers... To America, yes, indeed! Perhaps it would mean her death, but her son would have a chance to begin living again, to forget and obliterate his youthful error inspired by his bad companions, like that Russian or Pole or whatever he was, a madman, a guzzler who had come to Rome to bring ruin to so many honest families. Young ruffians, as everybody knows! Invited to the home of this very rich and dissolute foreigner, they had done foolish things. There was plenty of wine and some cheap women around. They would get drunk... When that rich fellow got drunk, he would insist on playing cards for money, and he would lose... He brought on his ruin with his own hands. What did those guzzling companions he had gathered around him have to do with it? Still, he accused them of cheating and brought them to court and created a scandal that had attracted so much attention and defamed so many young men who, of course, were reckless but came from decent and respected families.

She thought she heard a sob coming from her son's room, and she called out,

"Diego!"

Silence. She stayed there a while, listening and focusing her eyes on the door.

Yes, he was still awake. But what was he doing?

She got up and tiptoed to the door to eavesdrop. Then she bent over to look through the keyhole. He was reading... Ah yes, of course! He was still reading those dreadful newspapers with the account of the trial... Why, oh why had she forgotten to destroy the papers she had purchased during the terrible days of the trial? Why is it that this night and this hour, as soon as he returned home, he had again picked them up and again began to read them?

"Diego!" she called out again, but this time softly. She then opened the door timidly.

He spun around as if frightened and asked,

"What do you want? Are you still up?"

"And what about you?" the mother answered. "You see, you're making me still regret my stupidity."

"No, that's not it. I'm just enjoying myself," he answered, stretching out his arms.

He got up and began pacing his room.

"Tear them up, throw them away, I beg you!" the mother pleaded with clasped hands. "Why do you insist on torturing yourself? Quit thinking about it!"

He paused in the middle of the room, smiled and said,

"Wonderful! As if by not thinking about it I could make others not think about it. So that I can live, we would all have to pretend that we're absentminded... I'm absentminded, and the others are too... When someone asks what's happened, I'll answer, 'Nothing. I've just been *on vacation* for three years. Let's change the subject...' But don't you see, don't you see how even you are looking at me?"

"Me?" exclaimed his mother. "How am I looking at you?"

"Like all the others!"

"No, Diego! I swear it! I was looking... I was looking at your suit and noticed that it was high time you saw a tailor... that's all!"

Diego Bronner looked at the suit he was wearing and again smiled.

'Yes, it's old. That's why everybody looks at me... And yet, I brush it well before going out and I groom myself carefully... I don't know, but I feel that I could pass for an average man, for one who can still take part in life with indifference... The trouble is those things over there," he added, pointing to the newspapers on the desk. "We've put on such a spectacle that, come now, it would be extreme modesty to presume that people could have forgotten about it. It was a spectacle of naked souls, weak and rather filthy—ashamed to show themselves in public, like consumptives at a levy. And each of us tried to cover his shame by snatching at the gown of our defending counsel. What peals of laughter from the public! Do you expect, for example, that people can forget we called that Russian 'Luculloff and that we dressed him up like an ancient Roman, with gold-rimmed glasses on his pug nose? When they saw him in court with that fat face of his and they learned how we treated him, that we yanked his buskins off his feet and beat him on his bald head, and that, under this punishment, he laughed; he guffawed in utter bliss..."

"Diego! Diego, for heaven's sake!" the mother implored.

"Yes, he was drunk. We made him drunk..."

"No, not you!"

"Come on! Yes, me too, with the others. It was fun! And then came the playing cards. As you can imagine, when you play cards with a drunkard, it's very easy to cheat."

"For heaven's sake, Diego!"

"We were just joking... I can swear to that! In court they all laughed when I told them about it—the officials, the presiding judge,even the policemen. But it's the truth. We stole, not knowing what we were doing, that is, we knew but we thought it was just a joke. It didn't seem like a swindle. It was the money of a disgusting lunatic who just threw it away... Besides, not even a red cent of it remained in our pockets. Like him, with him, we too threw it away crazily..."

He broke off, walked over to the bookcase and pulled out a book.

"Look! This is my only regret," he said. "One morning, with that money, I bought this book from a book vendor."

He flung the book on the desk. It was Ruskin's *The Crown of Wild Olive,* translated into French.

"I haven't even opened it," he added.

He stared at it, frowning. How is it that in those days it had entered his mind to buy that book? He had resolved never to read again nor to write another line. And he was going there, to that house, with those companions, to become brutish, to kill his childhood dream in himself and to drown it in revelry. For, the sad necessities of life prevented him from abandoning himself to it as he would have liked.

For a while the old woman, too, looked at that mysterious book. Then she asked gently,

"Why don't you start working? Why don't you write anymore like you used to?"

He cast an ugly glance at her, contorting his whole face as if in disgust.

His mother insisted humbly,

"If only you could withdraw a bit into yourself... Why give up hope? Do you think it's all over? You're only twenty-six. Who knows how many opportunities life will offer you to redeem yourself!..."

"Ah yes! This very night I was offered one!" he sneered. "But I stayed put like a sack of potatoes. I saw a man throw himself into the river..."

"You?"

"Me. I saw him place his hat on the parapet of the bridge. Then I saw him climb over the parapet as quietly as possible. And finally I heard the splash in the river. I didn't shout nor did I move. I was in the shadow of the trees and there I stayed, trying to catch sight of anyone who might have seen the incident. I let him drown. Yes, indeed. But then I spotted his hat there on the parapet of the bridge, under the lamp, and I ran away, terrified..."

"Oh, that's why..." muttered the old woman.

"What?" he asked. "I can't swim. Should I have dived into the water and tried to save him? The flight of steps leading down to the river was there, a few feet away. I looked at it, you know, and I pretended not to see it. I could have... but it was already useless... too late... He had disappeared!"

"Wasn't there anyone around?"

"No one; only me."

"What could you have done by yourself, my son? It was enough that you became so frightened and are now so upset... See? You're still trembling... Come now, go to bed, go to bed... It's very late. Don't think about it anymore!..."

The old woman took his hand and caressed it. He nodded affirmatively and smiled at her.

"Good night, Mother," he said.

"Sleep tight, eh?" she said, touched that he had allowed her to caress his hand. And wiping her eyes so as not to spoil this anguished tenderness, she left the room.

About an hour later, Diego Bronner was again sitting on the river bank in the same spot as before, his legs dangling.

The low, wispy, ash-colored clouds continued their flight through the sky. The stranger's hat was no longer on the parapet. Perhaps the night patrolmen had passed by and taken it.

Suddenly Diego turned toward the avenue, retracting his legs. He got down from the embankment and went onto the bridge. He took off his hat and put it in the same spot where the stranger had put his.

"This makes two!" he said.

But it was as if he were playfully trying to spite the patrolmen who had removed the other hat.

He went around to the other side of the lamp to see what effect his hat made, lit up like the other had been, all alone on the ledge. He stood there a while bent over the parapet, his neck thrust forward to contemplate it *as if he himself were no longer there.* Suddenly he laughed horribly. He saw himself lying in wait like a cat behind the lamp, and the mouse was his hat. "Oh, come now, this is utter nonsense!"

He climbed over the parapet. He felt his hair standing on end. He felt his hands tremble as they clung stiffly to the edge. He released his grasp and plunged into the void.

Into the Sketch

When Raffaella Osimo learned that the medical students would be returning to the hospital that morning, she begged the head nurse to bring her to the chief physician's hall, where lessons in semiology were held.

The head nurse looked at her askance.

"Do you want the students to see you?"

"Yes, please. Take me."

"But don't you know that you look like a lizard?"

"Yes, but I don't care! Take me."

"How impudent! And what do you suppose they'll do to you in there?"

"What they did to Nannina," Osimo answered. "Isn't that so?"

Nannina had occupied the bed next to hers and had left the hospital the day before. But before leaving, and as soon as she had returned to the ward after the lesson in that back hall, she had shown Raffaella her body all marked up like a map; her lungs, heart, liver and spleen had been sketched in outline with a dermographic pencil.

"And you want to go there?" the nurse asked. "As far as I'm concerned, I'll do as you say. But, mind you, you won't be able to remove the sketches for many days, not even with soap."

Osimo shrugged her shoulders and said, smiling,

"Just bring me there and don't worry about it."

A little color had returned to her face but she was still very thin. She was all eyes and hair. However, her black and very beautiful eyes again shone brightly. And in that small bed her young, petite body could hardly be seen among the folds of the blankets.

To the head nurse, as well as to all the other hospital sisters, Raffaella Osimo was an old acquaintance.

The girl had been at that hospital already two other times. The first time, for... Oh, those blessed girls! They allow themselves to be taken advantage of, and then who's the loser? A poor innocent little baby who ends up in the home for foundlings.

To tell the truth, Osimo, too, had paid bitterly for her error. About two months after the delivery, she had returned to the hospital more dead than alive, with three pills of mercuric chloride in her body. This time she had been there for the past month because of her anemia. By dint of iron injections she had already recovered and within a few days she would be out of the hospital.

They were fond of her in that ward and were charitable and tolerant toward her for the timid and appealing charm of her goodness, though it was so disconsolate. Even the desperation within her was never displayed with somber moods or with tears.

The first time she had said, smiling, that at this point there was nothing left for her but death. However, since she had been a victim of a destiny common to too many young girls, she hadn't aroused either any particular pity or any particular fear concerning that obscure threat. It's common knowledge that all girls who have been seduced and abandoned threaten to commit suicide. These sorts of things shouldn't be taken so seriously.

Raffaella Osimo, however, had said it and attempted it.

In vain, then, the good sisters who assisted her had tried to comfort her with their faith. She had done what she was doing now. She listened attentively, smiled, said yes, but it was obvious that the pain wringing her heart was not being banished or soothed because of these exhortations.

Nothing could induce her to find hope in life anymore. She recognized the fact that she had deluded herself, that the real deception had come to her more from her inexperience, from her passionate and credulous nature, than from the young man she had yielded to and who could never be hers.

But as for resigning herself, no, *that* she could not do.

Because if for others her story had nothing special about it, that did not make it less painful for her. She had suffered so much. First the torture of seeing her father murdered treacherously, then the irreparable collapse of all her aspirations.

Now she was a poor seamstress, betrayed like so many others, abandoned like so many others. But some day... Yes, even the others, it's true, said the same thing, "But someday..." But they lied, because the need to lie arises spontaneously in an oppressed heart.

But she was not lying.

Still a young girl, she would certainly have gotten her teaching credentials if her father, who supported her schooling with so much love, had not suddenly passed away down there in Calabria. He had been assassinated but not directly out of hatred. During the political elections, he had been victimized at the hand of a hired assassin who remained anonymous and who had undoubtedly been paid by the faction opposing Baron Barni, to whom he was the zealous and faithful secretary.

Once elected deputy, Barni, knowing that the child's mother had also died and that she was alone, had taken her into his home in order to look charitable in the eyes of the electors.

So she had come to Rome in an uncertain state. They treated her as if she were one of the family, but meanwhile she acted as governess to the baron's youngest children and also as lady's companion to the baroness—of course, without a salary.

She worked and in the meantime Barni took credit for giving her charity.

But what did it matter to her then? She worked with all her heart to gain the paternal benevolence of her host, with a secret hope. It was her wish that her loving care, that is, her uncompensated services, after her father's sacrifice, might succeed in conquering the opposition that the baron perhaps would raise against his oldest son, Riccar-do, when the latter, as he had already promised her, would declare to him his love for her. Oh, Riccardo was quite certain that his father would willingly give his consent, but he was barely nineteen and still a high school student. He didn't feel the courage to make that announcement to his parents. It would be better to wait a few years.

And so, waiting... But was it possible, there, in the same house, always close to each other, among so many enticements, after so many promises, with so many vows...

Her passion had blinded her.

When finally her error could no longer be hidden, she was thrown out! Yes, she could say that she was really thrown out without any mercy, without any regard not even for her condition. Barni had written to an old aunt of hers telling her to come immediately to get her and take her away, down there to Calabria. He promised a pension, but the aunt begged the baron to wait at least until her niece had delivered in Rome, so as not to have to face a scandal in the small town. Barni had given in on the condition that his son know nothing of this and that he think that they were outside Rome already. However, after the delivery, Raffaella refused to return to Calabria. Then the baron in his rage threatened to terminate the pension and, in feet, he did so after her attempted suicide. Riccardo left for Florence. She, miraculously saved, began to work as an apprentice seamstress to support herself and her aunt. A year went by and Riccardo returned to Rome, but she didn't attempt to see him again. Her violent plan having foiled, she got it into her head to let herself die gradually. One fine day her aunt lost patience and returned to Calabria. A month before, after having feinted in the house of the seamstress who employed her, Raffaella was brought to the hospital and had remained there to be treated for anemia.

Meanwhile, the other day, from her bed, Raffaella Osimo saw the medical students who were taking a course in semiology pass through the ward. Among these students she again saw Riccardo, after almost two years. Beside him was a young lady who probably was also a student. She was blond, beautiful and looked like a foreigner. From the way he looked at her—ah, Raffaella could not be mistaken!—it appeared clear that he was in love with her. How she smiled at him, almost hanging upon his eyes...

She had followed them with her eyes, right to the back of the ward. Then she had remained there with her eyes wide open, propped up on an elbow. Nannina, who occupied the bed next to hers, had started laughing.

"What did you see?"

"Nothing..."

And she, too, had smiled, dropping back on her bed because her heart was beating as if it were about to leap out of her chest.

Then the head nurse had come to ask Nannina to get dressed because the professor wanted her in the hall for the lesson he was teaching the students.

"What'll they do to me?" Nannina asked.

"They'll eat you! What do you expect them to do to you?" the head nurse answered. "It's your turn now. The others will get theirs some other time. Anyway, tomorrow you'll be leaving."

At first, Raffaella trembled at the thought that her turn might also come. Having fallen so low and being so miserable, how could she reappear before him? For certain errors, when beauty has vanished, there is neither pity nor empathy.

Certainly, in seeing her so down and out, Riccardo's colleagues would make fun of him.

"What! You went with that little lizard?"

It would not have been a vendetta. Besides, she didn't want to avenge herself.

However, when, after about half an hour, Nannina had returned to her little bed and explained to her what they did to her in the hall and showed her body all marked up, Raffaella suddenly changed her mind. Lo and behold, she was now trembling with impatience, awaiting the arrival of the students.

They finally arrived around ten o'clock. Riccardo was there and, like the other day, was next to that foreign student. They were looking and smiling at each other.

"Shall I get dressed?" Raffaella asked the head nurse, bouncing excitedly on her bed as soon as the students entered the hall at the far end of the ward.

"Oh, what hurry! Lie down!" the head nurse commanded her. "Wait until the professor gives us the order."

But Raffaella, as if the nurse had said "Get dressed!" began to dress secretly.

She was already quite ready under the blankets when the head nurse came to call her.

As pale as a ghost, her miserable little body all feverish, her lips smiling, her eyes sparkling and her hair cascading every which way, she entered the hall.

Riccardo Barni was talking with the young student and, at first, did not notice her since she was lost among the many young people. She was looking for him with her eyes and didn't hear the chief physician, a university lecturer in semiotics, who was saying to her,

"Here, here, my dear girl."

Upon hearing the professor's voice, Barni turned and saw Raffaella, who was staring at him, her face now flushed. He was shocked. He turned very pale and his eyes clouded over.

"For heaven's sake!" shouted the professor. "Here!"

Raffaella heard all the students laugh and she was startled and continuously more bewildered. She saw that Riccardo was retreating to the far end of the room, toward the window. She looked around, smiled nervously and asked,

"What am I supposed to do?"

"Here, here, here, lie down over here!" ordered the professor, who stood at the head of a little table covered with a sort of quilt.

"I'm ready, yes, sir!" Raffaella hastened to say, obeying him, but since she had difficulty pulling herself up to sit on the little table, she again smiled and said, '.'I can't manage..."

A student helped her climb up. Once she was seated, before lying down, she looked at the professor, who was a handsome man—tall, clean-shaven, with gold-rimmed eyeglasses—and said to him as she pointed to the foreign student,

"If you wouldn't mind having her do the marking..."

Another burst of laughter from the students. The professor himself smiled and asked,

"Why? Are you embarrassed?"

"No, sir, but I'd be more pleased."

She turned to look toward the window, there at the far end where Riccardo had crept into a corner with his back turned to the hall.

The blond student instinctively followed that look. She had noticed Barni's sudden turmoil. She now noticed that he had withdrawn over there, and she too became greatly troubled.

But the professor called her.

"Now then, Miss Orlitz, it's up to you. Let's please the patient."

Raffaella stretched out on the little table and looked at the student, who was lifting the little veil from her forehead. Oh, how beautiful, white and delicate she was with her very sweet sky-blue eyes. The student now removed her cloak. She took the dermographic pencil that the professor handed to her and was bending over her to uncover the patient's bosom with unsteady hands.

Raffaella Osimo shut her eyes, ashamed of her miserable bosom exposed to the glances of the many young people around the little table. She felt a cold hand being placed on her heart.

"It's beating too fast," suddenly said the young lady, with a marked exotic accent, as she withdrew her hand.

"How long have you been in the hospital?" asked the professor.

Raffaella answered without opening her eyes but with eyelids that were quivering nervously.

"Thirty-two days. I'm almost well."

"Listen and see if there's a heart murmur caused by anemia," continued the professor, handing the student the stethoscope.

Raffaella felt the cold instrument on her breast. Then she heard the voice of the young lady, who said,

"No murmur... Too much palpitation."

"Let's go do the percussion," the professor then ordered.

At the first tappings, Raffaella bent her head to one side, clenched her teeth and tried to open her eyes. She shut them again quickly, making a violent effort to contain herself. From time to time, as the young woman interrupted her percussion to mark a small line under her middle finger—she used a pencil dipped in a glass of water held by a student nearby—Raffaella painfully blew the breath she was holding, through her nostrils.

How long did this torture last? He was always there, near the window. Why wasn't the professor calling him? Why wasn't he asking him to see her heart, which his blond companion was tracing near that squalid bosom reduced to such an awful state because of him.

Finally, there! The percussion was finished. Now the young female student was joining all the little lines to complete the sketch. Raffaella was tempted to look at that heart of hers designed there, but suddenly she was unable to contain herself and she burst into sobs.

The professor, who was annoyed, sent her back to the ward, ordering the head nurse to bring in another patient who might be less hysterical and less foolish than the last one.

Osimo peacefully put up with the reprimands of the head nurse and, trembling all over, returned to her little bed to wait for the students to leave the ward.

Would he at least look for her with his eyes as he crossed the ward? Why no, no. At this point, what did it matter to her? She wouldn't even lift her head to have him notice her. He mustn't see her anymore. It was enough for her that she had showed him to what state she had been reduced because of him.

With trembling hands she took the edge of the sheet and pulled it over her face as if she were dead.

For three days Raffaella Osimo took great care to make sure that the sketch of the heart would not be erased from her bosom.

As soon as she left the hospital, she went in front of a small mirror in her shabby little room and drove a knife, which she pushed against the wall, into the very center of the sketch that her unwitting rival had made on her.

In Silence

"Waterloo! Waterloo! Good Lord, Waterloo! It's pronounced Waterloo!"
"Yes, sir, after St. Helena."
"After? What are you saying? What does St. Helena have to do with it?"
"Ah, yes! The Island of Elba."
"No, no! Forget the Island of Elba, dear Brei! Do you think you can improvise a history lesson? Now then, sit down!"

Cesarino Brei, pale and timid, sat down, and the teacher continued looking at him for a while, annoyed if not actually angry.

The boy had been the teacher's boast for the diligence and good will he demonstrated in his studies during his first two years of high school. But now—that is, from the time he had put on the uniform of the National Boarding School—even though he paid very close attention during the lessons, like the fine student he was, well, just look at him now. He couldn't even comprehend the real reasons why Napoleon Bonaparte had been defeated at Waterloo!

What had happened to him?

Not even Cesarino himself could come up with an explanation. He would study for hours and hours or, better put, he would sit in front of his open books, staring at them through the thick eyeglasses he wore for nearsightedness, but he could no longer concentrate on them since he was surprised and distracted by new and confused thoughts. This had been going on not only from the time he had entered boarding school, as the teachers thought, but from some time before that. In feet, Cesarino could have said that it was because of these very thoughts and certain strange impressions that he had allowed his mother to persuade him to enter that boarding school.

His mother (who called him Cesare, not Cesarino) had said to him without looking him in the eye,

"Cesare, you need to change your life style. You need to spend some time with fellows of your own age and to put a little order and discipline not only in your studies but in your pastimes too. I've thought, if you don't mind, of having you spend this final high school year as a boarder. Okay?"

He had hastened to answer yes without giving it a second thought, so great was the turmoil that the sight of his mother had caused him for the past several months.

An only son, he had not known his father, who must have died extremely young since his mother, who was thirty-seven, could still be called young. He himself was already eighteen, exactly the same age his mother was when she had gotten married.

It all tallied but, really, the fact that his mother was still young and had gotten married at eighteen did not necessarily mean that his father must have died very young. She could have married someone older than herself, perhaps even an old man, right? But Cesarino had little imagination. He couldn't imagine this like so many other things.

Besides, there wasn't a single portrait of his dad in the house nor any clue that he had ever existed. His mother had never spoken to him about the man, nor had he ever felt curious to know anything about him. He only knew that his father's name was Cesare—like him—and that was all. He knew this because in his school records there were the words: *"Brei, Cesarino, son of the late Cesare, born in Milan,"* etc. In Milan? Yes. But he didn't even know anything about the city of his birth or, better said, he knew that there was the Duomo in Milan, and that was all... the Duomo, the Galleria Vittorio Emanuele *panettone,* and that was all. His mother, also a Milanese, had come to settle in Rome immediately after her husband's death and his own birth.

To think of it, Cesarino could almost say that he didn't even know his mother very well. He hardly ever saw her during the day. From morning until two in the afternoon she was at the Vocational School, where she taught drawing and embroidery. She then ran around until six or seven and sometimes until eight p.m. to give private lessons in French and piano. In the evening she would return home tired, but even at home, in that brief time before supper, she had other tasks, certain household chores that the servant girl could not do. Then, right after supper, there was the job of correcting the homework of her young private students.

They had furniture that was more than respectable, all the modern conveniences, a wardrobe full of clothes, a well-stocked pantry. Ah yes, naturally, because his dear, indefatigable mom worked very hard! But also what sadness and what silence in that house!

Cesarino, mulling over all this at the boarding school, still felt a pang of anguish in his heart. As soon as he returned from school, he ate lunch alone without appetite in the richly furnished but poorly lit dining room. He would sit there with an open book in front of him, which he propped against the water bottle on the rectangular white tablecloth spread out hastily over the old walnut table. Then he would shut himself up in his room to study. Finally, in the evening, when they called him for supper, he would come out all hunched up, benumbed and sullen, with his eyes squinting behind those glasses he wore for nearsightedness.

At supper, mother and son exchanged only a few words. She would ask him some questions about school. How had he spent the day? Often she would scold him for the way he was living, which was not very youthful. She wanted him to rouse himself. She would urge him to move around a bit during the day, out of doors. To be more lively. Yes, more like a man! He should study, yes, but he also needed some diversions. Yes, indeed, she suffered in seeing him so gloomy, pale and without appetite. He gave her brief replies such as yes and no. He would coldly promise to change. Then he would impatiently wait for supper to end so that he could go to bed as soon as possible because he habitually got up early in the morning.

Having grown up always alone, he was not on familiar terms with his mother. He noticed, or sensed, that she was different from him. She was so lively, energetic and spontaneous. Perhaps he resembled his father. The void left by his father so long ago stood between him and his mother and had grown steadily as the years went by. His mother, even in his presence, always appeared distant to him.

Now, this feeling had grown to the point of causing him the strangest feeling of embarrassment when, because of a conversation with two schoolmates, his first childhood illusions had collapsed, suddenly revealing certain shameful secrets of life that he hadn't suspected until then. At that moment it was as if his mother had jumped to a place even farther away. To be sure, this was happening very late but Cesarino, as we know, had little imagination. During the last days he spent at home, he had noticed that, despite the great deal of work she attended to without pause from morning to night, she continued to look beautiful—very beautiful and healthy—and that she took great care to preserve this beauty. Every morning she fixed her hair with long and loving care. She dressed with refined simplicity and uncommon elegance. He now felt almost offended by the perfume she wore, which he had never noticed before in quite the same way.

Precisely in an effort to rid himself of this strange attitude toward his mother, he had immediately accepted the proposal to go to boarding school. Had she become aware of it? What had prompted her to make such a proposal to him?

Cesarino was now thinking about that. He had always been obedient and studious ever since childhood. He had always done his duty without anyone's supervision. He was a bit frail, yes, but all the same he was healthy. The reasons brought forth by his mother did not at all convince him. Meanwhile he struggled with himself to suppress certain thoughts about which he later felt shame and remorse, and so much the more now that he knew his mother was sick. For several months she had not been coming to visit him on Sundays at the boarding school. The last few times she had come, she complained that she wasn't well. To be sure, she didn't seem as healthy to Cesarino as she had before. In feet, he had noticed that her hair was unusually neglected and that made him feel even more remorseful over the evil thoughts prompted by the excessive care that she had formerly devoted to it.

From the short letters his mother occasionally sent him to ask whether he needed anything, Cesarino learned that the doctor had ordered her to rest because she had worked too much and for too long. He had also forbidden her to go out, assuring her, nevertheless, that there was nothing seriously wrong with her and, if she followed his prescriptions scrupulously, she would undoubtedly be cured. But the illness dragged on, and Cesarino was worried and could hardly wait for the school year to end.

Naturally in such a frame of mind, regardless of the efforts he made, he could not easily comprehend the real reasons why Napoleon Bonaparte had been defeated at Waterloo, as excogitated by the history professor.

One day, as soon as Cesarino arrived at school, he was summoned by the principal. He expected to receive some stern reprimand for his poor performance that school year; instead he found the principal quite cordial and friendly and also with a somewhat troubled expression on his face.

"Dear Brei," he said to him, placing a hand on his shoulder as he normally never did, "you know that your mother..."

"Is she worse?" Cesarino promptly broke in, raising his eyes to look at him, almost in terror. His cap fell out of his hand.

"It appears so, my dear son. You've got to go home immediately."

Cesarino stood there looking at him with a question in his suppliant eyes that his lips dared not utter.

"I don't know the details," said the principal, grasping that silent question. A little while ago, a woman came from your home to call you. Take courage, my dear boy! Go. I'll place the caretaker at your disposal."

Cesarino left the principal's office with his mind in a turmoil. He no longer knew what he should do, where to turn in order to rush back to his home. Where was the caretaker? And his cap? Where had he left his cap?

The principal handed it to him and told the caretaker to remain at the young man's disposal even for the rest of the day if necessary.

Cesarino ran to Via Finanze, where his house was. When he was a few feet away, he saw the main door ajar and felt his legs buckling beneath him.

"Take courage!" repeated the caretaker, who knew what had happened.

The entire house was in great disorder as if death had made a violent entrance.

Rushing in, Cesarino immediately cast a glance at the far end of his mother's room. He spotted his mother there... on the bed. She seemed long—this in his confusion was his first impression, a strange feeling of bewilderment—long, oh God, as if death had forcibly stretched her. She was stiff, paler than a ghost and, at the sides of her nose, under her eyes, her flesh was livid. She was unrecognizable!

"What?... What?..." he stammered, at first almost more curious than terrified by the sight, and hunching up his shoulders and stretching out his neck to see, as nearsighted people do.

From the other room, almost as an answer, came the raucous cry of a baby to horribly shatter that deathly silence.

Cesarino spun around as if the cry had been a razor slash on his back. Trembling all over, he looked at the maid, who was kneeling beside the bed and crying silently.

"A baby?"

"In the next room...'•' she gestured.

"Hers?" he asked, more with his breath than with his voice. He was shocked.

The maid nodded yes.

He turned again to look at his mother but was unable to bear the sight. Upset by the sudden, atrocious revelation that stunned him and now wrung his heart with deep sorrow, he covered his eyes with his hands, while up from the troubled depths of his being came something like a scream, one which his throat, now choked with anguish, blocked.

In childbirth then? Dead in childbirth? How? So, it was because of that? Suddenly the suspicion flashed through his mind that in the room where the infant's cry had originated there was *someone*. He turned around to look at the maid scornfully.

"Who?... Who?"

He was unable to say anything else. With a trembling hand he tried to adjust his glasses, which were sliding down his nose because of the tears that meanwhile gushed inadvertently from his eyes.

"Come... come..." the maid said to him.

"No... Tell me..." he insisted.

Finally he noticed that in the room, around the bed, there were other people whom he didn't know and who looked at him with piteous astonishment. Without uttering a word, he let the maid accompany him to the little room that he had occupied before entering the boarding school.

In there he found only the midwife, who had just taken the infant, swollen and purplish, out of the bath.

Cesarino looked at it with disgust and turned again to the maid.

"No one?" he said almost to himself. "This baby?"

"Oh, my dear young man!" cried the maid, clasping her hands. "What can I tell you? I don't know anything. I was just telling that to the midwife here... I don't know anything at all! No one ever came here; I can swear to that!"

"Didn't she tell you?"

"Never, anything! She never confided anything to me, and I, of course, couldn't ask her... She would cry, you know. Oh, quite a lot. Secretly... She stopped going out when it began to show... You know what I mean..."

Cesarino, horrified, raised his hands to signal to the maid to keep silent. Although he felt an overwhelming need to know in the dreadful void that her sudden death had flung him, he also did not want to. The shame was too great. His mother had died from it and was still in the next room.

He pressed his hands on his face, drawing near to the window to make his suppositions alone in the darkness of his mind.

For as long as he had been at home, he, too, did not remember ever seeing any man who could arouse any suspicion in him. But, elsewhere? His mother had lived so little at home! What did he know about the life she had led elsewhere? What was his mother beyond the very limited relations that she had had with him before, there, in the evenings, at supper? An entire life from which he had always remained cut off. Certainly she must have spent some time with someone... But with whom?... He was crying. So then this fellow had abandoned her, unwilling or unable to marry her. That's why she had locked him up in a boarding school, to avoid and have him avoid an inevitable shame. But afterwards? He would certainly have left the boarding school next July. And then? Had she perhaps intended to erase every trace of her shameful deed?

He uncovered his eyes to look at the baby again. There he was. The midwife had swaddled him and laid him out on the little bed in which he himself used to sleep when he lived at home. That little bonnet, that little shirt, that little bib... But no, look. She had intended to keep the baby. Certainly she herself had prepared that layette. So, when he left the boarding school, he would have found that newborn infant at home. What would his mother have told him then? Ah yes, that's why she had died! Who knows what tremendous secret torture she had suffered during those months! Ah, how cowardly, how cowardly the man who had inflicted it on her had been in abandoning her after having shamed her! She had shut herself in the house to hide her condition. Perhaps she had lost her teaching position at the Vocational School... How had she gotten by during those months? Undoubtedly with the savings she had accumulated over the many years she had worked. But what now?

Cesarino suddenly felt the void gaping blacker and vaster around him. He saw himself alone, alone in life, helpless, without any relatives, either close or distant. He was alone with that little baby who had killed his mother by coming into the world and who remained in the same void, abandoned to the same fate, fatherless... like himself.

Like himself? Ah, yes, perhaps he too... Why had he never thought of it before? Perhaps he too had been born like that! What did he know about his father? Who had that Cesare Brei been? *Bret?* But wasn't that his mother's last name? Yes. Enrica Brei. That's how she signed her name, and everybody knew her as Maestra Brei. If she had been a widow when she came to Rome and became a teacher, wouldn't she have again used her own last name, perhaps followed by that of her husband? But no, Brei was his mother's last name, and he, therefore, bore only her last name. The late Cesare, about whom he knew nothing, and of whom not. a trace had been left, perhaps had never existed. Cesare, perhaps, but not Brei... Who knows what his father's last name had really been! How come he had never thought about these things until now?

"Listen, poor young man!" said the maid. "The midwife here would like to tell you... This little baby..."

"Ah, yes," interrupted the midwife. "This baby needs milk now. Who will provide it?"

Cesarino looked at her, perplexed.

"You see," continued the midwife, "I was just saying that... since he was born like this... and his mother, poor thing, is no longer living... and you're a poor boy who can't look after this innocent child... I was just saying that..."

"He should be taken away?" asked Cesarino, frowning.

"Because, see," she continued, "I should report it to the City Registry... I've got to know what you intend to do."

"Yes," said Cesarino, again perplexed. "Yes... Wait... I want, I first want to see..."

He looked around as if searching for something. The maid came to his aid.

"The keys?" she asked him softly.

"What keys?" said Cesarino, who hadn't been thinking of anything.

"Do you want the little bunch of keys, to see... I don't know what! Look, they're over there, on the dressing table, in your mother's room."

Cesarino made a move to go but he suddenly stopped at the thought of seeing his mother again, now that he knew. The maid, who had begun to follow him, added even softer,

"My dear young man, it'll be necessary to think about so many things. I know you're feeling lost. You are so alone, you poor innocent soul... The doctor came. I rushed to the pharmacy... I got a lot of things... This is the least of our worries. But now we also have to think about your poor mother, right? What are we to do? Look into that..."

Cesarino went to get the keys. He saw his mother stretched out long and stiff on the bed and, as if attracted by the sight, he went up to her. Oh, how silent those Hps were, silent now and silent forever. From them he would have liked to find out so many things! She had taken away with her, in the horrible silence of death, the mystery of that baby over there and the other mystery of his birth... But perhaps by searching, by rummaging... Where were the keys?"

He took them out of the dressing table and followed the maid into his mother's small study.

"Yes... look there, in that cabinet."

He found a little more than one hundred lire, which perhaps were what was left of her savings.

"Nothing else?"

"Nothing, wait..."

He had spotted some letters in the cabinet. He wanted to read them right away. But they (three, in all) had been written by a teacher at the Vocational School and were addressed to his mother at Rio Freddo, where she had spent her summer vacation with him two years before. And the following year, that teacher, a colleague of his mother, had died. Suddenly, from the last of those letters, a small piece of paper fell to the floor, which the maid hastened to pick up.

"Give it to me! Give it to me!"

It was written in pencil, without a heading, without a date, and said the following:

Impossible today. Maybe Friday.
Alberto

"Alberto..." he repeated, looking at the maid. "He's the one! Alberto... Do you know him? Do you know anything about him? Really nothing? Speak up!"

"Nothing, my dear young man, as I've told you!"

He again looked in the cabinet, then in the drawers of her wardrobes, everywhere, throwing everything into disorder. He found nothing. Only that name! Only this bit of information: The baby's father was named Alberto. And his own father, Cesare... Two names. Nothing else. In the next room, she was dead. All the furniture in the house was oblivious, impassive. And in that void, he was now without any support, with that baby over there who, as soon as he was born, no longer belonged to anyone. At least he himself up till now had had a mother. Get rid of him? No... no, poor little thing!

Moved by an impetuous sense of pity, that already was almost fraternal tenderness, he felt a desperate energy awakening within him. He took a few of his mother's jewels out of the cabinet and gave them to the maid so that she could try to get some money with them for the time being. He went to the living room to beg the caretaker, who had accompanied him, to take care of what still had to be done for his mother. He went back to the midwife to beg her to look for a wet nurse immediately. He rushed over to get his boarding school cap in the bedroom where his dead mother was lying and, after promising her in his heart that her baby would not perish, and neither would he, he ran to the boarding school to speak with the principal.

He had completely changed in a few seconds. Without complaining he explained his case, his plan to the principal, asking him for help. He did so with assurance, firmly convinced that no one would be able to deny it to him because, at this point, he had a sacred right to it for all the wrong which he, an innocent, had been forced to suffer from his own mother, from that unknown man who had given him life and from that other unknown man who had taken his mother from him and left a newborn baby in his arms.

The principal, open-mouthed and with eyes full of tears, stood there listening to him. Immediately the man reassured him that he would do all he could to obtain some help as soon as possible and that he would never, never, abandon him. He hugged him, cried with him, told him that that very evening he would come and pay him a visit at his home and, hopefully, bring some good news.

"That's good. Yes, sir, I'll wait for you."

He returned home in a hurry.

The help, though slight, arrived promptly, but Cesarino hardly noticed it because it immediately served to pay for the burial of his mother's corpse, which others took care of.

He no longer thought about anything but the baby. How to keep him at his side, outside, outside that sad house where so much affluence (who knows how it had gotten there and where it had come from?) had ended up confusing him. Furniture, drapes, carpets, kitchen utensils, all those furnishings that, if not actually luxurious, were certainly costly. He looked at them almost with rancor because of the secret that they preserved of their origin. He had to get rid of them as soon as possible. He would keep only the humblest and most necessary things to furnish the three modest rooms rented outside the city with the principal's help.

On the advice of his fellow tenants he turned to merchants of used furniture and to junk dealers, and he negotiated the sale with fury because—strange!—it seemed to him that they belonged above all to the baby, those household goods, now that his mother had died, making the shame behind that affluence evident to everyone. And, by God, one could at least grant the baby the right not to feel that shame. Someone had to defend the interests of that tiny and ignorant creature.

He would also have sold the clothes and many of his mother's remaining fineries to a melancholy, sickly secondhand dealer who presented herself all dolled up and droopy from exhaustion and affectation. But she, speaking softly amid sweet smiles, hinted to what sort of clientele she planned to resell his mother's clothes and fineries... He threw her out. The clothes were almost still alive for him. How greatly they preserved the perfume that had disturbed him so much recently! It now seemed to him that he could smell the breath of the baby in the bundle he made to put them back again. It was a confirmation of his strange impression that everything, everything there, belonged to the baby that was powdered and wrapped in that luxurious layette that she had prepared before dying. Yes, it now seemed like a precious thing, precious and dear, that baby. He was no longer only to be saved but also to be protected with all the care and attention that his mother certainly would have lavished on him. Cesarino was happy to feel her beautiful and courageous alacrity suddenly rekindled in himself.

He did not notice, as others did, that the lively spontaneity of his mother appeared like a desperate effort in him, given the ungainly thinness of his small body, which made him irritable, suspicious and even cruel. Yes, even cruel, as he showed himself to be in dismissing Rosa, the old maidservant, who had been so good to him in that confusion. But nobody could dislike him for what he did or said. It was right, after all, that he should dismiss the maid since he had to sustain the enormous expense of the wet nurse for the baby. Yes, he could have done it some other way but one forgave him even this. Rosa herself had forgiven him. Poor fellow, perhaps he couldn't even begin to suspect that he was being cruel to others. In that moment and in that measure he was himself experiencing the terrible cruelty of destiny. If compassion had not hindered them, at the most they might have smiled in seeing him so downtrodden, with those narrow and greatly hunched shoulders, his little face, pale and hard, always ready to blunt an attack, and his sharp eyes peering through the thick lenses he wore for nearsightedness. Breathless, anguished by the fear of never arriving on time, he ran here and there in order to take advantage of everything. People would help him and he wouldn't even thank them. He didn't even thank the principal of the boarding school when the man came to his new home, after he had moved, to inform him that he had found him a position as a junior clerk at the Ministry of Public Education.

"Yes, it's not much but in the evenings, after you leave the ministry, you'll be able to come to the boarding school to give private lessons to the boarders, young students in junior high school. You'll see that it'll be enough. You're resourceful."

"Yes, sir, but what about a suit?"

"What suit?"

"I certainly can't go to the ministry still dressed like a boarding school student."

"You can wear one of the suits you had before entering the boarding school."

"No, sir, I can't. They're all like my mother had wanted them— with short pants. Besides, they're not even black."

Every difficulty that confronted him (and there were so many) irritated him more than it dismayed him. He wanted to succeed. He had to succeed. But the duty of making him succeed seemed to belong to others, the more he showed the will to do so. At the ministry, when the other clerks, all mature or old men, spent their time joking despite their superiors' threats to eliminate that office because of its meager output, he would fidget in his chair, panting, or would stamp his foot. Then he would turn around suddenly to look at them from his desk and pound his fist on the back of his chair. He would do that not because their stupid negligence seemed dishonest to him but because, not feeling any obligation to work with him and almost for him, they put him in the position of risking his job. In seeing themselves recalled to duty like that by a young lad, it was natural that they should laugh and tease him. He would leap to his feet. He would threaten to report them and then he would do worse because, yes, they would challenge him to do it. So he would have to recognize that he himself could precipitate the damage that they would all suffer. He would stay there looking at them as if they had ripped open his abdomen with their laughs. Then he would once again hunch over his desk and madly recopy as many documents as he could, and review even the few recopied by the others, to eliminate their errors. He would be deaf to the jests with which those others now amused themselves to tease him. Certain evenings, in order to finish the work assigned by the office, he would leave the ministry one hour after the others. The principal would see him arrive at the boarding school, out of breath, panting, with his eyes hardened by the continuous torment arising from his inability to defend himself from the difficulties and adversities of fete, to which, unfortunately, was now joined the ill will of the men.

"Why, no, no," the principal would say to comfort him, and sometimes he would even reproach him kindly.

But he was indifferent both to the man's comforting words and his reproaches, just as he never saw anything in the morning while running from his distant house outside the city to get to the office on time, or at noon, to return way over there to have lunch and then to get to the office punctually at three. He always went on foot, both to save the streetcar fare and out of fear of being late if he were to wait for the streetcar to arrive. In the evening he would be exhausted. He felt so tired, he didn't even have the strength to stand up while holding Ninni in his arms. He first had to sit down.

Sitting on the small balcony with its rusty iron railing that he at first had thought was so beautiful with its view of the suburban gardens, he would now have liked to reward himself for all the running around he had done, for the toils and troubles of the entire day. But the baby, who was already about three months old, didn't want to stay with him perhaps because, hardly ever seeing him during the day, the child still didn't recognize him. Perhaps also it was because Cesarino didn't know how to hold him well in his arms or because the baby was already sleepy, as the wet nurse would say to excuse him.

"Come now, give him back to me. I'll rock him to sleep and then I'll see to your supper."

Waiting for supper as he sat there on the little balcony, in the last cold glimmer of dusk, he looked (perhaps without even seeing) at the portion of moon already lit in the dull, empty sky. Then he lowered his eyes to the filthy, deserted little street bordered on one side by a dry and dusty hedge that protected the gardens. He felt his heart overcome in that tiredness by a sorrowful dreariness, but as soon as tears threatened to sting his eyes, he clenched his teeth, squeezed the iron rod of the railing in his fist and fixed his eyes on the only light in the little street—a light with two glass panes that the neighborhood boys had broken with stones. Deliberately he started thinking evil thoughts about the young students of the boarding school, even about the principal, now that he no longer felt he could have faith in him as before. He realized that the man was helping him, yes, but almost more for himself, for the satisfaction of feeling good, which now gave him, in receiving that help, something like a feeling of humiliation. Not to speak of those office companions with their filthy talk and certain lewd questions that were meant to humiliate him. They asked him *if and how he did it* and *whether he had ever done it.* And, lo and behold, a sudden gush of tears assailed him at the memory of an evening when, rushing as usual down the street like a blind man, he happened to bump into a streetwalker. She had pretended to block him and had suddenly pressed him to her bosom with both her arms, forcing him to inhale—with his nostrils pressed obscenely against her living flesh—her perfume, that same perfume his mother had worn. Therefore, moaning, he had torn himself away from her and had run away. He now felt lashed by the mockery of his colleagues. It seemed he could still hear them shouting,

"Little virgin! Little virgin!" and so he continued to tighten his grip on the bar of the railing and to clench his teeth. No, he would never be able to *do it,* not him, because he would forever... forever have in his nostrils, filling him with horror, that perfume his mother wore.

Now, in the silence, he heard the blunt thuds made by the chair's legs on the brick floor, first the two front ones; then the two back ones, as the wet nurse rocked the baby to sleep. And from beyond the hedge, there was the swishing sound of water coming out fanlike from the long, serpentine hose with which the gardener watered the vegetable garden. He liked this swishing sound. It refreshed his spirit. He did not want too much water to fell on any one spot if the gardener had a moment of distraction. He would notice it right away from the noise it made on the ground that became like clay and appeared flooded. Why did that small damask tablecloth now come to his mind, the one with the pale blue edge and the very tight fringes which his mother used to spread over a little table in offering tea to some friend of hers on the rare occasions when she happened to be home around five o'clock? That nice tablecloth... Ninni's layette... the elegance, the good taste, his mother's scrupulous cleanliness. Now look. Spread out on the table, there was a filthy rag of a tablecloth, and dinner was not yet prepared. His bed in the adjoining room was still not made up from the morning. If the baby at least were well cared for—but, no sir. The baby's smock was dirty, his little bib was dirty. He knew that if he should direct the slightest reprimand to the wet nurse, he was sure to anger her, and there would be the risk that she might vent her scorn on that innocent infant as soon as he, Cesarino, was absent. She would immediately have the double excuse that, having to look after the baby, she did not have time neither to put the house in order or to attend to the kitchen or that, if the baby lacked some attention, this stemmed from the feets that she also had to serve both as maid and cook. She was an ugly, boorish woman who had come up from the country and looked as rugged as a tree trunk. She now thought she would make herself beautiful by doing up her hair and adorning herself with frills. But patience! Her milk was good. The baby, though neglected, was thriving. Oh, how he resembled his mother! The same eyes and that small nose, that little mouth... The wet nurse tried to make him believe that the baby looked like him! Nonsense! Who knows whom he resembled! But by now he did not care to know. It was enough for him that Ninni looked like his mother. In feet, this made him happy because like that he wouldn't have to kiss any feature on that little face that might remind him of that unknown man whom at this point he not care to discover.

After supper, on the same table that had just been cleared, he began to study with the intention of taking his final examinations for his high school diploma the following year and then to enter the university with a tuition waver, if they would grant him one. He would enroll in law and, if he succeeded in obtaining a degree that would allow him to take some civil service examination for a secretarial position at the same Ministry of Public Education. He wanted to rise up as soon as possible from that wretched and not very secure position as copyist. But while studying certain evenings, he was gradually overwhelmed and overcome by a feeling of gloomy discouragement. The things he had to study seemed so remote from his present troubles! His mind wandered in that remoteness and he felt as if his anguish itself was vain and that it would not and could not ever end. The silence of those three almost bare rooms was so great that it made him notice even the buzzing of the kerosene lamp that he had taken from where it was hanging and placed on the table so that he might see better. He would take his glasses off his nose. He would stare at the flame with his eyes half-shut, and large tears would then gush from his eyes and fall onto the open book under his chin.

These were only fleeting moments. The next morning he would return to his torturous studies more obstinately than ever, stretching out his head from between his curved little shoulders the way nearsighted people do. His bony, waxen face would be strained and sweaty with that sleek, sickly hair which had grown too much between his ears and his cheeks. And his powerful lenses seemed to glaze his small, shiny and intense eyes, pinching and bruising the delicate sides of his nose.

From time to time Rosa, his former maid, would come by to pay him a little visit. Very quietly she too would point out all the defects of the wet nurse and, to put him on his guard, she would relate what the women of the neighborhood were saying about her. Cesarino would shrug his shoulders. He suspected that Rosa spoke out of rancor, because, from the very beginning, in an effort not be sent away, she had suggested that the baby be raised on sterilized milk, as she had seen many mothers do who were then quite pleased with the results. But finally he had to admit that she was right, when he found himself suddenly obliged to throw out the wet nurse, who was already two months pregnant. Luckily the baby did not suffer from the change in the way he was being weaned, also because of the loving care of the good old woman, who appeared very happy to return to the service of those two abandoned souls...

Now, finally, Cesarino could really savor the sweetness of a peace acquired with so much suffering. He knew that his Ninni was in good hands, and so he could work and study very serenely. In the evening, when he returned home, he found everything in order. And Ninni was as neat and clean as a bridegroom. His dinner was very tasty and his bed was soft. It was happiness itself. The first little screams, certain graceful little gestures of Ninni made him mad with joy. He would send him to be weighed every two days for fear that he might lose weight because of the artificial nursing, despite Rosa's continual reassurances:

"But can't you see that he's beginning to weigh more than I do? He's always got his trumpet in his mouth!"

— The trumpet was his feeding bottle.

"Come on, Ninni, play yourself a little tune!"

And Ninni would do so at once. He didn't have to be told twice. It wasn't good enough that others should hold the "trumpet" for him either. He wanted to do so by himself like a good trumpeter, and he would half shut his dear little eyes out of languid, sensual pleasure. The two of them would look at him in ecstasy and, since the baby would often fell asleep before he finished sucking, they would get up very quietly and go on tiptoe to put him back in his crib, holding their breath as they did so.

In the evening, he resumed his studies with redoubled effort, already sure of success. Cesarino now comprehended very well the real reasons why Napoleon Bonaparte had been defeated at Waterloo.

One evening, however, returning home—in a hurry, as usual, and almost thirsting for a kiss from his Ninni—he was stopped at the doorstep by Rosa who, all upset, informed him that there was a gentleman in the other room who wanted to speak to him and who had been waiting for him for a good half hour.

Cesarino found himself in front of a man who was about fifty years old. He was tall, well set and dressed entirely in black for very recent mourning. He was gray-haired, dark-complexioned and had a gloomy, serious air. He had gotten up at the sound of the doorbell and was waiting for him in the dining room.

"You'd like to talk to me?" asked Cesarino, observing him, anxious and bewildered.

"Yes, privately, if you would allow me."

"Come, go on in."

And Cesarino pointed to the door of his little room and let him go in ahead of him. Then, having closed the door with hands already shaking, he turned, his face changed and very pale, his eyes blinking behind his glasses and his brow knitted. He ventured the question:

"Alberto?"

"Rocchi, yes. I've come..."

Cesarino drew close to him, feverish and transfigured as if he was about to rail against him.

"To do what? In my house?"

The man drew back, growing pale and containing himself.

"Let me talk. I've come with good intentions."

"What intentions? My mother is dead!"

"I know."

"Ah, you know? And isn't that enough for you? Go away immediately or I'll make you regret it!"

"I beg your pardon!"

"Regret, regret coming here to inflict on me the shame..."

"No, no... pardon me..."

"The shame of the sight of you! Yes, sir. What do you want from me?"

"Pardon me, but if you don't let me talk... Calm down!" added the man, confounded by that outburst. "I understand... But it's necessary that I tell you..."

"No!" yelled Cesarino, resolute, trembling, raising his delicate fists. "Look, I don't want to know anything! I don't want any explanations! Let it be enough for you that you dared appear before me! Go away!"

"But my son is here..." then said the man, disturbed and out of patience.

"Your son?" railed Cesarino. "Ah, is that why you've come here? Now you remember that your son is here?"

"I couldn't before... If you don't let me explain..."

"What do you want to explain? Go away! Go away! You made my mother die! Go away or I'll call for help!"

Rocchi half closed his eyes. He took a breath that swelled his chest, heaved a deep sigh and said,

"All right. That means I'll have to go elsewhere to assert my rights."

And he started to go.

"Rights? You?" Cesarino yelled after the man, losing his temper. "Scoundrel! You killed my mother and now you want to assert your rights? You, against me? Rights?"

The gentleman turned to look at him glumly but then opened his mouth in a smile that expressed both disdain and pity for the frailty of the young man who was insulting him.

"We'll see," he said.

And away he went.

Cesarino remained in the dark, behind the door of that little room, trembling all over from the violence aroused in him, timid and weak, by the rancor, the shame, the fear of losing his adored young one. Composing himself as best he could, he went to knock on Rosa's door. The old woman, who had locked herself in with a key, was holding the baby tightly in her arms.

"I understand! I understand!" Rosa said to him.

"He wanted Ninni."

"Him?"

"Yes. And he wants to assert his rights, understand? He wants to..."

"Him? And who would say he's right?"

"He's the father. But can he possibly take Ninni from me now? I threw him out like a dog! I told him that... that he killed my mother and that I made a home for the baby... and that now he is mine... mine and no one can tear him away from my arms! Mine! Mine!... Can you imagine?... That miserable... mur... murderer..."

"Why, yes! Why, of course! Calm down, young man!" said Rosa, more afflicted and dismayed than he. "He certainly can't come to take the baby away from you by force. Undoubtedly you too can make yourself heard. I'd like to see him try to take away Ninni, whom we have raised. But don't worry, don't worry, he won't show up anymore, not after the fine reception you've given him."

But neither these nor other assurances repeated by the good old woman during the course of the evening sufficed to calm Cesarino. The next day, there at the ministry, he experienced a real, eternal torment. At noon he rushed home, trembling and breathless. He did not want to go back to the office for the three hours he was supposed to work in the afternoon, but Rosa urged to him to go, promising that she would keep the door bolted and would not open it for anyone, and that she wouldn't leave Ninni alone, not even for a minute. So he went, but he returned at six of clock without going to the boarding school to teach his young pupils.

Seeing him before her so dazed, depressed and bewildered, Rosa tried in every which way to rouse him, but it was in vain. Cesarino had a presentment that was gnawing at his heart and gave him no rest. He spent the entire night, sleepless.

The next day he did not return home at noon for lunch. Old Rosa was unable to understand why he was late. Finally, around four o'clock, she saw him arrive, panting, livid and with a grim stare in his eyes.

"I have to give him the baby. They called me to the police station. He was there, too. He showed my mother's letters. The baby is his."

He said this by fits and starts without raising his eyes to look at the baby, whom Rosa was holding in her arms.

"Oh, my sweetheart!" she exclaimed, hugging Ninni to her breast. "But how? What did he say? How could the judicial authorities?..."

"He's the father! He's the father!" replied Cesarino. "Therefore, the baby is his!"

"And you?" asked Rosa. "What will you do?"

"Me? I'll go with him. We'll go together."

"You're going with Ninni to his house?"

"Yes, to his house."

"Ah, like that?... Both together, then? Ah, that's good like that! You won't leave him... And what about me, young man, this poor Rosa?"

In order not to answer her directly, Cesarino took the baby in his arms, pressed him to his chest and, crying, began saying to him,

"What about poor Rosa, Ninni? She too, together with us? It's not right! We can't! We'll leave everything to poor Rosa. The few things that are here. We lived so well together, the three of us, isn't that so, my dear Ninni? But they've decided against it... they've decided..."

"All right," said Rosa, swallowing her tears. "Do you want to distress yourself like that for me now, young man? I'm old; I don't count anymore. God will provide for me. As long as the two of you are happy... Besides, tell me, won't I be able to come and see you and this little angel of mine? They surely won't send me away if I come. After all, why shouldn't it be like this? When this moment has passed, it'll perhaps even be a good thing for you, young man, right?"

"Perhaps," said Cesarino. "Meanwhile, Rosa, you've got to prepare everything quickly... everything we've gotten for Ninni, my things and yours too. We're going away this evening. We're expected for dinner. Listen, I'm leaving it all to you..."

"What are you saying, my dear young man!" exclaimed Rosa.

"All... all of the small amount of money that I have with me. I owe you a great deal more for all the affection... Quiet, quiet! Let's not speak of it. You know it, and I know it. Enough said. Even those few pieces of furniture... We'll find another house over there. You can do whatever you wish with this one. Don't thank me. Prepare everything, and let's go. You first... I wouldn't be able to go away, leaving you here. Then tomorrow you'll come to visit me and I'll leave you the key and everything else."

Old Rosa obeyed without answering. Her heart was so heavy that if she had opened her mouth to speak, sobs, certainly, not words, would have come out. She prepared everything, even her few personal belongings.

"May I leave them here?" she asked. "Anyhow, if I'll be coming back tomorrow..."

"Yes, certainly," answered Cesarino. "And now, here you are. Kiss Ninni... Kiss him and good-by."

Rosa took the baby in her arms, and he looked around, a little dismayed. But at first she couldn't loss him. She first had to pour out her heart a bit, remarking,

"It's foolish to cry... because tomorrow... Here, young man... take him. And take courage, eh? A kiss for you too... See you tomorrow!"

She left without looking back, smothering her sobs in her handkerchief.

Immediately Cesarino bolted the door. He ran his hand over his hair, which stood on end. He went to place Ninni on the bed. He put his silver watch in the baby's hand to keep him quiet. Very swiftly he wrote a few lines on a piece of paper, bequeathing to Rosa the shabby household goods. Then he ran off to the kitchen. Quickly, very quickly, he made a good fire in a brazier which he brought into the room. He closed the shutters and the door. Then, by the light of the little lamp that old Rosa always kept lit in front of an image of the Madonna, he stretched out on the bed next to Ninni. The baby let the watch fall onto the bed and—as usual—raised his hand to snatch the glasses off his brother's face. This time Cesarino let him snatch them. He shut his eyes and hugged the baby to his chest.

"Hushaby, Ninni, hushaby... Sleepy time, my pretty child, sleepy time."

The Trip

For the past thirteen years Adriana Braggi no longer left the old house steeped in cloisteral silence that she had entered as a young bride. She was no longer to be seen, not even behind the windowpanes, by the few passersby who from time to time climbed the steep, slippery, half-crumbling street that was so deserted that weeds grew in clusters between the cobblestones.

At age twenty-two when her husband had died, after only four years of marriage, she too was all but dead as far as the world was concerned. She was now thirty-five and still wore black as she had the first day of the tragedy. A black silk kerchief hid her beautiful brown hair, no longer arranged but roughly gathered into two bands and knotted at the back of her neck. Nevertheless, a sad yet sweet serenity shone in her pale, delicate face.

No one wondered at this reclusive existence in that small mountain town in Sicily's interior. Strict local customs virtually required that a wife follow her husband to the grave. Widows were supposed to stay locked up like this, in perpetual mourning, until death.

Moreover, the women of the few respectable families, the unmarried as well as the married, were hardly ever seen on the street. They went out only on Sundays to go to Mass and, on rare occasions, to exchange visits. At such times they vied with one another in showing off their richest and most fashionable dresses, brought in from the finest shops in Palermo and Catania, as well as their precious jewels and gold ornaments. This was not done out of coquettishness. In fact, they would walk along with a serious demeanor, their cheeks blushing and their eyes downcast, close beside their husband, father or older brother. This ostentatious display was almost obligatory. These visits and those few steps to the church were major expeditions to be prepared for one a day in advance. The family's dignity was at stake and the men concerned themselves with this matter. Indeed, they were the real sticklers because they wanted to show that they knew how to spend for their women and had what it takes to do so.

Ever submissive and obedient, the women dressed up as the men desired, so as not to make them cut a poor figure. After these brief appearances, they would return peacefully to their household chores and, if they were married, they would devote themselves to the task of having as many children as God might send (this was their cross). If they were young and single, they would wait for the day when their family would say to them, "Here you go, marry this one," and that's the one they would marry, and their men would be satisfied and content to receive their servile and loveless fidelity.

Only a blind faith in the rewards of the hereafter could keep them from despairing and help them endure the dreary boredom in which their days went by, one after another. A boredom in which each day was like every other in that small mountain town which was so silent, under that intense and ardent blue sky, that it seemed almost deserted. It was a town with narrow, badly-cobbled streets that ran between the small rustic stone houses with their clay conduits and uncovered tin gutters.

If you went to the very end of these little streets and looked out over that rolling expanse of land scorched by the sulphur mines, the sight would make your heart sink. The sky was arid and so was the earth. In that motionless silence lulled by the buzzing of insects, the chirping of crickets, the distant crowing of a rooster or the barking of a dog, there arose from the earth, in the dazzling noonday sun, the odor of a multitude of withered grasses, mingled with the smell of manure emanating from the stables.

All the houses, even the few that belonged to the rich, lacked water. In the vast courtyards, as well as at the ends of the streets, there were old cisterns that stood at the mercy of the heavens. Even in the winter it rained little and when it did it was a holiday. All the women would then set out buckets and basins, tubs and small casks, and would stand in their doorways, their dresses of woven goat hair tucked between their legs, to watch the rain as it flowed in torrents down the steep paths, and to listen to it as it gurgled in the gutters and through the downspouts and pipes of the cisterns. It washed the cobblestones, it washed the walls of the houses, and everything seemed to breathe more freely in the fragrant freshness of the wet earth.

The men found some way or another to amuse themselves in their various business affairs, in the struggles of the town's political parties, in the cafes or at the casino in the evenings. But the loveless married women, who ever since childhood had been forced to stifle every instinct for vanity, after having attended like servants to their monotonous household chores, languished miserably with a baby on their laps or a rosary in their hands as they waited for their man, their master, to arrive home.

Adriana Braggi had never loved her husband at all.

Having a very weak constitution and being in a constant state of agitation because of his delicate health, her husband had oppressed and tormented her for four years. He was very jealous even of his older brother, whom he knew he had grievously wronged, or rather, actually betrayed, in marrying her. Once again tradition had strict dictates. It demanded that of all the male children of a wealthy family, only one, the oldest, was to marry, so that the family's fortune would not be dissipated among a great number of heirs.

Cesare Braggi, the older brother, had never shown any sign of resenting this betrayal, possibly because his father, who had died shortly before the wedding, had arranged that he remain the head of the family and that the second-born, Adriana's husband, should obey his brother totally.

When she had entered the old Braggi house, Adriana experienced some humiliation in discovering that she was subject to her brother-in-law in that way. Her situation had become doubly burdensome and irritating when her husband told her in a fit of jealousy that Cesare himself had previously intended to marry her. She no longer knew how to behave in her brother-in-law's presence, and the less Cesare allowed her to feel the weight of his authority, the more her embarrassment grew. From the first day he had received her with kindness and sincere cordiality and treated her like a real sister.

He was gentle and polite. He displayed an exquisite, unaffected refinement in his way of speaking and dressing, and in every other respect. Neither his contacts with the uncouth townsfolk, nor his daily tasks, nor those slovenly habits which that empty and miserable provincial life induced for so many months of the year had ever succeeded in hardening him or even changing him a single bit.

Besides, each year for several days and often for longer than a month, Cesare would leave the little town and his business. He would go to Palermo, Naples, Rome and Milano, and plunge into each city's life in order—as he put it—to bathe in civilization. And he always returned from these trips mentally and physically rejuvenated.

When Adriana, who had never set foot outside her native town, saw him return that way to the large and ancient house where time stagnated in a deathly silence, she always felt a sense of secret, indescribable turmoil.

Her brother-in-law brought back with him the spirit of a world that she couldn't even imagine.

Her turmoil would only grow when she heard her husband's guffaws as he listened in the other room to his brother's racy adventures. This turmoil would turn into indignation and then revulsion, in the evenings, when her husband, after listening to his brother's stories, would come to join her in the bedroom, all flushed, overexcited and restless. Her indignation and revulsion were for her husband, and these feelings became stronger the more she saw her brother-in-law's respect, or rather reverence, for her.

When her husband died, Adriana had experienced a sense of anguish and great fear at the thought of having to remain alone with Cesare in that house. Yes, she did have the two little ones born during those four years but, although she was a mother, she hadn't been able to overcome her instinctive youthful shyness in her brother-in-law's presence. In reality, this shyness had never been a serious problem but now it was, and she blamed her jealous husband for it since he had oppressed her with a most suspicious and insidious surveillance.

Cesare Braggi, with exquisite solicitude, had then invited Adriana's mother to come and stay with her widowed daughter. So gradually Adriana, freed from her husband's odious tyranny, had been able to find, if not complete serenity, at least a little peace of mind with the help of her mother's companionship. She devoted herself with utter abandon to the care of her sons, lavishing upon them all the love and tenderness that had found no outlet in her unfortunate marriage.

Each year Cesare continued to take his month-long trip to the mainland, bringing back gifts for her and the grandmother, and also for his little nephews, toward whom he always demonstrated the most gentle fatherly care.

Without the protection of a man, the women were afraid in the house, especially at night. During the days he was absent, Adriana felt that the silence, which had become deeper and gloomier, was holding a great and mysterious disaster in suspense above the house. So she would become extremely frightened when she would hear the creaking of the old cistern pulley at the end of the solitary, steep street when a breath of wind happened to shake its rope. But could she expect him, after a year of work and boredom, to deprive himself of his only entertainment for the sake of two women and two little ones who, after all, were not his? He could have decided not to look after them at all and live a free and selfish life, because, after all, his brother had prevented him from having a family of his own. Instead—how could she help noticing it?—as soon as those brief vacations were over, he devoted himself entirely to the house and to his fatherless nephews and nieces.

With time the resentment dulled in Adriana's heart. Her children were growing, and she was happy they were growing under their uncle's guidance. At this point her dedication had become almost total, so that she marveled if her brother-in-law or her children resisted some excessive care that she gave them. She felt she never did enough. What was she to think of, if not of them?

Her mother's death had been a great sorrow for her. She had been deprived of her sole companion. For quite some time she had spoken with her as if with a sister. Nevertheless, when her mother was beside her she could think of herself as still young, which, in feet, she was. But with her mother gone and both children almost grown up—one sixteen, the other fourteen, and each as tall as their uncle—she began to feel old and to consider herself in that way.

She was in this frame of mind when, for the first time, she felt a vague malaise, a feeling of tiredness, a slight heaviness in one shoulder and in the chest, a certain dull pain that sometimes affected her entire left arm and that from time to time became piercing and took her breath away.

She didn't complain, and perhaps no one would ever have known about it if one day at table she had not had one of those sudden acute attacks.

The old family doctor was called in and, from the very beginning he was dismayed by the symptoms. His dismay increased after his long and careful examination of the sick woman.

The trouble was in the pleura. But what exactly was it? The old doctor attempted an exploratory puncture with the help of a colleague but without any result. Then, noting a certain hardening of the upper and lower scapular glands, he advised Braggi to bring his sister-in-law immediately to Palermo, giving him clearly to understand that he feared it was an internal tumor that, perhaps, was incurable.

It was impossible to depart immediately. Adriana, after thirteen years of cloistered life, lacked the clothes she needed for appearing in public and for traveling. They had to write to Palermo to provide her with a new wardrobe as soon as possible.

Adriana tried to counter the idea in every way possible, assuring her brother-in-law and her children that she did not feel all that bad. A trip? The very thought of it gave her the shudders. And then it was precisely the time when Cesare customarily took his month-long vacation. If she left with him, she would take away his freedom and spoil any fun he might have. No, no, she would not do that under any condition! And then, how and to whom would she leave the children? To whom would she entrust the house? She put forth all these objections but her brother-in-law and her children demolished them with a laugh. She stubbornly insisted that the trip would certainly do her more harm than good. Oh, good Lord, she no longer even knew what streets looked like! She wouldn't know how to take her first step! For goodness sake, for goodness sake, would they leave her in peace!

When the dresses and hats arrived from Palermo, her two sons were overjoyed.

With the large boxes wrapped in oilcloth, they exultantly entered their mother's room, shouting and screaming that she must try the clothes on immediately. They wanted to see their dear mother look beautiful, such as they had never seen her before. They begged her in every which way, so that she had to yield to them and satisfy their wishes.

The dresses were black for mourning but were very elegant and tailored with marvelous skill. Having become completely ignorant and inexperienced regarding the latest fashions, she did not know how to put them on. Where and how should she join the many small hooks she found here and there? That collar—oh good Lord, was it supposed to be so high? And those sleeves with all those puffs... Is that how they were wearing them now?

Meanwhile, behind the door, the children were kicking up a storm impatiently.

"Mamma, are you finished? Not yet?"

As if their mamma was in there dressing for a party! They no longer thought of the reason why those clothes had arrived, and actually at that moment she herself didn't think about it either.

When she raised her eyes in her confusion and excitement and saw herself in the wardrobe mirror, she experienced an extremely violent feeling that was almost one of shame. This dress that elegantly but provocatively put into relief her hips and bosom made her look as slim and lively as a young girl. She had felt already old but now, suddenly, she found herself in that mirror, young and beautiful. A new person!

"Oh no! No! Impossible!" she shouted, twisting her neck and raising her hand to block her view.

The children, hearing this exclamation, began to knock even louder on the door, with their hands, with their feet, and to push against it, shouting for her to open up, to let them see her.

Oh no! No! She was embarrassed. She looked ludicrous! Oh no.

But they threatened to break down the door, so she had to open it.

At first, the children too were dazzled by this sudden transformation. Their mother tried to defend herself by repeating, "Oh no, leave me alone! No, no! Impossible! Are all of you crazy?" when the brother-in-law unexpectedly appeared. Oh, for goodness sake! She tried to run away, to hide herself as if he had caught her naked. But her sons held her back and showed her to their uncle, who laughed at her embarrassment.

"But it really looks nice on you" he said at last, becoming serious again. "Come on, let us see you."

She tried to raise her head.

"I feel I'm wearing a costume..."

"Oh no! Why? On the contrary, it looks very nice on you. Turn around a little... like that, sideways..."

She obeyed, forcing herself to appear calm, but her bosom, well outlined by the dress, rose and fell with her frequent breathing, betraying her inner commotion caused by his calm and attentive examination, that of an expert connoisseur.

"It really looks nice.—And the hats?"

"Those awful baskets!" exclaimed Adriana, almost appalled.

"Oh yes, it's fashionable to wear them very large."

"How can I get them on my head? I'll have to comb my hair some other way."

Cesare, calm and smiling, again looked at her, then said,

"Why yes, you've got a lot of hair..."

"'Yes, yes, dear Mother! Comb your hair right away!" said the children, approvingly.

Adriana smiled sadly.

"See what you're making me do?" she said, addressing her brother-in-law as well.

The departure was set for the following morning.

—Alone with him!

She was accompanying him on one of those trips that she had once thought about with such turmoil. She had only one fear now, that of appearing troubled in front of the man who stood before her, completely attentive to her but calm as always.

This calm of his, which was very natural, would have made her consider her turmoil as something unworthy and such as to make her blush over it, if she had not had recourse to a half-conscious fiction. Precisely so as not to be ashamed of it and to give herself courage, she ascribed it to something else, to the novelty of the trip itself, to the assault of so many strange impressions on her closed and bashful soul. She adduced the effort she made to control this turmoil (which, after all, interpreted like that, wouldn't have been at all reproachable) to the propriety of not making herself appear so impressionable, so astonished in the presence of one who, being an expert in everything and the master of himself for so many years, might feel annoyed and displeased by her behavior. In feet, she might even appear ridiculous at her age, for that almost childish wonderment that glowed in her eyes.

Therefore, she forced herself to restrain the cheerful, feverish eagerness of her glance and not turn her head continually from one window to the other, as she was tempted to do, in order not to miss any of the many, many things upon which her darting eyes rested for a brief moment and for the first time. She forced herself to hide her wonderment, to control her curiosity which, actually, she should have kept alive and alert to overcome the stupefaction and dizziness caused by the rhythmic rumble of the wheels and the illusory flight of hedges, trees and hills.

She was traveling on a train for the first time. At every moment, at every revolution of the wheels, she had the impression of penetrating, of advancing, into an unknown world that was suddenly being created in her soul. It was a world of images that, however close they may have been to her, all the same seemed far and gave her, together with the delight she felt in seeing them, a most subtle and indescribable feeling of pain, the pain caused by the realization that they had always existed beyond and outside her existence and her imagination—the pain of being a stranger among them and just passing through, and knowing that without her they would continue living for themselves, caught up in their own lives.

There, before her eyes, were the humble houses of a village, roofs and windows and doors and steps and streets. The people living there were like she herself had been for so many years in her small town. They were shut in there, on that speck of land, with their own habits and occupations. Beyond what their eyes managed to see, nothing else existed for those people. For them the world was a dream. So many of them were born there, grew up and died there without having seen anything of what she was going to see on this trip, which was very little when compared to the immensity of the world, but which, all the same, seemed already so much to her.

Now and then, as she looked around, she would encounter the glance and smile of her brother-in-law, who asked,

"How do you feel?"

She would reply with a nod of the head,

"Fine."

More than once her brother-in-law came to sit beside her, to point out and mention the name of a distant town where he had been,—and that mountain there with its menacing appearance, every feature in the landscape that stood out and that he imagined would especially attract her attention. He didn't realize that every single thing, even the most insignificant, those that were the commonest for him, were meanwhile arousing a raging flood of new sensations in her. All the information, the explanations he gave her, rather than increasing her interest, diminished and cooled that lively, floating image of grandeur that she, in her bewilderment, and still with a feeling of indescribable pain, was creating for herself at the sight of this immense, unknown world.

Moreover, amid this inner flood of sensations, his voice, rather than casting light, almost overwhelmed her with violent darkness that brought on cold shivers. Then the feeling of pain in her became sharper and more distinct. She saw herself as wretchedly ignorant and she felt an obscure and almost hostile resentment toward all those things which suddenly, too late for her, filled her eyes with tears and entered her soul.

In Palermo, the following day, she descended the stairs of the chief clinician's office after an extremely long visit. From the effort her brother-in-law made to hide his profound dismay, from the exaggerated solicitude with which he again wanted to be shown how the prescribed medicine was to be taken and from the manner in which the doctor had answered him—from all this she clearly understood that the doctor had pronounced a death sentence on her. The poisonous mixture, to be taken with great care in drops twice a day before meals, was nothing more than a merciful deception or the viaticum of a slow agony.

She was still a bit dazed and nauseated by the diffused odor of ether in the doctor's house when she left the shadow of the stairs and was on the street, there in the light of the dazzling setting sun, beneath a flaming sky which launched from the marina what seemed like an immense cloud over the very long Corso. In that golden glow, among the carriages, she saw the noisy, swarming crowd of people whose feces and clothes were lit up with purple reflections, flickers of light and colored flashes—like those from precious stones—that came from the windows, signs and mirrors of the shops, and she felt life, life, only life, violently entering her soul. It came through her overexcited senses as if from a divine intoxication. Nor did she feel any anguish. She didn't give a fleeting thought to death, which was near at hand and inevitable, to death, which was already within her, there under her left shoulder where she periodically felt the pains more sharply. No, no, she thought of life, only life! Meanwhile, this inner turmoil that threw her mind into confusion assailed her throat where something (she didn't know what), something like an old pain stirred up from the depths of her being suddenly choked her up and now made her burst into tears, even amid so much joy.

"It's nothing... nothing..." she said to her brother-in-law, with a smile that shone very brightly in her eyes, through her tears. "It seems I'm... I don't know... Let's go, let's go..."

"To the hotel?"

"No... no..."

"Then let's go have dinner at the "Chalet" by the sea, at the Foro Italico. Would you enjoy that?"

"Yes, wherever you'd like!"

"Very well. Let's go! Then we'll see the promenade at the Foro. We'll hear the music..."

They took a carriage and headed for that gleaming, blinding cloud...

Ah, what an evening that was for her at the "Chalet" by the sea, under the moon, in view of the illuminated Foro traversed by the continuous clatter of scintillating carriages, amid the odor of seaweed that came from the sea and the scent of orange blossoms that emanated from the gardens! Bewildered as if in a superhuman spell to which a certain anguish hindered her from abandoning herself totally—an anguish occasioned by the doubt that what she was seeing wasn't real—she felt distant, distant even from herself, bereft of memory, consciousness and thought, in an infinitely distant dream.

This sensation of infinite distance became more intense the following morning as she rode in a carriage through the endless deserted lanes of

Parco della Favorita. At a certain point, heaving an extremely deep sigh, she was almost able to come back to herself from that distance and measure it without even breaking the spell or disturbing the intoxication of that sunlit dream among the plants that seemed themselves absorbed in the endless dream.

Unwittingly she turned to look at her brother-in-law and smiled at him out of gratitude.

However, that smile abruptly roused in her a vivid and profound compassion for herself, condemned as she was to die now that so many marvelous and beautiful things were unfolding before her astonished eyes like the receding promise of a life that could have also been hers, as it was for the many, many people who lived there. She felt that it had perhaps been a cruel thing to make her take that trip.

But a little later the carriage finally stopped at the far end of a remote lane. Then, with his assistance, she got off to see the Fountain of Hercules from up close. She stood there, in front of the fountain, under the cobalt blue sky, which was so intense that it almost seemed black around the fulgent marble statue of the demigod atop the tall column that rose from the middle of the large basin. She bent over to look at the glassy water upon which a few leaves and some greenish algae were floating, their shadows reflected at the bottom of the conch. Then, at each slight ripple of the water, she saw a sort of fine mist arise over the impossible faces of the sphinxes that guard the basin, and she felt the shadow of a thought passing over her own face, which came like a cool breath of air from the water. At once a great astonishing silence enlarged her spirit immeasurably and, as if a light had suddenly come from other heavens to brighten that incommensurable void, she now felt as if she was almost touching eternity and acquiring a lucid, boundless knowledge of everything, of that infinity that lurks in the depths of the mysterious soul. She felt as if she had lived and that this would be enough for her because for an instant, *that* instant, she had experienced eternity.

She suggested to her brother-in-law that they go back that very day. She wanted to return home in order to leave him free after those four days taken away from his vacation. He would lose one more day in escorting her home, then he could resume his trip, his annual jaunt to towns farther away, beyond that boundless deep blue sea. He could do so without worrying because she would not die so soon, surely not during this month that he was on vacation.

She didn't tell him any of this; she only thought it, and asked him if he would kindly bring her back to their town.

"Oh no, why?" he answered. "We're here now. You'll come with me to Naples. We'll consult some other doctors down there, just to be doubly sure."

"No, no, for heaven's sake, Cesare! Let me go back home. It's no use!"

"Why? Not at all. It would be better. To be doubly sure."

"Isn't what we found out here enough? There's nothing wrong with me. I feel fine, see? I'll take the medicine. That'll be enough."

He looked at her gravely and said,

"Adriana, this is what I want."

And so she could make no further reply. She saw herself as the typical woman of her town who must never question what a man decides is just and proper. She thought that he wanted to have the personal satisfaction of knowing that he had not relied on one opinion alone, the satisfaction of knowing that the others in town might say after she died: "He did everything he could to save her. He brought her to Palermo, and to Naples too..." Or perhaps he really hoped that another doctor, a better doctor from some more distant place, might find her illness curable and have a remedy to save her. Or perhaps... why yes, this is what she ought to believe... Knowing that she was irremediably lost, perhaps he wished to give her this final and extraordinary diversion as a slight compensation for her cruel fate.

But she was frightened, yes, frightened of that great stretch of sea to be crossed. The very sight of it, with this thought in mind, took her breath away. It was as if she had to swim across it.

"But no, you'll see," he reassured her, smiling. "You won't even notice you're at sea in this season. See how calm it is? And then, you'll experience life aboard a steamboat... You won't feel anything."

Could she confess to him the obscure presentment that troubled her at the sight of the sea? What if she were to leave, if she were to pull away from the shores of the island that already seemed so far from her small town and so new, and where she had already experienced so much and such strange turmoil? If she were to venture with him still farther, lost with him in that tremendous and mysterious expanse of sea—if she were to do this, she most certainly would not return to her home, she would never again cross that water. At least, not alive. No, she couldn't confess this even to herself. She, too, believed that she feared the sea itself, for the sole reason that never before had she even so much as seen it from afar, and now to have to cross it...

That very evening they embarked for Naples.

As soon as the steamer moved away from the dock and left the harbor, Adriana recovered from her dizziness brought on by the bustle and confusion of the many people who were shouting as they went up and down the gangplank, and by the creaking of the cranes on the holds. She saw everything gradually becoming smaller and more distant: the people on the wharf who kept on waving their handkerchiefs, the dock, the houses. Finally, the entire city became a blurred white stripe, spangled here and there with dim lights, under the large encircling chain of reddish gray mountains. Once again she felt lost in a dream, another marvelous dream that, nevertheless, made her eyes open wide in dismay. And so much more so because on that ship that was so large, yes, but perhaps fragile, since it vibrated like that at the hollow and rhythmical splashes of the propellers, she was entering the two measureless immensities of sky and sea.

He smiled at her dismay and invited her to get up. Then, with an intimacy that she had never before permitted, he slipped an arm under hers to hold her up and led her to the deck itself to see the shiny, powerful steel pistons that drove the propellers. But already upset by that unaccustomed intimacy, she could not bear the sight and, experiencing the hot air and heavy stench that emanated from there, she was about to feint. She leaned back and almost rested her head on his shoulder but suddenly restrained herself, terrified by an instinctive desire to abandon herself, to which she had almost yielded.

And again he asked her, this time with greater concern,

"Do you feel sick?"

Unable to speak, she replied with a shake of the head. Then the two, arm in arm, walked toward the stern to gaze at the seething long phosphorescent wake in the sea that had already turned black under the star-dusted sky, as the enormous smokestack belched forth its slow, dense smoke that almost glowed from the heat of the engine. Finally, to complete the spell, the moon emerged from the sea. Appearing at first amid the mist on the horizon, it seemed like a lugubrious fiery mask that rose menacingly to watch over its watery dominions in the frightful silence; then gradually it brightened and contracted neatly within its snow-white splendor that shone over the broad, shining expanse of endless silver. And then, more than ever, Adriana felt increasing within her all the anguish and dismay that came from the ecstasy that ravished her and led her irresistibly, exhausted as she was, to bury her face in his chest.

It happened in Naples, in an instant, as they were leaving a "cafe-chantant" where they had dined and spent the evening. Accustomed as he was, on his annual trips, to leaving such night spots with a lady under his arm, he now offered her this gesture of courtesy. And in so doing he suddenly spotted, under her large black feathery hat, the glint of ardent eyes and immediately, almost unwittingly, with his arm, he quickly and forcefully pressed her arm against his chest. That was all. The fire suddenly blazed forth.

In the darkness of the carriage that was bringing them back to the hotel, joined mouth to mouth insatiably, they said everything to each other in a few moments, everything that he, in an instant, in a flash, had deduced from the glint in her eyes: her entire life of silent martyrdom. She told him how she had loved him—always, always, without wanting to, without even knowing that she did. He told her how much he had desired her ever since she was a very young girl, and how he dreamed of making her his, like this—his, his!

It was a delirium, a frenzy fueled by their violent, untiring craving to compensate, in those few days remaining to them because of her death sentence, for all those lost years of stifled passion and hidden feverish love. It was also fueled by their need to blind themselves, lose themselves, not see themselves as they had been to each other during those many years, with their falsely honest appearances down there in that small town of rigid customs where their love, their subsequent marriage, would appear as an unheard of sacrilege.

Their marriage? No! Why should she force him into an act that was sacrilegious to everyone? Why bind him to herself, she who now had so little time to live? No, no. She would resign herself to love, a frenetic love, for the few days that the trip would last. It would be a one-way love trip ending in death.

She could no longer return and face her children. She had strongly sensed this when she departed. She had known that if she crossed the sea, it would all end for her. Now, away, away, she would go away, farther north, arm in arm with him like this--blind until her death.

So they passed through Rome, then Florence, then Milan, hardly seeing anything. Death, which lurked inside her with its attacks and piercing pain, spurred them, stirring up their ardent love.

"It's nothing!" she would say at every attack, at every pang. "It's nothing..."

She would offer him her mouth, with the pallor of death on her face.

"Adriana, you're suffering..."

"No, it's nothing! What does it matter to me?"

On the last day, in Milan, shortly before departing for Venice, she saw her haggard face in the mirror. And when, after the night trip, in the silence of the dawn, there opened before her the dreamlike vision of the city emerging splendid and melancholic from the water, she understood that she had reached her destiny, that her trip had to end there.

Nevertheless, she wanted to have her day in Venice. All day until evening, until nightfall, she drifted through the silent canals in a gondola. And all night long she stayed awake with a strange impression of that day—a day of velvet.

The velvet upholstery of the gondola? The velvet shadows of certain canals? Who knows? Perhaps even the velvet lining of a coffin.

The following morning, when he left the hotel to mail some letters to Sicily, she entered his room. She spotted a torn envelope on the night stand. She recognized the handwriting of her older son. She brought the envelope to her lips and kissed it in desperation. Then she went back to her own room and took from her leather purse the bottle with the poisonous mixture still intact. She threw herself on the unmade bed and drank the contents in one gulp.

The Stuffed Bird

Except for their father, who died of pneumonia at age fifty, everyone else in the family—mother and brothers and sisters and maternal aunts and uncles—died quite young of consumption, one after another.

What a fine procession of coffins!

Only the two of them were still holding out, Marco and Annibale Picotti, and they appeared determined not to give in to the disease that had wiped out both sides of the family.

They watched each other with constant vigilance and trepidation, and followed their doctors' orders with utmost rigor not only as to the quantity and quality of their food and the various supplements to be taken either as pills or with a spoon but also as to the clothes to wear according to each season and the slightest variation in temperature, when to go to bed and when to get up, and the short walks to be taken and what were the other minor and permissible diversions, all of which themselves smacked of treatment and prescription.

By living in this manner, they hoped that both of them—first Marco, then Annibale—would exceed in perfect health the maximum age reached by all of their relatives, except for their father, who had died of another disease.

When they eventually succeeded, they thought that they had attained a great victory.

But Annibale, the younger of the two, became so bold that he began to relax somewhat those most rigorous restraints that up till then he had imposed on himself and gradually to allow himself to commit some not so minor transgressions.

His brother Marco tried to call him to order with the authority of his two or three years. But Annibale, as if he could now afford to guard less against death since it had not overtaken him at the age it did the rest of the family, refused to listen.

Yes, they had the same physique, short and rather sturdy, with a pudgy, turned-up nose, slanted eyes, narrow forehead and big mustache. But he, Annibale, though younger, was more robust than his brother. In feet, he had a fairly large potbelly, of which he was quite proud, a larger chest and broader shoulders. Now then, if Marco, though frailer, was getting along so well, couldn't he permit himself some minor transgressions and waste with impunity what he had more of?

After doing his duty as his conscience dictated, Marco put aside his warnings and reprimands in order to see—without any risk to himself—what effect these transgressions would have on his brother's health. Because, if in the long run they caused no harm, perhaps he too might allow them for himself, a little at a time. He could at least try.

What! No, no! Horrors! One day Annibale came to tell him that he had fallen in love and wanted to get married. Imbecile! Get married, with that terrible threat hanging over his head? Get married... to whom? Death? Besides, it would have been a crime, by God, to bring into the world other unfortunates! And who was the wretch who was lending herself to such a crime? To a double, double crime?

Annibale got angry. He told his brother that he absolutely could not allow him to use such words regarding the woman who would soon be his wife. Besides, if he had to preserve his life like that, on the condition that he did not live it, it was just as well that he lose it. A little sooner, a little later, what did it matter? He was sick and tired of this. Yes, and enough is enough.

His brother stood there looking at him, his face assuming an expression of pity and scorn as he shook his head slightly, ever so slightly.

That fool! To live... not to live... As if that were the question! It was necessary not to die! And not at all for fear of death, but because this was a terrible injustice against which his entire being rebelled. And not only for himself but also for all his deceased relatives whom he, with his hard, stubborn resistance, had to avenge.

Enough, yes, enough. He didn't want to get angry. He even regretted having initially become upset and excited. Never again! Never again!

If Annibale wanted to get married, he was as free as the wind! As for himself, he alone would be left to look death in the eye without allowing himself to be enticed by life's traps.

Set terms, though. To live together—nothing doing. Troubles, worries—nothing doing. If Annibale wanted to get married—out! Out, because he, Marco, was the older brother, the head of the house and, therefore, the house was his by right. Everything else would be divided equally. Even the household furniture, yes indeed. He could take away every piece he wanted, but very slowly and gently, without raising dust, because he, yes he, wanted to take care of his health.

That wardrobe? Why yes, and that chest of drawers too, and the dressing table and the chairs and the washstand... yes... yes... Those curtains? Why yes, those too... and, of course, the big dining room table for all the thriving children he would have, and the glass cabinet with all the china as well. Provided, in short, that he didn't touch his room, with those huge old armchairs and the couch—both upholstered in fake leather—that he was so fond of, and those two bookcases full of old books and the desk. Not those; those he wanted for himself.

"This too?" asked Annibale with a smile.

And he pointed to a large stuffed bird standing erect on a parrot perch between the two bookcases. It was so old that you could no longer tell what sort of bird it was from its faded feathers.

"This too. Everything in here," said Marco. "What's so funny? It's a stuffed bird, a family memento. Leave it alone!"

He didn't want to tell him that the bird, being so well preserved, seemed a good omen to him and, because of its age, gave him a certain sense of comfort whenever he looked at it.

When Annibale got married, Marco refused to take part in the wedding celebration. Only once, out of propriety, had he gone to the fiancee's home, and he hadn't even offered her a word of congratulations or an expression of best wishes. A cold five-minute visit. He certainly wasn't going to go to his brother's home after he returned from his honeymoon—or ever. Thinking of that marriage, he felt sick, a trembling in his leg.

"What ruin! What madness!" he repeated endlessly as he moved about the large and tightly-shut room that reeked of medicine, his eyes staring into space, his restless fingers running over the furniture left behind. "What ruin! What madness!"

Clearly visible on the old wallpaper were the outlines of the other pieces of furniture that his brother had taken away, and those outlines increased his sense of emptiness, an emptiness in which he felt almost obliterated and in which he wandered about like a soul in torment.

Come now, no! He should not get discouraged. He should no longer think about that ingrate, that madman! He would learn to depend only on himself.

And he began to whistle very softly or to drum on the windowpane as he peered outside at the trees of his little garden that had been stripped bare by the cold autumn wind, until he saw, there on the very same windowpane upon which he was drumming, oh God, a dead fly, withered but still hanging by one of its tiny legs.

Many months went by, almost a year since his brother's wedding.

On Christmas Eve, Marco heard the sound of bagpipes and a mouth harp coming from the street, and the chorus of women and children who had gathered for the last day of the novena in front of the small chapel adorned with leafy branches. He heard the crackling fire burning two large sheaves of straw next to the chapel and, terribly depressed, he got ready for bed at the usual time when a furious ringing of the doorbell made him jump with a start, almost along with everything else in the house.

A visit from Annibale and his sister-in-law. Annibale and Lillina.

They burst in all bundled up and puffing, and began stamping their feet from the cold. They laughed and laughed... How they laughed! They were lively, merry and in a festive mood.

They seemed drunk.

Oh, just a short ten-minute visit to wish him a happy holiday. They didn't want him to delay his going to bed for a single moment on their account. And... couldn't, meanwhile, even a little crack be opened to air the place out a bit? No? It couldn't, even for a minute? My God, and what was that ugly beast, that awful stuffed bird doing there on the perch? And this? Oh, it's a little scale. For medicines, right? Cute, cute. And Donna Fanny? Where was Donna Fanny?

Not for a second, during all those ten minutes, did Lillina stop jumping about here and there in her brother-in-law's room.

Marco Picotti was stunned as if by a violent gust of wind that had come to throw into disorder not only his old quiet room but his entire soul as well.

"And so... And so..." he began saying as he sat on his bed after they had left. And he scratched his forehead with both hands. "And so..."

He was unable to finish his sentence.

Was it possible? He had thought for sure that his brother, a week after the wedding, would immediately break down and fall to pieces. Instead, instead, there he was—and in great shape. He was doing quite well! And how cheerful! He was actually happy.

So then?... Was it really possible that he too did not need all those oppressive treatments and that frightful vigilance? Could he too escape the nightmare that was suffocating him? And live; live! Plunge into life like his brother?

Laughing, his brother had told him that he no longer followed any treatment or diet. Away with everything! To the devil with doctors and medications!

"What if I should try it too?"

He decided to do so and, for the first time, went to Annibale's home.

He was received so warmly that for a while he was stunned. He would shut his eyes and stretch out his hands as if to defend himself whenever Lillina made a motion of wanting to hug him. Oh, what a cute little devil, what a cute little devil, that Lillina! She was bubbly. She was life! She insisted on his staying for dinner with them. And how much she made him eat, and how much she made him drink! He got up tipsy, but more from joy than from the wine.

But in the evening, as soon as he got home, Marco Picotti felt ill. He came down with a bad cold in his chest and stomach that kept him bedridden for several days.

In vain Annibale tried to convince him that this had happened because he had worried too much and had not plunged into the foolish decision courageously and cheerfully. No, no! Never again! Never again! And he looked at his brother with such eyes that suddenly Annibale... no, why?

"What... what are you looking at?" Annibale asked his brother, turning pale and sporting a faded smile on his lips.

The poor wretch! Death... death... He already had the sign of it on his face, the unfailing sign!

Marco had noticed it when his brother had suddenly blanched.

His cheeks were still flushed, but as soon as his merriment had been extinguished, lo and behold, there on his cheekbones, the two fires of death, dark and vivid.

In fact, Annibale Picotti died about three years after his wedding.

For Marco it was a devastating blow.

He had foreseen it, yes indeed. He knew very well that it had to end like that for his brother. But, meanwhile, what a terrible warning for himself, and what a scare!

He even refused to accompany him to the cemetery; he would have been affected too deeply. And he would have felt too much scorn, or rather hatred, for the people who, on the one hand, would have pitied him but, on the other, would have stared sharply into his face to see if he too had the signs of the disease that had brought death to everyone in his family, including, now, his brother.

No, not himself; he must not die! Of all the members of his family, he alone would win! He was already forty-five years old. He would be satisfied if he made it into his sixties. And then death—but a different one, not the one that had befallen the members of his family!—could have the satisfaction of taking him away. It would no longer matter at all to him.

He redoubled his treatments and vigilance. However, at the same time, he didn't want that constant worry, that spying on himself every moment, to hurt him. Therefore, he went so far as to pretend to himself that he no longer thought about it. Yes, indeed, from time to time certain expressions such as "It's warm" or "Fine weather" would come to his lips automatically, really automatically, not consciously, not that he wanted to utter them in order to hear if his voice had become slightly hoarse.

And he wandered about the vast empty rooms of his old house, swinging the tassel of his velvet nightcap and whistling.

Little Fanny, his maid—who didn't yet feel so old and, after many years in his service, hadn't yet managed to get it out of her head that her master had some designs on her but, being shy, couldn't tell her so—seeing him wandering about the house like that, would smile at him and ask,

"Do you need something, my dear man?"

Marco Picotti would look down his nose at her and answer dryly,

"I don't need a thing. Blow your nose!"

Fanny would twist and turn and add,

"I understand, I understand... You, Master, are scolding me because you love me."

"I don't love anybody!" he would then scream, his eyes wide open. "I'm telling you to blow your nose because you take snuff! And when you take snuff, you shouldn't let drops hang from your nose."

He would turn his back on her and begin to whistle again as he swung his tassel and wandered about.

One day his brother's widowed wife had the awful notion of paying him a visit.

"For heaven's sake, no!" he shouted at the woman, pressing his hands tightly over his face so as not to see her cry, dressed as she was in mourning. "Go, go away! For heaven's sake, don't you dare come here again! Do you want to make me die? I beg you, go away immediately! I can't look at you! I can't look at you!"

He viewed the visit as an outrage. But what in the world was that woman thinking? That he no longer thought about his brother? He did think about him. He certainly did... He only pretended not to because he didn't have to, he didn't have to yet!

He felt sick about it for an entire day. And even when he awoke that night, he had a violent fit of crying that he pretended not to remember the following morning. He was cheerful, yes, cheerful that morning; he whistled like a blackbird and periodically would utter,

"It's warm... Fine weather..."

When his mustache, which had remained obstinately black, began to turn gray, as the hair on his temples already had, instead of being upset, he was happy, very happy. Since all his relatives had died quite young, he associated consumption with youth. The further he got away from it, the more he felt secure. He wanted... he *had* to grow old. Along with youth he detested everything connected with it, such as love and spring. Above all, he hated spring. He knew that for those with chest ailments this was the most frightful season. And with silent anger he saw the trees in his little garden turn green again and bud.

In the spring he would no longer leave his house. After dinner he would remain at the table and amuse himself by making the glasses chime. If Fanny, hearing the sound, rushed over like a little butterfly attracted to light, he would send her away harshly.

Poor Fanny! It was really true that her horrible master did not love her. She realized it all the more when she become gravely ill and was sent away to die in the hospital. Marco Picotti grieved over this only because he had to get another maid. And he had to change so many of them in so few years! In the end, since none of them satisfied him anymore, and all of them got tired of him, he ended up living alone, doing everything for himself.

And so he reached his sixtieth birthday.

At that time the tension that had gripped his mind for such a long time suddenly decreased.

Marco Picotti felt appeased. His lifetime goal had been achieved.

And now?

Now he could die. Ah yes, die, die, because he was fed up, nauseated, sickened. He asked for nothing more! What more could life be for him? Without that goal anymore, without that task —tiredness, boredom, dullness.

He began to live without any rules at all, to get up much earlier than usual, to go out in the evening, to frequent a few taverns, to eat every sort of food. He ruined his stomach a little, got angry and more irritable than ever at the sight of the people who continued to congratulate him on the fine state of his health.

The boredom, the nausea increased so much that finally one day he became convinced that he had to do something. He was not quiet sure yet precisely what, but certainly something to free himself from the nightmare that was still suffocating him. Hadn't he already won? No. He felt he hadn't yet.

It was that stuffed bird standing upright on the parrot perch between the two bookcases that told him so and showed him why, marvelously.

"Straw... straw," Marco Picotti began saying as he looked at it that day.

He snatched it from the perch and, pulling a penknife out of his vest pocket, slashed its belly.

"Here it is, straw... straw..."

He looked about the room; he saw the huge old armchairs of fake leather and the couch, and, with that same penknife, he began slashing the upholstery and pulling out the stuffing by the fists-full, repeating with a face expressing both spite and nausea,

"Here it is, straw... straw..."

What did he mean by that? Why, simply this. He went to sit at his desk, took the revolver out of a drawer and aimed it at his temple. This is what he meant. Only like this could he really have won.

When the news of Mario Picotti's suicide spread through the town, no one at first wanted to believe it since it seemed so contrary to the stubborn, narrow passion with which he had kept himself alive until old age. A good many people who saw the slashes on the armchairs and the couch in that room, unable to explain either the suicide or the slashes, believed instead that a crime had been committed and suspected that the slashes were the work of one or more thieves. Judicial authority entertained this suspicion before anyone else and it immediately began to conduct an investigation and research the incident.

Among the numerous exhibits, that stuffed bird found a place of honor, and as if it could help shed light on the case, a good ornithologist was given the task of determining what sort of bird it was.

The Lonely Man

Now that the season permitted it, they would meet outdoors around a small table in a cafe under the trees on Via Veneto. The first to arrive were the Groas, father and son. Their loneliness was so great that even though they were quite close to each other they seemed miles apart. As soon as they sat down, they would fall into a deep, bewildering silence that estranged them even from everything around them, so that if something happened to fall under their glances, they had to squint slightly to look at it. Finally the other two, Filippo Romelli and Carlo Spina, would arrive together. Romelli was a widower for the past five months. Spina was a bachelor. Mariano Groa was separated from his wife for about a year and had kept his only son, Torellino, with him. The boy, already a high school student, was slim and all nose. Moreover, he had small sunken eyes that were dark and a bit sullen.

Seated there around the little table, they rarely exchanged words after the usual greetings. They would sip their small pilsners, drink syrupy sodas through a straw and remain there looking, looking at all the women who passed down the street, whether they were alone, in couples or accompanied by their husbands: the married ones, the young girls, the young mothers with their children, those getting off the streetcars on their way to Villa Borghese, those who were returning from there in carriages and the foreigners entering or leaving the large hotel across the street on foot or by car.

They would scarcely take their eyes off one of them, when they would immediately fix them on another and follow her with their eyes, studying every motion she made or staring at some particular feature of hers: her breasts, hips, neck or rosy arms, the latter perceivable through her lacy sleeves. They were dazzled and inebriated by all this swarming, by this bustling of life, by such a variety of appearances, colors and expressions, and they were suspended in painful anxiety, with a confusion of feelings, thoughts, regrets and desires, when they managed to catch an obliging and furtive glance or a feint promising smile from this one or that, amid the hubbub of vehicles and the dense, continuous chirping coming from the gardens of the nearby villas.

All four of them, each in his own way, felt the same burning need for a woman, for the good that only a woman can provide in life, a good that so many of these women already provided with their love, presence and care, perhaps without being dutifully recompensed by their ungrateful men.

As soon as the sad air of one of these women would make this doubt arise within them, they hastened with their glances to express intense sorrow or bitter condemnation or compassionate adoration. And the young ladies? Who knows how ready and willing they were to give the joy that their bodies could provide! Instead they had to waste away in perhaps useless expectation, falsely prudish in public and who knows how ardent in private.

Each of the men, viewing that spellbinding sight before him, and thinking about his own house—empty, squalid and silent —would be stricken by a profound feeling of bitterness and would sigh.

Filippo Romelli, the widower, rather small in stature, was neatly dressed in his black mourning suit, which still hadn't a single wrinkle. With the fine, perfect features of a small, good-looking man caressed by his wife, he would go to the cemetery every Sunday to bring flowers to his deceased wife. He, more than the other two, felt the ache of having a home steeped in memories. Each object there, clothed in shadow and silence, seemed still to be waiting for the woman who could never again return, the woman who had always welcomed him so cheerfully and took take care of him, made a fuss over him and repeated with laughing eyes how happy she was to be his wife.

In all the women he now saw pass down the street, he endeavored to catch a graceful move that would return the loving image of his wife, not as she had been recently but as she once was when she had given him the same joy that these women now rekindled pungently in his memory. He would immediately tighten his lips from the surge of emotion that bitterly rose to his throat, and half close his eyes as solitary birds do on a branch when there is wind.

Even with his wife, in those final days, he had loved the remembrance of past joys that could never again be his. No woman would ever love him again for his own sake. He was already almost fifty years old.

Ah yes, fete had really been cruel to him! To see his companion torn away from him at that point, on the threshold of old age, when he needed her the most and when even love, which is always restless in youth, made one begin to value only the peace of a faithful nest! And now it was his lot again to feel the restlessness of love, which was untimely and, therefore, ridiculous and desperate.

On several occasions he had said to Spina, his faithful friend for so many years,

"It's the pure truth, my friend. A man cannot be at peace if he hasn't secured three things: his daily bread, a home and love. You can find women now. I would even concede that, as far as that goes, you are better off than I— for the time being. But youth, my dear friend, is much shorter than old age. A bachelor enjoys himself when he's young but suffers when he's old. For the married man it's the opposite. He has more time to enjoy himself, as you can imagine."

Yes sir. Fate had given him a great answer! Spina, now an old bachelor, began to suffer the emptiness of his life in a rented room, among cheap furniture that wasn't even his. But he could at least say that he had enjoyed himself in his own fashion during his youth, and that he himself had wanted his old age to be solitary, without the comfort of female attentions and the usual affections. Not so himself!

And yet, perhaps cruder than his own destiny was that of Mariano Groa. It sufficed to look at him, poor man, to understand that.

Romelli, though depressed, still found the inner strength even now to spruce up, to dress neatly, to trim his thin, gray mustache, while that poor fellow Groa... There he was, potbellied and untidy. He had a grim, bespectacled face that looked like the snout of a mastiff, bristly hair on a face who knows how many days unshaven, a jacket without buttons, a wrinkled collar yellowed with sweat and a filthy tie knotted backwards.

As for Mariano Groa, he looked at the women with savage frowns almost as if he was about to devour them.

Now and then, as he stared at one of them, he would pant as if his nose was tickling. He would rouse himself, making his chair creak, and would assume an appearance not less grim than before, with the knob of his cane pressed deeply under his double chin, shiny with sweat.

For many years he knew that his wife—a small affected woman with a tiny turned-up nose, two impertinent dimples on her cheeks and extremely lively ferret-like eyes—was betraying him. Finally one terrible day, he was forced to face it and he got a legal separation from her. He regretted it immediately afterwards, but she would have nothing more to do with him, being happy to receive the two hundred lire he passed on to her each month through his son, who went to visit her every other day.

The poor man was consumed with a desire to have her back. He still loved her madly and could not live without her. He could have no peace!

Often his son, Torellino, who slept in a bed nearby, would hear him crying or sobbing with his face buried in his pillow. The boy would then raise himself on his elbow and try to comfort him affectionately.

"Papa, Papa..."

But the boy would often become tired of seeing him so restless. On the days he had to visit his mother, he would groan every single time his father would start suggesting all the things he wanted him to tell her so as to move her to pity: the fact that he, at his age, was not being looked after, his desperation, his crying spells, the fact that he couldn't sleep and that he was at his wit's end and didn't know what to do.

It was a torment for Torellino! It was also his shame, and it thoroughly upset him and made him break out in a cold sweat. What's more, the messages he delivered served no purpose because, already on several occasions, his mother, who was unyielding, had made him tell his father that she didn't even want to hear anything about him.

It was another torment every time he returned from those visits. His father would wait for him at the foot of the stairs, panting, his face flushed, his eyes tense with pain and glazed with tears. As soon as he would see his son, he would immediately bombard him with questions:

"How is she? How is she? What did she tell you? How did you find her?"

At every answer, he would wrinkle his nose, shut his eyes and open his mouth wide as if he was being stabbed.

"Ah, so she's all right? Didn't she say anything? Ah, so she said she's doing well? And you, what did you answer her?"

"Me? Nothing, Papa..."

"Ah, nothing, is that so?" And he would bite his hands from rage. Then he would burst out, saying,

"Ah yes! Ah yes! Keep it up! Keep it up! It's convenient. Keep it up like that, you too, my dear boy! Of course... You don't lack anything. There's an ox here working for both of you... Keep it up, keep it up, without any concern for me! But for God's sake, don't you understand that I can't live like this anymore? That I need help? That this is killing me? Don't you understand that? Don't you understand that?"

"But what can I do about it, Papa?" Torellino would finally say, shrugging his shoulders in exasperation.

"Nothing! Nothing! Keep it up!" Mariano Groa would retort, holding back his tears.

"But don't you at least think it's a crime to make me die like this? Because, you know, I'm really dying! I'll leave you both out in the street and I'll put an end to myself! I'll put an end to myself! I'll put an end to myself!"

He would immediately regret these outbursts and compensate his son with caresses and gifts. He would spoil the boy, lavishing on him all the attentions of a mother and he would neglect himself, his clothes, shoes and linen, so that his son would be well dressed from head to foot and would appear before his mother every two days dressed according to the latest fashion.

He himself would be moved to pity by his own kindness, which not only was not reciprocated but not even commiserated by anybody. In feet, everybody trampled on it. His tender pity would devour him. He felt precisely as if his heart, wracked with pain, wasted away with anxiety, was breaking apart within him.

He felt he had never done anything wrong to that awful woman who had treated him so poorly!

How could he help it if that fat, ugly body had grown around his tender and simple heart, the heart of a child? Cut out for a domestic life, for adoring only one woman in life who would love him—not a lot, not a lot, just a little!—how greatly he would have repaid her for this bit of affection!

With eyes glassy from the tears he could scarcely contain, he now sat there observing every married couple on the street which he believed were in love and got along well. He would have fallen on his knees before every honest and wise wife who was the smile and the godsend of a home and who loved her husband tenderly and looked after the children.

It was just his luck, just his luck, to have a woman like that! Who knows how many good women there were, there among the ones walking down the street, how many of them who would have brought him happiness, because he was hot asking for much, just a little affection, just a little!

With those eyes of his that seemed fierce, he begged for it from all the women he saw passing by. But not because he wanted it from them. He wanted it from only one woman, from *that* woman, since she alone could give it to him honestly, bound as he was by the ties of matrimony and with that poor son of his at his side.

In the shadow of the large trees lining the street, life seethed that evening with a more intense throbbing.

His two friends, Spina and Romelli, still hadn't shown up.

The air, saturated with all the fragrances of the nearby villas, seemed to sizzle with a golden glow, and the feces of all the women, lit up by purple reflections, smiled under haughty large hats. With that smile they presented to the admiring and desirous men their bodies, clearly outlined by their tight-fitting dresses.

The roses of a flower shop nearby, behind Groa, gave off a perfume so voluptuous that the poor man experienced a powerful sense of inebriation. All that seething life assumed vaporous, dreamy outlines and made him almost question the reality of what he was seeing. The muffled noises reached his ears as though coming from afar and not from that great, marvelous dream before him.

At long last the other two arrived. They were having a lively discussion. Romelli, small in stature, dressed in black, was nervous and upset. At intervals he twitched as if he were getting a shock, and Spina, who was all excited, tried to calm him down and convince him of something.

"'Yes, two sisters, two sisters! Leave it to me. It's still early. Let's sit down now."

With his eyes, Groa signaled to the two not to speak of such things in front of his son. Then, realizing that they would not be able to contain themselves, so excited as they were, he turned to Torellino and told him to go take a little walk over there in Villa Borghese.

The boy reluctantly set out, grumbling.

After taking a few steps, Torellino turned and saw that the three men, their heads joined, were mysteriously chatting around the little table. His father, however, was shaking his head and saying, "No, no..."

Undoubtedly Spina was tempting them.

When Torellino returned, half an hour later, the two friends, Romelli and Spina, had gone away. The boy's father, in a state of desperate loneliness, was there alone, waiting for him. His face was so changed, his eyes so full of pain and gloom, that the boy stood there a while to observe him in dismay.

"Shall we go, Papa?"

It seemed that Groa could not hear him. He looked at him. And as he tightened his lips with a sort of childish, tearful grimace, he was assailed by a fit of muffled sobs. Then he got up, clutched his son's arm and squeezed it with all his strength as if to communicate something that he could not and knew not how to say. As they walked, they headed in the direction of Porta Pinciana.

Torellino felt himself dragged toward the house where his mother lived. Yes, they would be there shortly. It was there at the end of the second lane, where a streetlight was burning. Gradually he stiffened his arm against the arm of his father, who, noticing his resistance, looked at him anxiously to move him to pity.

"Oh, God! Oh God!" thought Torellino. "The usual story! The usual torment! Go up, right? Beg his mother to finally give up, and hear her say 'No, no' again?"

And there in front of the lane, under the streetlight, he resolved not to go up, and obstinately said to his father,

"No, listen, Papa, I'm not going up! I'm not going up!"

Groa looked at his son with dreadful eyes.

"No?" he said with anger in his voice. "No?"

He pushed the boy away gently without adding a word. Left alone there in the middle of the deserted street, Torellino, at first a bit dazed, felt for a moment that his father had left him forever, since he suddenly reappeared there in the distance. He felt that his father would be lost forever in the crowd, a stranger among so many strangers who walked down that sloping street. Then, filled with dismay, he began to follow him from a distance.

Without allowing himself to be seen, he followed him down Via Capo le Case, down Via Due Macelli, Via Condotti, Via Fontanella di

Borghese and across Piazza Nicosia. When he came to Via di Tordi-nona, he stopped.

Romelli and Spina were coming out of a small dark lane, and the boy's father was joining them. Romelli had a black-edged handkerchief on his eyes and was sobbing. All three of them were going over to lean against the parapet along the bank of the Tiber.

"You fool! Why?" shouted Spina, shaking Romelli by the shoulder. "She's so pretty! So attractive!"

Romelli, sobbing, replied,

"It's impossible! Impossible! You can't understand... It's a question of decency! The sanctity of the home!"

Spina was then turning to the boy's father.

In that clear, moonlit evening in May, close to the waters of the river that still seemed to retain the light of the day gone by, one could clearly distinguish all the gestures and even the facial features of those three troubled men.

Spina was now trying to convince Groa that Romelli was wrong, while Romelli continued wiping his tears, some distance away. The boy's father stood there looking at Spina with fierce, dilated eyes. Suddenly Groa seized Spina by the collar of his jacket, gave him a mighty shake and sent him fleeing in the distance. Then he jumped onto the parapet and, looking unusually huge, he shouted with arms upraised,

"Look! This is how it's done!"

Then down he went into the river. A splash. Two screams followed by another from a distance. The third scream, more piercing than the others, was uttered by the boy, who was unable to rush to his father's assistance, his legs nearly giving way from terror.

The Trap

No, no, how can I resign myself? And why should I? If I had any responsibilities toward others, perhaps I would but I don't! So, why should I?

Listen to me. You can't say I'm wrong. No one reasoning in the abstract like this can say I'm wrong. What I'm feeling, you and everyone else feels too.

Why are all of you so afraid of waking up at night? Because for you, the reasons for living are strengthened by the light of day, by the illusions produced by that light.

Darkness and silence terrify you. You light a candle but the candlelight seems dismal to you because that's not the kind of light you need, right? The sun! The sun! All of you desperately seek the sun because illusions no longer arise spontaneously with the artificial light you yourselves procure with a trembling hand.

Like your hand, all your reality trembles. It reveals itself to you to be fake and flimsy. Artificial like that candlelight. All your senses keep watch, painfully tense in the fear that beneath the reality that you discover to be flimsy and hollow, another reality may be revealed to you: an obscure and horrible one—the real one. A breath of air... What's that? What's that creaking sound?

Suspended in the horror of that uncertain wait, amid chills and sweat, you see your daytime illusions in that light. They move about the room with the appearance and gait of ghosts. Look at them carefully. They have the same puffy and watery bags under their eyes that you have, the same jaundiced look brought on by your insomnia, and your arthritic pains too. Yes, the same dull torment caused by the gout in the joints of your fingers.

What a strange appearance, what a strange appearance the pieces of furniture in your room assume! They too seem suspended in a bewildering stillness that troubles you.

You slept with them around you.

But they do not sleep. They remain there both day and night.

For now, it's your hand that opens and closes them. But tomorrow it'll be another hand. Who knows whose other hand!... But for them it's all the same. For now they contain your clothes: empty forms that have been hung up and that have taken on the shape and wrinkles of your tired knees and bony elbows. Tomorrow they'll contain someone else's forms hanging there. The mirror on the wardrobe reflects your image now, but it doesn't preserve a trace of it nor will it preserve a trace of someone else's image tomorrow.

The mirror itself cannot see. The mirror is like truth.

Do you think that I'm delirious, that I'm talking nonsense? Come on, you understand me, and you understand even what I am not saying since I find it very hard to express this obscure feeling that rules me and overwhelms me.

You know how I've lived up till now. You know that I've always felt revulsion and horror about giving myself some sort of form, becoming congealed and fixing myself even momentarily in it.

I've always made my friends laugh because of the great many... what do you call them? Alterations? Yes, alterations in my personal characteristics. But you've been able to laugh at them because you've never condescended to consider my urgent need to look at myself in the mirror, with a different appearance; to trick myself in believing that I was not always the same person, to see myself as someone else!

But of course! What could I alter? It's true that I went so far as to shave my head to see myself bald before my time. At times I shaved off my mustache, leaving my beard, or vice versa. At times I shaved off my mustache and beard, or I let my beard grow now one way, now another. A goatee, parted on the chin or running along the line of the jaw...

I played around with the bristles.

I couldn't at all alter my eyes, nose, mouth, ears, torso, legs, arms or hands. Did I put on make-up like a theater actor? I sometimes had that temptation. But then I thought that, under my mask, my body always remained the same... and was growing old!

I tried to make up for it with my spirit. Oh yes, with my spirit I was able to play around better!

Above all, you value and never tire of praising the constancy of feelings and the coherence of personality. Why? Always for the same reason! Because you are cowards. Because you're afraid of yourselves. That is, you're afraid that if you change, you'll lose the reality you have given yourselves and you'll recognize, therefore, that it was nothing more than an illusion of yours and, consequently, that no reality exists other than the one we give ourselves.

But, I ask, what does giving oneself a reality mean if not fixing oneself in a feeling, becoming congealed, stiff and encrusted in it? Therefore, arresting in ourselves the perpetual vital movement, making of ourselves so many small miserable pools destined for putrefaction, while life is a continuous flux, incandescent and indistinct.

See, this is the thought that perturbs me and makes me furious!

Life is wind. Life is sea. Life is fire. Not earth, which becomes encrusted and takes on form.

All form is death.

All that is removed from the state of fusion and congeals amid this continuous flux--which is incandescent and indistinct, is death.

We are all beings that have been caught in the trap, separated from the ceaseless flux and fixed to die.

The movement of this flux in us, in our form, which is separated, detached and fixed, and will last for a brief moment more. But, see, little by little it slows down. The fire cools down. The form dries up and finally movement ceases completely in the form, which has become rigid.

We have finished dying and we have called this life!

I feel caught in this death trap that has separated me from the flux of life in which I flowed without form, and has fixed me in time, in this time!

Why in this time?

I could still have flowed on and become fixed a little later, at least in another form, a little later... You think it would have been the same, right? Well, yes, sooner or later... But I would have been someone else a little later. Who knows who and who knows how! Trapped in another fate. I would have seen other things or, perhaps, the same things but with different appearances, arranged differently.

You can't imagine what hatred the things I see arouse in me, the things caught with me in the trap of this time that is mine. All the things that end up dying with me, a little at a time! Both hatred and pity! But more hatred, perhaps, than pity.

Yes, it's true, if I had fallen into the trap a little later, I would then have hated that other form as I now hate this one. I would have hated that other time as I do this one now, and all the illusions of life that *we the dead of all time* fabricate for ourselves with that small amount of movement and heat that remains shut up within us and that comes from that continuous flux that is true life and that never stops.

We are so many busy corpses who are deceiving ourselves into believing that we are creating our lives.

We copulate, a dead man with a dead woman, and we think we are giving life but we give death... Another being in the trap!

"Here, my dear, here. Begin to die, dear... Begin to die... You're crying, eh? You're crying and wriggling about... You would have liked to flow on some more? Relax, my dear! What can you do about it? Caught, co-ag-u-la-ted, fixed... It won't last but a short while! Relax..."

Oh, as long as we're very young, as long as our body is fresh and grows and weighs little, we do not clearly realize that we are caught in the trap! But then the body becomes a tangled mass and we begin to feel its weight. We begin to feel that we can no longer move as we did before.

With disgust I see my spirit struggling in this trap to avoid, it too, being fixed in a body already worn out by the years and grown heavy. I immediately drive away every idea that might become stale in me. I immediately interrupt every act that might become a habit in me. I don't want responsibilities, I don't want tender attachments and I don't want my spirit to harden into a crust of concepts either. But I feel that from day to day my body finds it ever more difficult to follow my restless spirit. It continually slumps. It has tired knees and heavy hands... It wants rest! I'll give it that.

No, no, I'm unwilling and unable to resign myself to offering, me too, the miserable spectacle given by all those old people who end up dying slowly. No. But first... I don't know what, but I'd like to do something enormous, something unheard of, to give vent to this rage that's devouring me.

I'd like at least... See these fingernails? I'd like to dig them into the face of every beautiful woman who passes down the street, teasing men provocatively.

What stupid, miserable and thoughtless creatures all women are! They dress up, put on their fineries, turn their laughing eyes here and there and show off their provocative shapes as much as they can. But they don't realize that they too are in the trap and are fixedly formed to die, and have the trap in themselves for those that are to come!

For us men the trap is in them, in women. For a moment they put us once again in a state of incandescence to wrest from us another being who is sentenced to death. They say and do so much until they finally make us fall, blind, passionate and violent, into their trap.

Me too! Me too! They made me fall too! In feet, most recently. That's why I'm so furious.

An abominable trap! If only I had seen it... A demure young lady. Timid, humble. As soon she would see me, she would lower her eyes and blush because she knew that otherwise I would never have fallen.

She used to come here to put into practice one of the seven corporal works of mercy: to visit the sick. She used to come for my father, not for me. She used to come to help my old governess look after and clean my poor father, who's in the other room...

She used to live here in the adjoining apartment and had become friends with my governess, to whom she would complain about her idiotic husband, who always reproached her for not being able to give him a son.

But do you understand how it is? When you begin to stiffen and you can no longer move as before, you want to see other small corpses around, very young corpses that still move as you did when you were very young; other small corpses that resemble you and do all those little things that you can no longer do.

There's nothing more amusing than to wash the faces of small corpses that still don't know they are caught in the trap, and to comb their hair and take them out for a little stroll.

As I was saying, she used to come here.

"I can imagine," she would say, blushing, her eyes downcast, "I can imagine what a torment it must be, Signor Fabrizio, to see your father in this condition for so many years!"

"Yes, Signora," I would answer gruffly and I would turn around and go away.

I'm certain now that as soon as I would turn around and go away, she would laugh to herself, biting her lip to hold back her laughter.

I would go away because, in spite of myself, I felt that I admired that woman. Not indeed because of her beauty—she was very beautiful, and the more she showed she had no regard for her beauty, the more seductive she was—but because she didn't give her husband the satisfaction of putting another unfortunate in the trap.

I thought she was the one. Instead, no, it wasn't her problem. It was his. And she knew it or, at least, if she didn't actually have the certainty, she must have entertained the suspicion. That's why she laughed. She laughed at me because I admired her for that presumed incapacity of hers. She laughed silently in her evil heart and waited. Until one evening...

It happened here, in this room.

I was here in the dark. You know that I like to go to the window and watch the day die and let myself be taken and wrapped gradually by the darkness, and to think, "I'm no longer here!" To think, "If there were someone in this room, he would get up and light a lamp. I won't light the lamp because I'm no longer here. I'm like the chairs in this room, like the little table, the drapes, the wardrobe, the couch, that don't need light and don't know and don't see that I'm here. I want to be like them and not see myself and forget I'm here."

Now then, I was here in the dark. She came tiptoeing in from my father's room, where she had left a small night lamp lit whose glimmer came through the small opening in the door and faintly spread through the darkness, almost without diminishing it.

I didn't see her. I didn't see that she was about to bump into me. Perhaps she didn't see me either. When we collided, she let out a cry and pretended to faint in my arms, on my chest. I lowered my head. My cheek brushed up against hers. I felt the ardor of her eager mouth, and...

After a while, her laugh roused me. A diabolical laugh. I can still hear it! She laughed and laughed as she ran off, that wicked woman! She laughed because she had set a trap for me with her modesty. She laughed because my ferocity was vanquished. And she laughed because of something else that I learned about later.

She went away three months ago with her husband, who was assigned to the position of high school teacher in Sardinia.

Certain assignments come in the nick of time.

I will never see my remorse. I will not see it. But at certain moments I am tempted to run off and find that wicked woman and choke her before she puts into the trap that unfortunate whom she wrested from me with such treachery.

My friend, I'm happy I never knew my mother. Perhaps if I had known her, this ferocious thought would not have arisen in me. But since it has, I'm happy I never knew my mother.

Come, come; come here with me into this other room. Look!

This is my father.

For seven years he has been here. He's nothing anymore. Two eyes that cry, a mouth that eats. He can't speak, can't hear and can't move anymore. He eats and cries. He is spoon-fed. He cries in private without reason or, perhaps, because there's still something in him, a vestige of something that, though it began to die seventy-six years ago, doesn't want to end yet.

Don't you find it atrocious to remain still caught in the trap like that because of a single remaining moment and not to be able to free yourself?

He cannot think of his father who, seventy-six years ago, fixed him for death, which is so frightfully late in coming. But I, I can think about him, and I think about the fact that I am a germ of this man who can no longer move, and that if I am trapped in this time and not in another, I owe it to him!

He's crying, see? He always cries like that... and he makes me cry too! Perhaps he wants to be freed. I'll free him some evening together with myself. It's now beginning to get cold. One of these evenings we'll light a little fire... If you'd like to join us...

No, eh? You're thanking me? Yes, yes, let's go outside, let's go outside, my friend. I can see that you need to see the sun again, on the street.

The Imbecile

"But what on earth had Mazzarini—the deputy Guido Mazzarini—to do with Pulino's suicide?"

"Pulino? What! Did Pulino kill himself?"

"Yes, Lulu Pulino, two hours ago. They found him in his house, hanging from the light fixture in the kitchen."

"Hanging?" "Yes, hanging. What a sight! All black, with his eyes bulging, his tongue sticking out and his fingers all shriveled up."

"Oh, poor Lulu!"

"But what had Mazzarini to do with it?"

Nobody could figure anything out. A score of maniacs were shouting in the cafe, waving their arms in the air. Some had even climbed on their chairs. They were all gathered around Leopoldo Paroni, president of the Republican Club of Costanova, who was shouting louder than any of them.

"That imbecile! Yes, yes, I say it and I'll continue to say it. That imbecile! That imbecile! Why, I would have paid for his trip! Yours truly would have paid for it! When someone no longer knows what to do with his life, by God, if he doesn't do something like that, he's an imbecile!"

"Excuse me, what happened?" asked a newcomer, almost deafened and somewhat puzzled by all the shouting, as he approached a customer sitting in a dark corner of the room, away from the others. The latter, all hunched over, had a woolen scarf over his shoulders and wore a traveler's cap with a wide visor that cast a shadow over half of his face.

Before answering, the customer took his emaciated hand off the knob of his cane and brought a handkerchief rolled into a ball to his mouth, over his grimy, drooping moustache. As he did so, he showed his gaunt, sallow race with its sickly, scraggly growth of beard. His mouth covered, he struggled silently for some time with his throat, from which a deep racking cough burst forth, cutting his words into syllables. Finally he said in a cavernous voice,

"You caused a draft as you approached me. Excuse me, sir, but you're not from Costanova, right?"

(And he collected and hid something in his handkerchief.) The stranger, who was sorry, ashamed and embarrassed because of the revulsion he felt but was unable to conceal, answered,

"No, I'm just passing through."

"We're all passing through, my dear sir."

He opened his mouth as he said this, and showed his teeth in a cold, silent sneer that contracted the yellow cartilage of his bony face into tight wrinkles about his sharp eyes.

"Guido Mazzarini," he then slowly went on, "is the deputy of

Costanova, a great man."

He rubbed the thumb and forefinger of his hand to indicate the reason for this greatness.

"The political elections in Costanova have been over for seven months now, and, as you can see, dear sir, they're still boiling over with indignation against him because, while everyone opposed him here, he nevertheless managed to win with well-paid votes from the other constituencies. The fury hasn't yet subsided because Mazzarini, to avenge himself, arranged to have sent to the municipality of Costanova...—stand back, stand back a little; I need some air—a Royal commissioner. Thanks. Of course! A Royal commissioner. Something... something of great importance... Yes, indeed, a Royal commissioner."

He stretched out his hand and, under the eyes of the stranger who gazed at him in astonishment, he made a fist, leaving out only his very thin little finger. Then he pursed his lips and stood there for a while, staring quite intently at his black and blue nail.

"Costanova is a great town," he then said. "The universe, all of it, gravitates around Costanova. The stars in the heavens do nothing but peer down at Costanova; and there are some who say that they laugh; and others who say that each of them is dying of jealousy to have a city like Costanova on its surface. Do you know what the fate of the universe depends on? On the Republican Party of Costanova, which never has a moment of respite, with Mazzarini on one side, and the former major of Cappadonna, who acts like a king, on the other. Now the city council has been dissolved and, consequently, the entire universe is in turmoil. There they are. Do you hear them? The one who's yelling the loudest is Paroni. Yes, the one over there with the goatee, the red tie and the Homburg. He's yelling like that because he wants the life of the universe, and even its death, to be at the service of the Republicans of Costanova. Even its death, yes sir. Pulino killed himself... Do you know who Pulino was? A poor sick man like me. Here in Costanova there are a lot of us, sick like him. And we ought to be good for something. Today, poor Pulino, tired of suffering..."

"Hanged himself?"

"From the light fixture in his kitchen. Hey, but that way, no, I don't like it. Too much effort, to hang oneself. There are revolvers, my dear sir. A quicker death. Fine, but can you hear what Paroni is saying? He's saying that Pulino was an imbecile not because he hanged himself but because, before hanging himself, he didn't go to Rome to murder Guido Mazzarini! Of course! So that Costanova and, consequently, the universe, might breathe again. When someone no longer knows what to do with his life, if he doesn't do something like that, if before killing himself he doesn't murder someone like Mazzarini, he's an imbecile. He, Paroni, would have paid for his trip, he says. With your permission, my dear sir."

He sprang to his feet and, with both hands, he tightened the ends of his scarf around his face, all the way to the visor of his cap. Then, all bundled like that, hunched over and casting dirty looks at the howling group, he left the cafe.

The transient stranger sat there in bewilderment and, with his eyes, followed the man to the door. Then he turned to the old waiter of the cafe and asked him with extreme dismay,

"Who is he?"

The old waiter nodded dolefully, tapped his chest with one finger and replied with a sigh,

"He too... eh, he too doesn't have much time left. It's a family trait! Already two brothers and a sister... He's a student. His name is Fazio, Luca Fazio. The fault of his awful mother, you know. The woman married a consumptive for money, knowing that he was a consumptive. And now she lives out in the country, big and fat like an abbess, while her poor children, one after another... What a shame! If you only knew how smart this fellow is! How much he has studied! He's learned, everyone says so. He just got back from Rome, where he was studying. What a shame!"

And the old waiter rushed over to the group of shouting men who, after paying for their drinks, got ready to leave the cafe, with Leopoldo Paroni leading the way.

A dreadfully humid November evening. The fog was so thick you could cut it with a knife. The pavement of the square was wet, and there was a large halo around every streetlight.

As soon as they were outside the cafe, they all turned up their coat collars and, saying good night to one another, they set out, each on his own way.

Leopoldo Paroni, with the usual haughty, scowling expression on his face, threw back his head to one side and, with his goatee in the air, crossed the square. Twirling his cane as he walked, he took the street opposite the cafe, then turned right at the first lane, at the end of which stood his house.

Two whimpering little lamps engulfed in the fog, one at either end of the lane, were scarcely able to dispel the darkness from that filthy alley.

Paroni was only halfway down the dark lane but already began to look forward to the brightness of the still distant streetlight, a feint glimmer of which was now visible. He thought he could make out someone waiting at the end of the lane, directly in front of his own house. He felt his blood run cold throughout his body and he stopped.

Who could be there at this hour? Undoubtedly someone was there and was obviously waiting. Right in front of the door of his house. The person was obviously waiting for him but certainly not to rob him, because everyone knew he was as poor as a church mouse. Then because of political hatred... Someone sent by Mazzarini or by the Royal commissioner? Was that possible? To go so far as that?

The haughty Republican turned to look behind him, in doubt as to whether he should go back to the cafe or run off to join the friends whom he had just left, if for no other reason than to have them witness the cowardice, the infamy, of his opponent. But he noticed that the man waiting there, having evidently heard his footsteps in the silence as soon as he had entered the lane, was coming toward him where there was the greatest darkness. There he was; now he could see him well. He was all bundled up. Paroni managed with difficulty to overcome his fear and the temptation to take to this heels. He coughed and shouted loudly,

"Hey, there!"

"Paroni...," the man called out in a cavernous voice.

In recognizing the voice, Paroni was filled with a sudden joy that lifted his spirits.

"Oh, Luca Fazio... you? I thought so! But what's this? You're here, my friend? So you've returned from Rome?"

"Yes, today," replied Luca Fazio, glumly.

"You were waiting for me, my dear fellow?"

"Yes, I was at the cafe. Didn't you see me?"

"No, not at all. Ah, so you were at the cafe? How are you, how are you, my Mend?"

"Not well. Don't touch me."

"Do you have something to tell me?"

"Yes, something serious."

"Serious? Well, here I am!"

"Not here. Up there in your house."

"But... what *is* it? What's wrong, Luca? "Whatever I can do for you, my friend..."

"I told you not to touch me. I'm not well."

They went over to the house. Paroni took the key out of his pocket, opened the door, struck a match and began climbing the steep little flight of stairs, followed by Fazio.

"Careful... Watch out for the steps..."

They crossed a small room and entered the study, which reeked with the pungent, stale odor of pipe smoke. Paroni lit a greasy enameled kerosene lamp on the paper-strewn desk and turned anxiously to Fazio. But he found him with his eyes bulging out of their sockets, and his handkerchief pressed with both hands against his mouth. That tobacco stench gave him another coughing fit, a terrible one.

"My God... you're really sick, Luca..."

Fazio had to wait a while before answering. He nodded his head several times. He had become as white as a corpse.

"Don't call me friend. Stand back," he finally began to say. "I'm on the verge of death. No, I'll remain... I'll remain standing... But you? Stand back."

"But... but I'm not afraid," protested Paroni.

"You're not afraid? Wait..." sneered Luca Fazio. "You say that too easily. In Rome, seeing myself at the end like this, I squandered everything I had; I only saved a few lire to buy myself this revolver."

He thrust his hand into the pocket of his overcoat and pulled out a large revolver.

Seeing the weapon in the hand of a man in that frightful state, Leopoldo Paroni turned as white as a sheet, raised his hands and stammered,

"Is... is it loaded? Come on now, Luca..."

"Loaded," replied Luca coldly. "You said you weren't afraid."

"No... but God help us if..."

"Stand back! Wait... I had locked myself in my room, in Rome, to end my life, when, with the revolver already aimed at my temple, I heard a knock at the door."

"You were in Rome?"

"Yes, in Rome. I opened the door. Who do you think I saw there in front of me? Guido Mazzarini."

"Him? At your home?"

Luca Fazio nodded his head repeatedly as if to say yes, then continued,

"He saw me with the revolver in my hand, and immediately, from the expression on my face as well, he realized what I was about to do. He ran up to me, grabbed me by the arm, shook me and shouted, *What? You're killing yourself like that? Oh Luca, how can you be such an imbecile! Come on... if you intend doing that... I'll pay for your trip. Run down to Costanova and first kill Leopoldo Paroni for me!'"

Paroni, who up till then had been listening most attentively to these grim and strange words, and whose mind was thrown into confusion by the terrible prospect of some dreadful violence occurring there and then, suddenly felt faint; he opened his mouth with a pitiful, hollow smile and asked,

"Are you joking?"

Luca Fazio stepped back; a sort of nervous tic developed in one of his cheeks, near his nose, and he said with a contorted mouth,

"I'm not joking. Mazzarini has paid for my trip, and here I am. Now, first I'll kill you, then I'll kill myself."

And in so saying, he raised the hand holding the weapon and took aim.

Paroni, terrified, his hands in front of his face, tried to evade the line of fire, all the while shouting,

"Are you crazy? Luca... are you crazy?"

"Don't move!" commanded Luca Fazio. "Crazy, eh? Do I seem crazy to you? And wasn't that you shouting for three hours in the cafe that Pulino was an imbecile because he hadn't gone to Rome to kill Mazzarini before hanging himself?"

Leopoldo Paroni tried to protest.

"By God, but I'm not Mazzarini! There's a difference."

"A difference?" exclaimed Fazio, as he continued aiming at Paroni. "What difference do you think there is between you and Mazzarino for someone like me or Pulini, who no longer care a thing about your lives and all your clowneries? Killing you or someone else, the first person to walk down the street, it's all the same to us! Ah, so you consider us imbeciles if in the end we don't become the tools of your hatred—or that of someone else—and of your many rivalries and buffooneries. Well then, I don't want to be an imbecile like Pulino, so I'm going to kill you!"

"For God's sake, Luca... what are you doing?" Paroni implored, as he squirmed to avoid the muzzle of the revolver.

A mad temptation to squeeze the trigger actually flashed in Fazio's eyes.

"See," said Fazio, with the usual cold sneer on his lips, "when someone no longer knows what to do with his life... Buffoon! Relax, I'm not going to kill you. Since you're a fine Republican, you're probably a freethinker, eh? An atheist! Of course... If you weren't one, you wouldn't have called Pulino an imbecile. And now you're thinking that I'm not going to kill you because I'm hoping for joys and rewards in a life to come. No, that's not it. It would be the most dreadful thing for me to believe that I'll have to bring elsewhere the burden of all the experiences that it has been my fete to have during the twenty-six years of my life. I don't believe in anything! All the same, I'm not going to kill you and I don't believe I'm an imbecile if I don't. I pity you... I pity you for your buffoonery, that's all. I see you as if from a distance, and you seem so small and miserable to me. But as for your buffoonery, *that* I'd like to copyright."

"What?" said Paroni, cupping his hand over his ear, not having heard the last word since he had fallen into a state of utter amazement.

"Cop-y-right," repeated Fabio, breaking the word into syllables. "I've got the right to it since I've arrived at death's door. And you can do nothing about it. Sit there and write."

With the revolver, he pointed to the desk, or rather, he virtually seized Paroni and forced him to sit down, pointing the weapon at his chest.

"Wha... what do you want me to write?" stammered Paroni, utterly crushed.

"What I'm going to dictate. You're depressed now, but tomorrow, when you'll find out that I've killed myself, you'll get cocky. I know it well. And at the cafe you'll shout that I too was an imbecile. Right? But I'm not doing this for my own sake. What in the world do I care about your opinion? I want to avenge Pulino. So, write... There, there, that's fine. A couple of words. A short deposition. *I, the undersigned, am sorry...*' Oh no, for God's sake! Write, understand? Only under this condition will I save your life! Either you write or I'll kill you... *'I am sorry I called Pulino an imbecile, this evening at the cafe, among friends, for not having gone to Rome to kill Mazzarini before killing himself.*' That's the truth and nothing but the truth. Actually I'm even leaving out your being willing to pay his way. Have you written that? Now go on: *'Luca Fazio, before killing himself, came to see me...*' Would you add *'armed with a revolver!'* Go ahead and add *'armed with a revolver.'* Anyway, I won't have to pay the fine for unlawfully carrying a weapon. Well then, *'Luca Fazio came to see me, armed with a revolver'*—have you written that? —*'and told me that, consequently, he too, so that he might not be called an imbecile by Mazzarini or someone else, should have murdered me like a dog.'* Did you write *'like a dog!'* Good. New paragraph: *'He could've done it, but he didn't do it. He didn't do it because my fear filled him with disgust and moved him to take pity on me. He was satisfied with my declaration that the real imbecile is me.'*"

At this point, Paroni, his face flushed, pushed the paper aside furiously and drew back in protest.

"Oh no, not..."

"*...that the real imbecile is me,*" repeated Luca Fazio, coldly and decisively. 'You'll save your dignity more easily, my dear fellow, if you keep your eyes on the paper you're writing on, rather than on this weapon I'm holding over your head. Are you through? Now sign it."

He made him hand him the paper. Then he read it attentively and said, "That's fine. They'll find it on me tomorrow."

He folded it in four and put it in his pocket.

"Leopoldo, console yourself with the thought that I'm now going to do something a bit more difficult than what you've just done. Good night."

The Fish Trap

Drunk? No! He had scarcely had three glasses. Perhaps the wine was exciting him more than usual because of the mood he had been in since morning and also because of what he intended to do, even though he wasn't quite certain what it would be.

For quite some time now he had been harboring a certain secret thought that seemed to be lying in wait, ready to spring forth at the right moment.

He kept it concealed as if he were hiding it from all his duties that stood like irritating sentinels guarding the prison of his conscience. For about twenty years he had been locked up in this prison to pay for a crime that, after all, had harmed no one but himself.

Why yes! Whom had he killed, after all, if not himself? Whose life had he stifled, if not his own?

In addition, there was this prison. For the past twenty years. He had locked himself in it. He had made all those irritating duties stand guard over himself with fixed bayonets, so that not only did they never allow him to spot a probable remote way out but they didn't even let him breathe.

Some pretty girl had smiled at him on the street?
"Sentry, atten—tion!"
"Ye-e-s, sir!"
Some friend had suggested that he run off with him to America?
"Sentry, atten—tion!"
"Ye-e-s, sir!"

And what had he become? Someone who disgusted him, really disgusted him when he compared himself to the person he could have and should have been.

A great painter! Yes sir, not at all like the kind who paint just to paint... trees, houses... mountains, seascapes... rivers, gardens and nude women. Ideas: that's what he wanted to paint, living ideas embodied in living images. Like the masters!

Drunk? Well, yes, he was a little drunk but, all the same, he was speaking well.

"Nardino, you speak well."

Nardino... That's what his wife called him. Good God, what nerve! A name like his, Bernardo Morasco, became simply Nardino in his wife's mouth.

But, poor woman, that's how she viewed him, as a diminutive, .ino, ...ino, ...ino, ...ino.

As Bernardo Morasco crossed the bridge from Ripetta to Lungotevere dei Mellini, with one hand he pulled his shabby hat over his thick, curly and already grizzled hair. He fixed his wide-open, cheerful, eloquent eyes on the face of a poor middle-aged woman who passed beside him, followed by a small, black, teary-eyed poodle holding a package in its mouth.

The woman jumped from fright, and the package dropped out of the poodle's mouth.

Morasco stood there for a moment, embarrassed and perplexed. Had he said anything to the woman? Oh God! He hadn't had the slightest intention of offending her. He was talking to himself. He was talking about his wife... She too was a poor woman!

He roused himself. A poor woman? Not now! Now his wife was rich, and his four children were rich. His father-in-law had finally croaked. So, after spending twenty years in jail, he had finally served his time.

Twenty years ago, when he was twenty-five, he had run off with the daughter of a miser. Poor thing, what a sorry sight! She was very timid and very pale, and her right shoulder was a bit higher than the other. But he had to think of Art, not women. He had never been able to stand women. For the little he might have needed from a woman, that poor thing, even that poor thing, sufficed. Once in a while, with his eyes closed, there you are, and that's it.

But the dowry he had expected didn't come. After the abduction, that miserly father-in-law didn't give in, and since the coup had failed, everyone expected him to abandon the unfortunate girl to the rage of her father and to *dishonor!* Those fools! Just like in an opera libretto. Him? Never! This instead is how he ended up so as not to give that satisfaction to those people and to that wicked miser!

Not only had he never uttered a harsh word to that poor thing but, in order to put food on the table, first for her and then for the four children that were born... Away with dreams! Away with Art! Away with everything!

So he painted flocks of thrushes for all the shopkeepers who sell cheap commercial paintings. He painted knights with plumed hats and silk clothes, dueling in a cellar. He painted cardinals in full regalia playing chess in a cloister, peasant girls from the Roman countryside flirting in Piazza di Spagna, cowboys on horseback behind a wooden fence, small temples of Vesta with egg yolk sunsets and ruins of aqueducts in tomato sauce. Then he made drawings of all the worse news events for the color pages of tabloids. Bulls on the run and bell towers collapsing, customs officers and smugglers battling one another, heroic rescues and fisticuffs in the Chamber of Deputies...

His wife and children were now spitting on these fine labors of his from which they had received such meager bread for so many years! What's more, he also had to put up with the derisive pity of all those for whom he had sacrificed, tortured and destroyed himself. Now that they had become rich, what respect, what consideration could they have for someone who had struggled to turn out disgusting puppets and caricatures for the pittance that for so many years had almost starved his family to death?

Ah yes, but, by God, he too wanted to have the pride, in his turn, to spit on that wealth and to despise it now that he could no longer make use of it to realize the dream that had once made him desire it. He too had been rich then, rich in spirit and dreams!

What a mockery his father-in-law's inheritance was—all that money—now that the feeling for life had hardened for him into a harsh and squalid reality that was like a patch of scrub full of thorny thistles and sharp rocks, a nest for snakes and owls! Now it rained gold on this land! A fine consolation! Who would give him the strength anymore to pull up all those thistles, to carry away all those rocks, to crush the heads of all those snakes, to shoo away all those owls? Who would give him the strength anymore to break up the land and rework it so that the flowers he had once dreamed of would bloom? Ah, *what* flowers! By now he had even lost the seeds! Over there, those thistles had heads on them...

Now everything was finished for him.

He became well aware of this as he wandered about that morning. He was finally free, out of his prison. His wife and children no longer needed him.

He had left his house with the firm intention of never returning to it again. But he didn't know yet what he would do nor where he would end up.

He wandered and wandered. He had been up to the Janiculum and had eaten in a small restaurant there, and yes, to tell the truth, he had drunk more than three glasses! He had also been to Villa Borghese. Feeling tired, he had stretched out on the grass in a field for several hours and... yes, perhaps because of the wine... he had even cried. He had felt as if lost in an infinitely remote place. It seemed he recalled so many things that perhaps had never existed for him.

Spring, the rapture of the first warm rays of the sun on the tender grass of the meadows, the first timid little flowers and the singing of the birds: When had the birds ever sung so joyously for him?

What torture it was to be in the midst of that vernal green, so vivid, fresh and youthful, and to realize that you've got gray hair and a scraggly beard. To know that you're old. To realize that a cry that had the joy of those trills, of that twittering could never again erupt from your soul;

that a thought, a feeling that had the gentle timidity of those first little flowers, the freshness of those first blades of grass in the meadows could never again blossom in your heart and mind. To realize that all that joy for youthful spirits was being converted into an infinite, agonizing regret for you.

His season had passed forever.

In winter, who can say which tree among so many is dead? They all seem dead. But as soon as spring arrives, first one, then another, then so many together blossom again. Only one of them, one that all the others up till then might have thought was like them, remains bare. Dead.

That was he.

Gloomy, distressed, he left Villa Borghese. He crossed Piazza del Popolo and turned into Via Ripetta. Then, feeling suffocated along this street, he crossed the bridge and went down Lungotevere dei Mellini.

Still embarrassed because of his unintentional rudeness toward the lady with the small black poodle, he came upon a funeral procession moving quite slowly under the now green trees, a musical band leading the way. God, how out of tune that band played! Thank goodness the deceased could no longer hear it. And that long line of mourners... Ah, life!

Yes, one could easily define life like this: a harmony between the bass drum and the cymbals. In funeral marches the bass drum and the cymbals no longer harmonize. Every now and then, the bass drum rolls on its own as if there were dogs inside. The cymbals *ching!* and *chang!* on their own, too.

After making this fine observation and greeting the deceased, he again set out.

When he arrived at Ponte Margherita, he stopped. Where was he going? He was so tired that his legs would no longer carry him. Why had he taken Via Ripetta? Crossing Ponte Margherita, he again found himself almost in front of Villa Borghese. No, no, he would follow the avenue along the Tiber from this other side until he reached the new Ponte Flaminio.

But why? What did he want to do anyway? Nothing... Just walk and walk as long as it was still light.

The embankment came to an end just beyond Ponte Flaminio, but the avenue continued to be wide, high above the river, forming a scarp over the natural banks, with a long wooden fence serving as its parapet. At a certain point Bernardo Morasco noticed a small path leading down to the river bank, through the thick grass of the slope. He passed under the fence and went down to the river bank, which was rather wide there; it too covered with thick grass. He lay down.

The last glimmers of the setting sun filtered through the cypress trees of Monte Mario. Almost directly in front of him, they cast a sort of very soft and gradually darkening glaze over the things that would maintain their colors for a short time longer in the falling darkness. They also cast mother-of-pearl reflections on the peaceful waters of the river.

There was a deep, almost astonishing silence. It was not broken, but animated, so to speak, by a sort of hollow, rhythmic splash, repeatedly followed by the lively sound of trickling water.

His curiosity aroused, Bernardo Morasco sat up to look, and saw what seemed like the tip of a black barge stretching out from the bank into the river. It ended in a solid axle that held two fish traps, two sorts of iron baskets rotating from the force of the water itself. As soon as one of the traps plunged into the water, the other emerged from the opposite side, all dripping wet.

He had never before seen this fishing apparatus. He did not know what it was nor what it meant, so he remained there a long time, looking at it in puzzled astonishment. He was stricken with a sense of mystery by the slow, rhythmic motion of those two fish traps that plunged one after the other into the water, to draw water, nothing but water.

The useless, monotonous rotation of such a large and gloomy contraption gave him a sense of infinite sadness.

Again he fell back onto the grass. He felt that everything in life was as useless as the rotation of those two fish traps in the water. He looked at the sky, where the first stars had already appeared. They were dim because the moon was about to rise.

A delightful May evening was being announced, but Bernardo Morasco's melancholy was becoming increasingly gloomy and bitter. Ah, who could ever remove those twenty years of prison from his shoulders so that he too might enjoy this delightful scene? Even if he managed to renew his spirit by getting rid of all those memories that would forever sour his meager pleasure of living, how would he be able to renew his already worn-out body? How could he go searching for love with that body? Without love, with no other blessings, his life had passed for him, a life that could have, ah yes, could have been beautiful! Before long it would end... No trace of him would remain, even though he had once dreamed of having the power to give a new expression, his own expression, to things... Ah no! Vanity! That fish trap which the river of time turned and plunged into the water, making it catch nothing but water...

Suddenly he got up. As soon as he was on his feet, it seemed strange to him that he had gotten up. He felt he had not gotten up by himself but had been brought to his feet by an internal stimulus that was not his own. Perhaps it was a result of that hidden thought that seemed to be lying in ambush within him for so many years.

So, had the moment arrived?

He looked around. There was no one. There was a silence that, formidably suspended, waited for the grass to rustle as soon as he would take his first step toward the river. And there were all those blades of grass that would remain exactly the same under the damp, soft light of the moon, even after his disappearance from the scene.

Bernardo Morasco walked to the river bank but only out of curiosity to observe that strange fishing device from up close. He got down onto the barge, where a pole was fixed vertically next to the two rotating fish traps.

That's it. By holding on to the pole, he could take a leap and fall into^ one of those fish traps and have himself dished out into the river.

Beautiful! Original! Yes... With both hands he grabbed hold of the pole as if to attempt it. Smiling nervously, he waited for one of the fish traps, which at that moment was plunging into the water a short distance away, to make its revolution. As soon as it emerged near him, progressively rising while the other was plunging, he actually leaped and thrust himself into it, his eyes shut, his teeth clenched, his whole face contracted in the agony of the horrible wait.

What! Had the weight of his body arrested the movement? Was he remaining in balance in the fish trap?

He opened his eyes, dazed by what had happened. He was trembling, almost laughing... Oh God, wasn't it moving anymore?

But no, see, see... the force of the river was winning... The fish trap was again beginning to rotate... Good Lord, no... He had waited too long... The hesitation, the momentary stopping of the contraption's motion on account of the weight of his body had seemed like a joke to him, and he had almost laughed about it... Oh God! While the fish trap rose again, he looked up and saw all the stars in the sky seemingly crashing downward. Then, instinctively, in an instant, overcome with terror, Bernardo Morasco stretched out his arm toward the pole—both his arms —and grabbed it with such desperate effort that in the end he flew out of the trap and landed on his feet on top of the barge.

The trap, with an extremely violent splash caused by the jolt, plunged again, squirting water on him.

He shuddered and laughed, and again, in a state of feverish excitement, he almost shivered audibly, looking about as if he had played a trick on the river, the moon and the cypress trees of Monte Mario.

He felt that he had rediscovered the enchantment of the night, with the stars quite steady and brilliant in the sky, and those river banks, that peace and that silence.

By Himself

A first-class coach with trimmed and crested horses, and with a coachman and footmen wearing wigs—*that* his relatives would certainly not get for him. But a second-class one, yes, to keep up appearances.

Two hundred fifty lire, the going rate.

And then the coffin, even though made of fir and not of walnut or beech, would certainly not be left completely bare (again for appearances).

When it is covered with red velvet--even of the lowest quality, with gilded studs and handles, at the very least that would come to four hundred lire.

Then, a generous tip to the person who would wash and dress his corpse (a fine task!): The expense of the silk skullcap and the cloth slippers. The expense of the four torches to be lit at the four corners of the bed. The tip to the undertakers who would carry the coffin on their shoulders up to the coach and then from the coach to the grave. The expense of the wreath of flowers —at least one, by God. Then, let's forget the municipal band —one could do without it; but a couple of dozen candles for the procession of the little orphans of the *Relief for the Poor,* who live on this, that is, on the fifty lire they are paid to accompany all the dead of the city. Who knows how many other small, unpredictable expenses...

All this Matteo Sinagra would save his relatives by going with his own two feet to the cemetery to kill himself—economically—in front of the little gate of his family tomb. So that, with very little expense, right there, after the police had arrived, they could thrust him in among four bare, planks, without even brushing him off, and lower him there where his father, mother, first wife and the two children she had borne him had been resting for quite some time.

The dead seem to believe that the difficult part is losing one's life and that everything ends with death. Undoubtedly that's true for them. But they don't think of the horrible, encumbering body that remains there stiff on the bed for one or two days and of the troubles and expenses of the living who, though they gather around it to cry, have to get rid of it. Knowing how much it costs to get rid of a body, those who intend to die by their own hand and are in good health such as he, could take a stroll to the cemetery and quietly put themselves away--all by themselves.

Yes, Matteo Sinagra no longer had anything else to think about. For him life had suddenly become devoid of all meaning. He could hardly remember what exactly he had done. But yes, certainly, he too had done all the foolish things that one usually does. Without realizing it. With a lot of frivolity and great ease. Yes, because he had also been rather fortunate, that is, until three years ago. Nothing had ever been difficult for him. Nor had he ever stopped, uncertain whether to do a certain thing, whether to choose this or that path. He had plunged with cheerful confidence into all of his ventures. He had traveled down every road and had always gone forward, overcoming obstacles that others perhaps would have found insurmountable.

Until three years ago.

Suddenly, who knows how, who knows why, that sort of creative impulse which for so many years had helped him and pushed him ahead, making him industrious and sure of himself, had died out. His cheerful confidence had collapsed and with it all the undertakings he had sustained by hook and by crook and that now, suddenly, he too, awestricken, was unable to account for.

From one day to the next everything had changed and darkened like that for him. Even the appearance of things and people. He suddenly found himself face to face with another self that he didn't know at all, in another world that, for the first time, revealed itself to be hard, obtuse, opaque, inert.

At first he was left with the sort of stupefaction that silence inflicts on those who live in the midst of noisy machines that are suddenly stopped. Then he had thought of the financial ruin, not only his own but also that of his father and his second wife's brother, who had entrusted large sums of money to him. But perhaps his father-in-law and brother-in-law, though suffering grave losses, would get back on their feet again. His financial ruin, instead, was total.

He locked himself in his house, crushed not so much by the weight of his misfortune as by his awareness of the fact that the mysterious damage so suddenly occurring in the mechanism of his life was irremediable.

Do something? And why? Why leave his home? Every act, every step, was useless. Even talking was useless.

Silent, hiding in a corner, he remained there like a madman, observing the frenzy and tears of his desperate wife. He became all beard and hair.

Until his brother-in-law, infuriated, shoved him out violently after having him forcibly shorn.

Something could be done. He could earn ten lire a day by becoming an errand boy in the employ of a small agrarian bank that had just opened. What was he doing, brooding there on that chair? Out! Out! Wasn't the damage he had done until now enough? Did he also want to live, with his wife and two small ones, at the expense of his victims? Out!

Out, so here he was. He had left his home several days before. He had become an errand boy for that small agrarian bank. A tattered hat, a faded suit, torn shoes and the look of an utter fool.

No one recognized him anymore.

"That's Matteo Sinagra?"

He didn't even recognize himself, to tell the truth. And that morning, finally...

It had been a friend, a dear friend from his better days, who clarified the situation for him.

Who was he now? Nobody. Not only because he had lost everything he had. Not only because he had been reduced to that miserable, humiliating state of errand boy with that faded suit, that tattered hat, those torn shoes. No, no. He was really no one now because there was no longer anything left, except for the physical appearance (and that too, so changed, unrecognizable!) of that Matteo Sinagra who he had been until three years ago. He didn't recognize himself in this errand boy who had just left home, nor did the others. And so, who was he? Someone else who still was not living. Someone who had to learn how to live a new life, if at all, a miserable, humiliating one on ten lire a day. And was it worth the effort? Matteo Sinagra, the real Matteo Sinagra, had died, absolutely died, three years ago.

The eyes of the friend he had run into that morning had told him that, with the most ingenuous cruelty.

This friend, having returned to town after an absence of almost six years, knew nothing of his misfortunes. Passing him by on the street, this friend hadn't recognized him.

"Matteo? But how can that be? You're Matteo Sinagra?"

"They say..."

"But how can that be?"

His eyes, those eyes, remained there staring at him with such an expression of bewilderment and, at the same time, with such pity and revulsion that suddenly he saw himself in them as being dead, absolutely dead, without even a little bit of the life that Matteo Sinagra had once had in himself.

So, as soon as this friend, no longer able to find a word, a glance, a smile to address to this shadow, had turned his back on him, he had had the strange sensation that suddenly everything had actually become devoid of meaning, that all of life had become empty.

But just now? No... Good Lord! It had been like this for the past three years... He had been dead for three years, for a good three years... And was he still there on his feet? Was he walking... breathing... looking?

But how could that be if he was no longer anything, no longer anyone! Dressed in that suit of three years ago... with those shoes of three years ago still on his feet...

Come, come now, wasn't he ashamed? A dead man still on his feet? He should bed down there in the cemetery!

Once they have disposed of the encumbrance, the relatives would look after the widow and the two little orphans.

Matteo Sinagra had felt around in his vest pocket for the revolver, his trusty companion for so many years. And, with nothing else, there he is on the road that leads to the cemetery.

It's really an amusing thing, an unheard of pleasure.

A dead man who goes on his own, with his own feet, ever so slowly, taking his own sweet time, to his fate.

Matteo Sinagra knows perfectly well that he's a dead man and what is more, an old dead man, someone who died three years ago and had all the time in the world to rid himself of every regret for his lost life.

He is now very light, as light as a feather! He has found himself. He has become the shadow of himself. Free from every obstacle, devoid of every affliction and immune from every hardship, he goes to rest comfortably.

Now, look! The road that leads to the cemetery, which he is walking down like that as a dead man, for the last time, without any possibility of returning, appears different to him, filling him with a sense of joyous freedom that truly is something already outside life, beyond life.

The dead, locked and sealed in a double coffin made of zinc and walnut, travel down that road in a coach. But he walks, breathes and can move his neck here and there to continue to look around.

With new eyes, he looks at the things that are no longer for him, that for him no longer have any meaning.

The trees... oh look! Were the trees like this? These were the very ones? And those mountains down there... why? Those blue mountains with the white cloud over them... The clouds... what strange things! There, in the distance, the sea... Was it like this? That's the sea?

Even the air that enters his lungs has a new fragrance, a pleasant coolness on his lips, in his nostrils... The air... ah, the air... What a delight! He breaths it... ah, he now drinks it in as never before in life, as no one still in life can drink it in! It's air just as air is, not as breath for living. The other dead certainly cannot have all this infinite delight that envelops him, the ones who travel down that road in a carriage, rigid, stretched out, plunged in the darkness of a coffin. Not even the living can have it, the living who do not know what it means to enjoy it *afterwards* like this, once and for all. A living, present, seething eternity!

There is still a lot of road ahead but he could already stop here. He is in eternity. He walks and breathes in this divine rapture unknown to the living.

"Do you want me? Bring me along..."

A stone. A stone from the road. Why not?

Matteo Sinagra bends down, picks it up, weighs it in his hand. A stone... Were stones like this? These were the very ones? Yes, look! A small fragment of rock, a piece of living earth, of all this living earth, a fragment of the universe... Here it is. Into his pocket. It'll go with him.

And that little flower?

Why yes, that too, right here in the buttonhole of this dead man who goes by himself, with his own two feet, to his grave. Being so carefree, peaceful and happy, he seems to be going to a party, with that little flower in his buttonhole.

Here's the entrance to the cemetery. Another twenty steps or so and the dead man will be at his own home. No tears. He's coming by himself with a brisk pace and that little flower in his buttonhole.

Those cypress trees standing like sentinels at the gate are a beautiful sight. Oh, it's a modest house at the top of a hillock, among the olive trees. There are probably a hundred family tombs, more or less, without any pretence to art: small chapels, each with a small altar, a small gate and a few flowers growing around them.

For the dead, this cemetery is really an enviable residence. Since it is far from the town, the living rarely comes here.

Matteo Sinagra enters and greets the old caretaker, who is sitting on the doorstep of his little house, to the right of the entrance, with his gray woolen shawl on his shoulders and his cap trimmed with braid on his nose.

"Hey there, Pignocco!"

Pignocco is sleeping.

And Matteo Sinagra stands there observing the sleep of the only living man among so many dead and—as a dead man—he feels displeasure, a certain irritation.

No matter what one says, it comforts the dead to think that a living man watches over their sleep and is bustling about over the ground that covers them. Sleep above, sleep below. Too much sleep. He had best wake Pignocco and say to him,

"Here I am. I'm one of yours. I've come by myself, with my own two feet, to make my relatives save a little money. But is this how you're taking care of us?"

Oh, come on, what sort of care, poor Pignocco! What need of care do the dead have? When Pignocco has watered a flower bed here and there, when he has gone to this or that family tomb and lit some small votive lamp that doesn't provide light for anyone, when he has swept the dead leaves from the paths, what else is left for him to do? No one in there is stirring. And so, the buzzing of the flies and the slow rustling of the soothing olive trees on the hillock coax him to sleep. He too is awaiting death, poor Pignocco, and in that wait, here he is, sleeping for the time being over so many dead who sleep forever below.

Perhaps he'll wake up before long when he hears the blunt shot of the revolver. But, perhaps, not even then. The revolver is very small, and he's sleeping very soundly. Later, toward dusk, when he'll go around to make his final inspection before closing the gate, he'll find something black blocking the path, there at the far end.

"Oh! What's all this?"

Nothing, Pignocco. Someone who has to go below. Call, call for some people to prepare him a bed down below as best they can, without much fuss. He came by himself to save his relatives the expense, and also for the pleasure of seeing himself beforehand like this, a dead man among the dead, already in his home, having arrived at his fate in good health, with his eyes open, perfectly conscious. Leave that stone in his pocket. It too is tired of staying in the sun, on the road. And leave that little flower in the dead man's buttonhole. It's the only vanity possible to him at this time. He picked it and offered it to himself for all the wreaths that his relatives and friends will not offer him. He's here, still above ground; but it's precisely as if he had come from below, after three years, to satisfy his curiosity to see what impression these things make on the hillock: the family tombs, the flower beds, the gravel paths, the black crosses and the tin wreaths in the pauper's field.

A fine impression, really.

Ever so quietly Matteo Sinagra, tiptoeing, without awakening Pignocco, goes in.

It's still early to go to bed. He'll wander down the paths until evening, looking about (as a dead man, naturally). He'll wait for the moon to rise, and then that'll be the end of it.

The Long Dress

It was Didi's first long trip. From Palermo to Zùnica, an eight-hour train ride, more or less. For Didi, Zùnica was a dreamland, far, far away and more distant in time than in space. In feet, when she was a child, it was from Zùnica that her father used to bring her certain fresh, fragrant and delicious fruits whose color, taste and fragrance she wasn't able to recognize later in the many others her father brought from there. He brought large berries in rustic earthenware jars sealed with vine leaves; small pears with crowns, pale on one side, blood-red on the other; and iridescent plums as well as pistachios and limes.

Even now, the very mention of Zùnica evoked in Didi's mind a deep wood of Saracen olive trees and vast expanses of very green vineyards and bright red gardens with hedges of sage buzzing with bees, whose mossy nurseries and citrus orchards were perfumed by orange blossoms and jasmine. Yet Didi knew, for quite some time, that Zùnica was a poverty-stricken, barren little town located in Sicily's hinterland. She also knew that it was completely surrounded by the black parched tuff of the sulphur mines and by rugged chalky rocks that shone under the fury of the sun, and that these fruits, unlike the ones she received in her childhood, came from an estate called "Ciumia," quite a few kilometers outside of the town.

She heard this from her father. She had never gone beyond Bagheria, near Palermo, for her vacation. Bagheria was a town of whitewashed houses scattered among the vegetation, under a brilliant deep blue sky. Last year she had gone on vacation even closer, among the orange groves of Santa Flavia, and at that time she was still wearing short dresses.

Now, for the long trip to Zùnica, she was wearing a long dress for the first time.

She felt she was already someone else: really and truly a young lady. She even seemed to have the train of her dress in her eyes, and from time to time she would raise her eyebrows as if to pull it up. She held her small bold nose and her dimpled chin high in the air and she kept her mouth closed. Hers was the mouth of a lady in a long dress, a mouth that hid her teeth, just like her long dress hid her small feet.

However, seated in front of her was Coco, her older brother. That mischievous Coco, his head flung back on the red back of the seat in the first-class coach, his eyes cast downward, a cigarette dangling from his upper lip, would occasionally say to her with a tired sigh,

"Didi, you make me laugh."

God, how angry that made her! God, how her fingers itched!

Now then, if Coco had not shaven off his mustache to suit the fashion, Didi would have pounced on him like a cat and torn it off.

Instead, smiling with upraised brows, she would answer him calmly,

"My dear, you're an idiot."

Imagine laughing at her long dress and, if you will, at the airs she was putting on after the serious talk he had had with her the evening before regarding this mysterious trip to Zunica...

This trip: was it or was it not a sort of expedition, an undertaking, something akin to the scaling of a well-fortified castle on top of a mountain? And her long dresses: were they or were they not machines of war for that scaling? So, what was there to laugh at if, feeling armed with them for the conquest, she periodically tried out these weapons by putting on those airs?

The evening before, Coed had told her that the time had finally come for them to look after their affairs seriously.

Didi had opened her eyes wide.

Their affairs? What affairs? Could there possibly be affairs that she, too, had to look after and give serious consideration to?

After an initial moment of surprise, she had burst into a hearty laugh.

She only knew one person who was expressly made to look after her own affairs as well as those of everyone else: Donna Sabetta, her governess, known as Donna Bebe, or Donna Be', as she called her for short. Donna Be' always looked after her own affairs. Assaulted, pushed and pulled by certain furious and sudden impulses, the poor old woman would pretend to start whimpering and, scratching her forehead with both hands, would moan,

"Oh, blessed be the name of the Lord, let me look after my affairs, young lady!"

Was Coco now taking her for another Donna Be'? No, he was not. The evening before, Coco had assured her that their precious "affairs" existed and that they were serious, quite serious, like her long dress for the trip.

Since childhood, Didi had seen her father go to Zùnica once and sometimes twice a week. Hearing talk about the Ciumia estate and the sulphur mines of Monte Diesi and of other locations, as well as about farms and houses, Didi had always thought that all these properties, the baronage of the Brillas, were her father's.

They belonged, instead, to the Nigrentis, the marquises of Zùnica. Her father, Baron Brilla, was only the judicial administrator. This administration, which had yielded her father great affluence for twenty years and which the two of them, Coco and Didi, had always enjoyed, was to end within a few months.

Didi had been born and raised amid this affluence. She was now a little more than sixteen years old. Coco, however, was twenty-six. Hence he retained a clear, though distant, memory of the dire poverty their father had struggled with before he had managed, through intrigues and quarrels of all sorts, to have himself appointed the judicial administrator of the vast estate of those marquises of Zùnica.

Now, there was great fear that they would once again fell into that poverty which, even if less severe, would seem harsher after their life of ease. In order for them to avert it, the battle plan engineered by the father had to succeed, to succeed well and in every respect. The present trip was the first move.

But not really the first. Coco had already gone to Zùnica with his father three months before to look into the situation. He had stayed there two weeks and had met the Nigrentis.

Excluding an error, this family was composed of three brothers and a sister. Excluding an error, because, in the ancient palace above the town, there were also two eighty-year-old women, two *zonne,* or spinster aunts. Cocó was uncertain whether they, too, were Nigrentis—that is, whether they were sisters of the marquis' grandfather or of his grandmother.

The marquis' name was Andrea. He was about forty-five years old and, as soon as the term of the judicial administration expired, he, in accordance with dispositions of the will, would become the principal heir. There were two other brothers. One was a priest, *Don Arzigogolo* [Rev. Daydreamer], as their father called him. The other, the so-called *Cavaliere,* was a boor. One had to be wary of both of these fellows and more so of the priest than of the boor. The sister was twenty-six, one year older than Coco, and her name was Agata, or "Titina." She was as frail as a Host and as white as a ghost. Her eyes were constantly full of anguish, and her long, cold, slender hands trembled from timidity because she was uncertain and bashful. She must have been purity and goodness personified, poor thing, because she never set foot outside the palace but always looked after the pair of eighty-year-old women, the *zonne.* She embroidered and played the piano "divinely."

Well then, their father's plan was this: Before leaving the judicial administration, he would arrange two marriages. He would have the Marquis Andrea marry Didi, and Agata would go to him, Coco.

As soon as Didi had heard of the plan, her face turned crimson and her eyes flashed with anger. Her anger had erupted in her not so much because of the thing itself but because of the cynical, resigned air with which Coco accepted it for himself and tendered it to her as a way out. Marry an old man for money, someone who was twenty-eight years older than she?

"No, not twenty-eight," Coco had said to her, laughing at her burst of anger. "Not twenty-eight, Didi! Twenty-seven, let's be honest, twenty-seven and some months."

"Coco, you make me sick! Yes, sick!" Didi had then yelled at him, trembling with rage and shaking her fists.

And Coco had added,

"I'm marrying Virtue, Didi, and I'm making you sick? She's also a year or so older than I but Virtue, my dear Didi, allow me to point this out, can't be very young. Besides I need it so much! I'm an awful rogue and I'm terribly depraved, you know. I'm a scoundrel, as Papa says. I'll become sensible. I'll have an extremely beautiful pair of embroidered slippers on my feet, with my initials in gold and my baronial crown. I'll wear a velvet cap on my head. It too will be embroidered and it'll have a nice long silk tassel. The young Baron Coco Virtue... How handsome I'll be, my dear Didi!"

And he had started walking back and forth like a real simpleton, his neck twisted, his eyes downcast, his mouth pursed, his hands, one on top of the other, hanging from his chin like a goat's beard.

Didi had unwittingly let out a guffaw.

Then Coco had tried to calm her down, caressing her and telling her about all the good he could do for that poor girl who was as frail as a Host and as pale as a ghost. After all, during his two month stay in Zùnica, she had shown that she viewed him as her savior, even though with the timidity that came natural to her. Why yes! Of course! It was in the best interest of her brothers and especially in the interest of that so-called *Cavaliere* (who maintained a prostitute outside the palace from whom he had had ten, fifteen, twenty... in a word, an unknown number of children) that she remain unmarried, holed up there to rot in the shadows. Well then, he would be her sunshine, her life. He would take her out of there and bring her to Palermo to live in a beautiful new house. There would be parties, theatrical performances, trips, car rides... She was a little ugly all right but, anyway, she would do as a wife. Besides, she was so good and, since she wasn't used to ever having anything, she would be satisfied even with little.

He had purposely kept on talking at length only about himself in this vein, that is, about the good he was resolved to do for her, with the result that Didi, provoked like this on the one hand and on the other, annoyed at seeing herself put aside, finally asked,

"And me?"

When her question had surfaced, Coco answered her with a profound sigh.

"Oh, for you, my dear Didi, the matter is very, very difficult, that is, much more difficult! You're not alone."

Didi had frowned and asked. "What does that mean?"

He had replied,

"It means... it means that there are others buzzing around the marquis, yes indeed. And especially one of them... one!"

With a most expressive gesture Coco had let her imagine a woman of extraordinary beauty.

"She's a widow, you know." he had said. "About thirty years old. What's more, she's his cousin..."

With his eyes half-shut, he had kissed the tips of his fingers.

Didi had erupted in a scornful outburst.

"Let her have him!"

But Coco immediately had said,

"Let her have him? That's easier said than done! Do you think that Marquis Andrea... (A fine name, Andrea! Listen to how well it sounds: *Marquis Andrea*... But in private you could call him Nenè, the way Agata—that is, Titina, his sister—calls him.) He's quite a man, this Nene, you know. It's enough for you to know that he had the... the strength of mind to stay locked up at home for twenty years. Twenty years, understand? It's no laughing matter... From the time his estate fell under the judicial administration. Imagine his hair, my dear Didi, how it must have grown during these twenty years! But he'll cut it. Rest assured, he'll cut it. Every morning, at dawn, he goes out by himself... You like that? He goes out by himself, wrapped in a cloak, and takes a long ride as far as the mountain. He goes on horseback, you know. His mare is rather old, and white, but he rides her divinely. Yes, divinely, as divinely as his sister plays the piano. And just think, oh yes, just think that when he was young, until he was twenty-five —that is, until they called him back to Zùnica because of the financial setback —he lived it up, and what a life it was, my dear sister! He went all over Europe. He went to Rome and to Florence. He traveled all over the world. He went to Paris and to London... It seems that, when he was young, he fell in love with this cousin I spoke to you about. Her name is Fana Lopes. I believe he even got engaged to her, but when the financial trouble came, she would have nothing more to do with him. She married someone else. Now that he's returning to his former state... you understand? But it is more likely that the marquis, to spite her, will marry another cousin. An old maid. A certain Tuza La Dia, who, I believe, has always pined for him in secret, praying to God. Given the marquis' moods and his long hair, after having lived like a recluse for these twenty years, even this old maid is a threat, my dear Didi. But enough of this," concluded Coco the evening before. "Now bend over, Didi, and with your fingertips take the hem of your dress and hold it up against your legs."

Stunned by this lengthy speech, Didi had bent over and asked,

"Why?"

And Coco had replied,

"I'm waving your legs good-by because they'll never be seen again."

He had looked at them and waved at them with both hands. Then, sighing, he had added,

"Roro! Do you remember Roro Campi, your little girlfriend? Do you remember that I waved good-by to her legs too, the last time she wore short dresses? I thought that I would never see them again. And yet I did see them again!"

Didi had turned extremely pale and serious.

"What do you mean?"

"Oh, you know, she died," Coco had hastened to answer. "Yes, I swear it. I saw them when she was dead. Poor Rord! They left the casket open when they brought her into the church in San Domenico. That morning I was there in the church. I saw the casket surrounded by candles and I went up to it. There were several peasant women around it, all of them admiring the sumptuous wedding gown in which her husband had wanted her dead body to be adorned. At one point, one of these women lifted the edge of the gown to examine the lace on her petticoat, so that's how I again saw poor Roro's legs."

That entire night Didi had tossed and turned in her bed, unable to sleep.

Before going to bed, she had wanted to try on her long dress once again in front of the wardrobe mirror. After the expressive gesture made by Coco to describe the woman's beauty—What was her name? Oh, yes, Fana... Fana Lopes...—she saw herself in the mirror as being too small, too thin and pitiful. Then she had pulled her dress up in the front to look at that small, that very small area of skin on her legs that up till now she had shown, and immediately she thought about Roro Campi's legs when the girl was dead.

In bed she had again wanted to look at her own stiff and skinny legs under the covers. She pictured herself also dead in a coffin with a wedding gown, after marrying the long-haired Marquis Andrea...

What sort of talk was that! That Coed!

On the train, Didi was now looking at her brother sprawled out on the opposite seat and she felt increasingly overwhelmed by a feeling of great pity for him.

Within a few years she had seen her brother's fresh, handsome face waste away. She had seen its look change, as well as the expression in his eyes and mouth. It seemed to her that he had a fire burning inside. She perceived this fire that burned within, this terrible fever in his glance, in his lips, in the dryness and redness of his skin, especially under his eyes. She knew that he came home very late every night and that he gambled.

She suspected he had other vices, worse ones, from the violent scolding her father often gave him in private while the two of them, father and son, were alone in the study. And what a strange impression, a mixture of sorrow and repulsion, she had felt for some time in seeing him approach her from that wicked, impenetrable life. She had an alarming thought: Though for her he was always a good and affectionate brother, outside the home he might be worse than a little rogue, a depraved fellow if not actually a scoundrel, as so many times her father had shouted in his face when angry. Why, why had he not had the same heart for others as he had for her? If in all truth he appeared so good to her, how could he, at the same time, be as wicked as the others painted him?

But perhaps his wickedness was out there, out there in the world, into which, at a certain age, after having left the peaceful and innocent affections of the family, men entered in long trousers and women in long dresses.

It must have been a disgusting wickedness since no one dared talk about it if not in a whisper and with sly winks that annoyed whoever, like herself, could not understand anything about it. It must have been a devouring wickedness if in such a short time her brother, once so fresh and innocent, had been reduced to such a state, and if Rorò Campi, her little girlfriend, died of it after scarcely one year...

Didi felt her long dress weighing down on her small feet, which, until the day before, were free and bare. And it gave her a feeling of restless annoyance. She felt overwhelmed by a feeling of suffocating anguish and she turned her gaze from her brother to her father, who sat at the other corner of the coach, busily reading some administrative documents taken from a small leather briefcase open on his knees.

In that small briefcase, lined with red cloth, there shone the frosted glass stopper of a vial. Didi stared at it and thought about her father, who for many years was living under the continuous threat of sudden death. From one moment to the next he could have a heart attack, to which he was prone and because of which he always brought along that vial.

If he were suddenly to die... Oh, God, no, why think about that? Even though he had that vial there in front of him, he himself never thought about it. He was reading his administrative papers and, from time to time, would adjust his glasses, which rested on the tip of his nose. Then, suddenly, he would run his plump hand, pale and hairy, over his very shiny bald head or he would take his eyes off what he was reading and stare into space, contracting a bit his fat puffy eyelids. His sky-blue oval eyes would then light up with a sharp malicious vitality that contrasted with his tired flabby face, plump and porous, from which there extended under his nose, his bristly short reddish mustache, already graying a bit and bushy.

For quite some time, that is, since her mother's death three months ago, Didi felt that her father had virtually turned away from her, or rather, had broken away to such an extent that she could now view him as a stranger. And not only her father but Coco too. She felt that only she had been left to continue living the life of the home, or rather, to feel its emptiness, after the death of the one who had filled it entirely and had kept everyone united.

Her father and her brother had started living on their own —outside the house, naturally. The activities of life that they continued to engage in together with her were almost only for appearances' sake. They no longer had that cordial intimacy of old from which there emanates that familial scent which sustains, consoles and reassures.

Didi still felt an anguished desire for that intimacy, which made her cry inconsolably as she knelt before the ancient chest where her mother's dresses were kept.

The familial scent was locked up in there, in that ancient walnut chest which was as long and narrow as a coffin. From it, from her mother's dresses, that scent emanated to sadly intoxicate her with the memories of her happy childhood.

It was as if her entire life had been rarefied and made useless by her mother's death. Everything seemed to have lost its corporeal reality and to have become a shadow. What would happen tomorrow? Would she forever feel this void, this longing in her uncertain wait for something that would fill that void and restore her confidence, her security and her rest?

The days had gone by for Didi like clouds passing in front of the moon.

How many evenings, without turning on the light in her silent bedroom, had she not stood behind the high windowpanes to gaze at the white and ashen clouds that shrouded the moon? It seemed that the moon was racing along to free itself from those shrouds. She had remained there at length, there in the shadows, to daydream with her intent yet vacant eyes. Afterwards her eyes unwittingly became filled with tears.

She did not want to be sad, no. She wanted, rather, to be happy, active and lively, but in her solitude, in that void, this desire found no vent other than in fits of true madness that astonished poor Bebe.

No longer having anyone to guide her nor anything substantial around her, Didi did not know what to do in life and where to turn next. One day she wanted to be one thing, the next day something else. She had even dreamed an entire night, after returning from the theater, of becoming a ballerina, yes, indeed, and a sister of charity the following morning when the nuns of the Relief for the Poor came by to beg for alms. At times she wanted to close herself completely in herself and go wandering about the world, absorbed in theosophy like Frau Wenzel, her German language and piano teacher. At other times she wanted to dedicate herself entirely to art and painting. But, no, not really to painting anymore. Painting now disgusted her. It was as if it had become embodied in that imbecile, Carlino Volpi, the son of her teacher, the painter Volpi, who had come to substitute for his sick father and teach the lesson. How had it gone?... At a certain point she had asked him,

"Vermilion or carmine?"

And that ugly dog had replied, "Young lady, it's Carmine... like this!"

He had kissed her on the mouth.

From that day on, and forever, no more easel, paint brushes or palette! She had overturned the palette on him and, not satisfied with that, had even flung a bunch of brushes in his face and had thrown him out without even giving him time to wash his impudent face, all besprinkled with green, yellow and red.

She was at the mercy of the first to come, yes, indeed... There was no longer anyone in the house to protect her. A rascal could easily enter the house and take the liberty, as easy as anything, to kiss her on the mouth. What disgust that kiss had caused her! She had rubbed her lips until she drew blood, and still now, when she but thought about it, she instinctively brought her hand to her mouth.

But did she really have a mouth? She didn't feel it! She squeezed her lip forcefully, very forcefully with two fingers and—there!—she didn't feel it. And the same went for her entire body. She didn't feel it. Was it perhaps because she was always distracted and distant?... Everything was suspended, fluid and restless within her.

Now they had put that long dress on her like that... on a body she could not feel. That dress weighed much more than her body! They imagined that there was someone, a woman, under that long dress, but instead, no, she, at the most, could not feel she was anything more than a child inside; yes, still now, hidden from everyone, the child she once was when everything around her had a reality for her, the reality of her sweet childhood, the secure reality that her mother bestowed on things with her breath and her love. The body of that child—yes, it had lived, nourished itself and grew under the caresses and the care of her mother. But when her mother had died, she began not to feel her body, almost as if it too had become rarefied like everything surrounding the life of the family, the reality that she no longer could feel in anything.

Now, this trip...

Looking again at her father and her brother, Didi suddenly felt a deep, violent sense of revulsion.

The two had fallen asleep in uncomfortable positions. Her father was displaying, on one side, under his chin, his flabby dewlap indented by his collar. His forehead was beaded with sweat and, as he breathed, his nose whistled a bit.

In the steep terrain, the train proceeded very slowly as if it were panting. It was traveling through desolate stretches of land without a trickle of water or a tuft of grass, under the intense and gloomy blueness of the sky. Nothing, never anything, passed in front of the window of the coach. Only, from time to time, a telegraph pole, it, too, arid, with its four strings of wires that sank slightly.

After leaving her so alone even on the train, where were those two bringing her? To a shameful venture. And they were sleeping! Yes, because perhaps all of life was that way, and no other way. They, who had already entered it, knew that. By now they were used to it and, as they traveled, letting the train carry them forward, they could sleep... They had made her put on that long dress to drag her there, to that disgusting venture that no longer made any impression on them. They were dragging her there to Zùnica, the dreamland of her happy childhood! Why? So that she would die from it a year later like her little friend, Rorò Campi?

Where and in what would the suspense, the restlessness of her spirit, have stopped? In a small dead city, in a gloomy ancient palace, at the side of an old husband with long hair... Perhaps she would have to take the place of her sister-in-law in the care of those two old women who were in their eighties, even if her father succeeded in his plot.

Staring into space, Didi saw the rooms of that gloomy palace. Hadn't she already been there once? Yes, once in a dream, and to stay there forever... Once? When? But now, yes... she had been there for quite some time and she would remain there forever, suffocated in the emptiness of a time made up of eternal minutes disturbed only by the perpetual buzzing, near and distant, of drowsy flies in the sun; a sun that yawned forth its light through the flyspecked windowpanes to the naked walls yellowed with age, or stamped itself on the dusty pavement of worn-out terracotta bricks...

Oh God, not to be able to run away... Not to be able to run away... bound as she was, here, by the sleep of those two, by the enormous slowness of this train, which was equal to the slowness of time in that ancient palace where there was nothing else to do but sleep as those two were sleeping...

Suddenly in the daydream that became a reality in her spirit, a great, ponderous, unbreakable reality, she suddenly felt a sense of emptiness so arid, a *taedium vitae* so stifling and dreadful that instinctively, really without wanting to, she cautiously reached out her hand to the small leather briefcase that her father had left open on the seat. The vial's frosted glass stopper with its iridescence had already attracted her attention.

Her father and her brother continued to sleep. Didi sat there for a while examining the vial that shone from its pink, poisonous contents. Then, almost without heeding what she was doing, she unstopped it ever so quietly and slowly brought it to her lips, keeping her eyes fixed on the two who were sleeping. While she drank, she saw her father lift a hand in his sleep to shoo away a fly that was running lightly down his forehead.

Suddenly, the hand holding the vial fell heavily on her lap. As if her ears had suddenly been unplugged, she noticed the huge, rumbling, deafening noise of the train. It was so loud that she feared it would muffle the cry that was issuing from her throat and lacerating it... No... look! Her father and brother were leaping out of their sleep... They were standing over her... How could she grab on to them now?

Didi stretched out her arms but grabbed nothing, saw nothing and no longer heard anything.

Three hours later, she, a small dead girl wearing that long dress, arrived in Zunica, the dreamland of her happy childhood.

Candelora

Nane Papa, his plump hands gripping his shapeless old panama, says to Candelora, "It's not in your best interest. Listen to me, dear. It's not in your best interest."

And Candelora, furious, yells at him,

"Then what is? To stay on with you? To croak here in a fit of rage and shame?"

Nane Papa, tugging his hat farther and farther down, calmly replies,

"Yes, dear, but without croaking. With a bit of patience. Look, to put it frankly, Chico..."

"I forbid you to call him that!"

"Don't you call him that?"

"Precisely because I call him that!"

"Oh, all right. I thought it would please you. Do you want me to call him 'the baron'?" The baron, then... As I was saying, the baron loves you, my dear Candelora, and he spends a lot on you..."

"Ah! He spends a lot on me? Fool! Scoundrel! Doesn't he spend much more on you?"

"But let me finish... The baron spends a lot on me *and on* you. But, don't you see, if he spends much more on me, what does it mean? Be reasonable. It means that he values you only because you receive your shine from me. *That* you can't deny."

"Shine?" Candelora asks, again yelling and now at the height of her rage. "Yes, the shine of these..."

She lifts her foot and shows him her shoe.

"It's shame I receive! Shame! Shame!"

Nane Papa smiles and more calmly than ever answers,

"No, pardon me. I'm the one who gets the shame, if anyone. I'm your husband. That's what it's all about, Loretta, believe me. If I weren't your husband and, above all, if you were no longer under this hospitable roof with me, all the gusto, understand, would vanish. Here they can all come to honor you with impunity, and their pleasure is all the greater the more you, shall we say, dishonor and shame me. Without me around, you, Loretta Papa, would suddenly become a small, insignificant thing of little value, and they'd have to take more of a risk That's why Chico... that is, the baron, doesn't spend as much... What are you doing? Crying? No, no, come on! I'm only joking..."

Nane goes up to Candelora and makes a motion to place his hand under her chin, but she grabs his arm, opens her mouth like a wild animal and bites down on it. She bites down hard without letting up, and furiously increases her grip.

Bending down to keep his arm at an easy reach of her mouth, Nane, too, grinds his teeth, but only to smile silently at the pain, which makes him blanch.

His eyes become increasingly sharp and bright.

Then, when Candelora's teeth lose their grip, blissful relief! He feels as though his arm has been branded.

He says nothing.

Slowly, ever so slowly he pulls up his jacket sleeve. The shirt sleeve under it remains where it is because the cloth has been pressed into his living flesh. The white sleeve is dappled in the middle with red. There's a bloody circle: the entire set of Candelora's strong teeth, each of them stamped there in great relief. She dares him to lift his sleeve. Finally, Nane manages to do so, all the while smiling and still quite pale. His arm is a pitiful sight. Each tooth has left its mark and inside the circle, the flesh is black and blue.

"See?" says Nane as he shows her his wound.

"That's how I'd bite into your heart if I could!" roars Candelora, huddled in her chair.

"I know," says Nane, "and that's precisely why you'll decide not to go away. Come on, take off your little hat and go get some iodine so it won't get infected. Go get me some phenolic cotton and a bandage too. Go, Loretta, they're in my desk drawer, the second to the right. I know you're one of those little beasts that bite, and that's precisely why I keep an emergency supply on hand."

Candelora lifts his arm but only to steal a glance at it.

Nane admires her as she does that.

Candelora is a marvel of shapes and colors, a spiteful challenge to his painter's eye, which finds her ever new and different.
Now, at noon, here in the garden of their little villa, under the dreadful August sun that casts violent shadows in every direction, Candelora looks frightful. Having returned that morning from her vacation at the beach, her skin is roughened and burned by the sun and the salt water. In her bright, smarting eyes, in her somewhat receding chin and in her course yellow hair, she has the air of a she-goat lulled by sensual pleasure. With those strong, bare, peeling arms and those powerful hips, her every movement threatens to rip open the flimsy, tight-fitting dress of blue voile, which clashes with her sunburned flesh.

How ridiculous that dress is!

Candelora has spent entire mornings swimming. She has lain naked on the deserted beach, where she has covered and dappled her firm flesh with sand, under the sun, while the cool, foamy seawater lapped the soles of her feet. How can that flimsy blue dress now hide her exuberant nudity. It is only worn for the sake of decency, and for a moment it actually makes her appear more indecent than if she were naked.

In her rage she notices the admiring look in his eyes, and instinctively a smile of satisfaction appears on her lips, which, however, immediately exasperates her. So at first the smile becomes a grin, but then the grin suddenly breaks into sobs.

Candelora runs to the villa.

Unwittingly, Nane Papa grins mischievously as he follows her with his eyes. Then he looks at his wounded arm, which stings painfully in the sun. He too feels tears inexplicably stinging his eyes.

It is truly dreadful to sense, during a brief pause in the middle of a sweltering August afternoon, that life is a burden full of shame and disgust, and while dripping with sweat, to feel compassion for a poor soul burdened with that shame and that disgust.

In the gloomy, torrid sunshine, in the garden shot through with shadows, Nane Papa now feels the oppressive, painful, almost disconcerting presence of so many immobile things that appear wondrously suspended around him: the trees, those tall acacias, the pond bordered with artificial rocks, the green, mirror-like surface of the stagnant water, the benches.

What are they waiting for?

He can move and he can even go away, and yet how strange! He feels as if he is being watched by all those motionless things around him. Indeed he feels as if he is being held by the hostile, almost ironic fascination that emanates from their astonishing stillness, a stillness that makes his ability to go away seem useless, stupid, even ridiculous.

This garden symbolizes Baron Chico's wealth. Nane Papa has been living here for nearly six months but only this morning, when Candelora returned from the beach, did he feel the irresistible need to point to his shame and to hers and to expose it completely. He had done so jokingly because Candelora had hoped to leave that shame behind while, as she put it, "we still can."

Of course they can! Now Nane Papa's paintings are selling well, and the value of his original and exceedingly personal art has become evident. Not because his work has really been understood but because those stupid, wealthy visitors who frequent art exhibits were forced by the critics to pause in front of his canvases.

Reviews? They're words, words that live only in the minds of the critics. What about the one to whom Candelora had gone in desperation one day, shouting in his face that it was not right that an artist like Nane Papa should starve to death? That critic, the most influential of them all, had written a masterly article to call the attention of those idiots to the original and exceedingly personal art of Nane Papa, but he had also decided to have his recognition of the artist, let's not say paid for, but graciously compensated by Candelora's deepest gratitude. And Candelora, intoxicated by the victory, which perhaps she thought must cost her who knows what, had immediately shown her extreme gratitude not only to that critic but to all of the most fanatic admirers of her husband's new art. She had extended her extreme gratitude to everyone, especially to Baron Chico, who, yes indeed, went so far as to put them up in his villa in order to have the honor of harboring this art prodigy, this child of glory... What receptions! What gifts! What parties!

If doing that had cost her nothing, no harm would have been done. Poor Candelora!

Poverty had frightened her, yes, that's it. But she denies it. She says it had angered not frightened her because that poverty was not hardship, not humiliation; given his merits, it was injustice. It was this injustice she wanted to avenge. How? This is how: by accepting the villa, the car, the boat, the gold jewelry, the precious stones, the trips, the clothes, the parties... And she felt great scorn for him because he remained just as he was, neither sad nor happy, as slovenly as before, with no other pleasure than his paints, with no other desire than that of digging deeper and deeper into his art for the ever insatiable need of getting to the bottom of it, or as much to the bottom as possible so as not to see any of life's ridiculous phantasmagoria swirling around him.

Perhaps, or rather certainly, this ridiculous phantasmagoria symbolizes his glory: the precious stones, Loretta's luxurious life, the invitations, the parties. His glory and also—why not?—his own shame. But what does it matter to him?

His whole life, all that is alive in him, he applies, he gives, he spends for the joy of seeing a leaf come alive on his canvas. He himself becomes the living substance, the fibers and veins of that leaf, or the hardness and bareness of a stone that becomes a real stone on his canvas. This is all that matters to him.

His shame? His life or the lives of others? Extraneous, transitory things, not worth worrying about. Only his art lives, a creation that wrests its form from the light and torment of his soul.

If this has been his destiny, that means that it could not have been any different. It already seems so far in the past to even think about it!

And so, that morning, as if speaking from a distance, he said to Loretta—casually of course—that he certainly would have liked to have a good lifetime companion at his side, a woman who would not have resented poverty so much, a meek and humble companion upon whose bosom he could find rest, one whose suffering could inspire him with the same pity his unrecognized work once did.

Naturally Loretta had turned on him like a wildcat.

But what is she doing now? Why isn't she coming back down with the iodine, the cotton and the bandage? She went upstairs, crying, poor thing...

Now Loretta wants to be loved, loved by him. Perhaps out of spite for his indifference. Isn't this madness? If he really loved her, he would kill her. He absolutely needs his indifference to endure the shame of having her at his side. Can he escape this shame? How can he any longer, since both of them have it inside, outside and all around them? The only thing to do is not to give it any importance. He has to continue painting, and she had to go on having a good time, with Chico now, then with someone else later, and even with Chico and someone else together. Happily. This is the only substance of life: foolishness... One way or another, it all passes, leaving no trace behind. Meanwhile, laugh at all ill-conceived things that remain to suffer in awkward or disgraceful forms until they eventually crumble to dust. Everything carries its own miserable form, the miserable form as it is, with no hope of ever again being otherwise. This is precisely what is new about his art: his ability to express this miserable form. He fully realizes that every humpback has to resign himself to having a hump, and that deeds are like forms. Once a deed is done, it is what it is and can never change. For example, however much Candelora may try, she can never go back to being pure as when she was poor. Although, perhaps, Candelora was never pure, even as a child, otherwise she would not have been able to do the things she did and still take pleasure in them.

But why this sudden yearning to be pure? Why did she now want to be alone with him, calm, modest, loving? With him, after all that had happened? As if he could now take anything in life seriously again. And then love! A love as crumpled as hers, with that ridiculous image of Chico it conjured up, and that critic and so many others who could encircle the idyllically embracing couple and play ring-around-a-rosy...

Look! Under the sun, the blood has clotted, forming a scab over the teeth marks. His wrist and even a bit his hand have become swollen, and his veins have stiffened.

Nane Papa rouses himself from his thoughts and starts to climb back up to the villa. He calls out twice, first from the foot of the stairs, then from the entrance hall,

"Candelora! Candelora!"

His voice resounds in the empty rooms. No one answers. He enters the room next to his study, where his desk is, and then jumps back. Motionless in the bright light of that white room, Candelora is stretched out on the floor, her clothes ruffled as though she had rolled. One of her thighs is uncovered. He runs over to her and lifts her head. Oh, God! What has she done? Her mouth, chin, neck and breast are stained a blackish yellow. She drank the entire bottle of iodine.

"It's nothing! It's nothing!" he cries out. "Oh, my dear Candelora, what foolish thing have you done? My baby... But it's nothing, really! It'll just burn your stomach a little... Come on, come on, get up!"

He tries to lift her but fails because the poor thing has stiffened in her agony. But he does not call her "poor thing" but rather "baby... baby..." because he thinks it a bit silly that she has drunk the iodine. "Baby," he cries out repeatedly and even calls her "my little fool," as he tries to pull down the flimsy blue dress over her bare thigh that offends him. He looks away so as not to see her black-stained mouth. The flimsy dress is ripped apart under his jittery hand, laying bare even more of her thigh.

Now he is alone in the villa. Loretta had dismissed the servants that morning before going to the beach. There is no one to help him lift her off the floor, no one to send out immediately for a car to bring her to a hospital for emergency care. Fortunately, he hears the horn of Baron Chico's car out on the street. And a little later, a bewildered Chico appears with his stupid, sallow, aging face and his youthful, lanky body dressed in very elegant clothes.

"Oh! What's this?"

Without thinking, he brings his monocle to his eye to stare at her bare thigh.

"Help me lift her, for the love of God!" Nane cries out, exasperated by his own futile efforts.

As soon as they lift her, a revolver in the hand that had remained compressed under her side, fells to the floor, and there on her side, a blood stain appears.

"Oh! Oh!" Nane groans at this point as he and Chico carry her to the bedroom.

Loretta has not stiffened from pain, but from death. After laying the body on the bed, Nane Papa, who is nearly out of his wits, screams at Chico,

"Who was at the beach with you? Tell me, who was at the beach with you this summer?"

Chico, perplexed, mentions a few names.

"Oh, for God's sake!" cries out Nane, his fury mounting as he comes straight for him, grabbing him by his lapels and shaking him violently. "Is it possible that every one of you has to be so stupid, you who have a little money?"

"So stupid? Us?" Chico utters, more perplexed than ever, shrinking back at every shake.

"Why yes! Yes! Yes!" Nane Papa keeps on railing. "So stupid as to make this poor girl want me to love her! Understand? Me! Me! Me to love her!"

Then, in his fit of desperation, he bursts into tears and falls on Loretta's body.

While the Heart Suffered

The fingers of the left hand started first. Initially it was the little finger which being the smallest was also the most restless. It had always been a torment not only for the poor languid ring finger, which had the misfortune of being next to it, but also a bit for the other three fingers.

Oddly shaped, with its terminal phalanx badly attached, bent inward, hard, almost inflexible, it seemed like a finger with a permanent twisted neck.

But this defect had never bothered it. On the contrary, it had always used it so as not to leave its companions on that hand in peace for a moment, and, as if it gloried in that, it often stood erect as if to say to everybody,

"Look! See? I'm like this!"

Instead of modestly hiding that crippled phalanx under the ball of the ring finger, it would arrogantly impose it on its back or, forcing it to stay up in an extremely uncomfortable position, it would stretch out to place it on the middle or index finger, or it would go with its crooked little fingernail to tease the large hard nail of the squatty thumb.

Sometimes the latter, sick and tired of that, would oppose it violently, jumping on its first phalanx, and it would hold it down, pressing on it with the help of the other three fingers, almost to the point of strangling it.

It wouldn't give up.

Pressed in this way, it would scratch the ball of the thumb as if to say,

"See? I can move! You're worse off than I."

In feet, the thumb, as if caught in a vise, would quickly release it.

But that day they were all in agreement.

That this funny little finger was very spiteful and arrogant and wouldn't stay quiet for a moment was something that the other four fingers, in fact, liked, since they were greatly afraid of growing in the self-forgetful abandon in which the whole body had been left for about a week.

Not only the fingers but also the toes, which were confined, and each foot and the legs and, up, up above, the chest, the shoulders, the arms, the neck and, in the head, the cheeks, the lips, the alae of the nose, the eyes, the eyebrows, the forehead—all noticed confusedly, in that long-protracted abandon, an obscure and fearful threat that each of them, for its own sake, tried to escape.

For the past several days, life seemed to have become alienated from them to settle gloomily in a profound, mysterious intimacy from which they were excluded, kept apart and as if in the distance. It was as if the decision secretly maturing in that profound and mysterious intimacy had nothing at all to do with them.

For several days they were left there on a Viennese armchair near the window, waiting for the decision to come to a head. And in that wait, so as not to grow torpid in that abandon, they, not knowing what to do, played on their own. They really played like madmen.

One should have seen how the legs danced, now one, now the other, now both of them together, with the tips of the feet on the floor and the heel suspended so that the tendon would quiver! And how, tired of that game, they would stretch out to start another, which consisted of a rhythmic opening and closing, first with the left foot on the right, then with the right on the left in order to stay under, each in his own turn, without any cheating! And even the shoes with their squeaking took part in that game.

But it was the hands that played the most, now braiding the fingers, now joining them by their tips and moving them like a lever so that they first stretched to make each finger touch the other, then sprang apart in a spring-like action. Or each hand played separately. But almost always what one did, the other repeated. If the right hand drummed on the right leg, the left hand would drum on the left leg as if it couldn't help doing that. If the right hand made a roll or a crack, the left hand, a little later, would make the same roll or the same crack. Or, still playing a game, one of them would squeeze the fingers of the other and vice versa, or would pinch them only then to stroke them with a very slow rubbing. Or that hand would start scratching where there was no itch, so that the scratched finger would rebel with a violent jerk. And then a sort of scuffle would break out between the two hands, a convulsive rubbing finally cut short when one of them would seize the other, and for a while, the two would keep themselves imprisoned ever so tightly. Then suddenly one of them would rise up either to stretch the lobe of an ear, the lower lip of the mouth or the swollen bag under an eye; or needlessly to scratch the bristly chin, unshaven for several days.

More pitiful than any were the eyes, the eyebrows and the forehead. They, too, would have liked to play, but the gloomy tension of the spirit kept the eyes in a state of bewilderment or gave them a hard, grim fixity. It also kept the eyebrows knit and the forehead wrinkled.

The eyes were able to look but not see. If they saw anything even vaguely, they were immediately distracted from the thing seen and condemned to turn elsewhere without focusing. But then, out of their corners, without seeming to, they followed the play of the legs or hands. They would hastily suggest to the latter to take, for example, the paper knife from the little table near the armchair, in order to start playing another game with it. The hands didn't have to be told twice. To entertain the eyes, they would start that game unobtrusively, almost secretly, making the paper knife turn over and over again in every which way.

Sometimes they would interrupt this game to call the spirit's attention to themselves with violent means, hurting themselves. The terrible little finger of the left hand would thrust its crooked terminal phalanx into one of the little holes in the seat of the Viennese armchair and, not being able to pull itself out again, forced the man to bend his whole body to one side in his effort to find a way to extract it without it getting scratched and without ruining the seat of the chair. At once the thumb and then all five fingers of the other hand would compensate it with little caresses and amorous rubbings for hurting itself for the sake of them all. At other times the thumb and the index finger of the right hand would pinch one of the legs to make the man notice that if he had a heart suffering within, he also had that leg, which was also quite sensitive; that is, it too was very capable, as a leg, of suffering from a pinch, yes, of suffering that stinging sensation that was ever more painful. No? He didn't want to notice it? So then? Nothing! The index finger would rub the leg as if to cancel the suffering needlessly inflicted on it. Then both hands would take it and bestride it on the other so that it might amuse itself a bit by rocking its foot.

Oh look! In the wardrobe mirror placed at an angle on the other side of the window, the tip of the swinging foot would appear and disappear with a glint on its patent leather toecap.

Another game. The frowning eyes would follow one of the feet, focusing on the corner of the mirror and waiting for the tip of that foot to appear. However, they would pretend not to notice it, knowing that if they were to show the slightest sign of paying attention to it, the man, completely absorbed in his sorrow, would put an end to the rocking with a grumble and make the body assume another position.

Who knows! Perhaps that wouldn't have been bad...

If an elbow was placed on the right armrest of the armchair and the neck extended a little, the entire head could be seen in the mirror and this— that is, the sight of his own face—would be enough to make the man jump to his feet, angry and fierce.

It very nearly happened. No, come on, that wouldn't do. It would be better to continue playing and not provoke the fierce inimical will which was immersed in that profound, mysterious intimacy where the obscure and fearful decision was coming to a head. There was the risk that the will, seeing the squalor of the troubled face, the bald head, those swollen bags under the eyes, that beard unshaven for several days, might suddenly counter the violence with another form of violence. It wasn't worth it.

But at this point the temptation of the mirror was too strong, and now no longer for the body but also for that inimical will which—look!—forced the eyes to stare at it sullenly.

Damn that foot that, rocking, had first been reflected in it! But no, damn those eyes, rather, that had spotted it!

Now, see... No, no! The body was reluctant; but the inimical will forced the man to get up from the armchair and confront himself in the mirror.

There he is!

What scorn, what hatred that enemy will had accumulated in those eyes! With what cruel pleasure had it revealed the irreparable ravages of time in that poor face: the slow, ungainly alterations of its features, the worn and yellowed skin on its temples and around the cheekbones, the depressions, the swellings, the humiliating baldness, the ridiculous and pitiful wretchedness of those few remaining hairs, combed almost one at a time over that shiny cranium which was pinker than the forehead with its many rough wrinkles!

And the face, which had been used to showing itself in the mirror mercifully, in the most favorable way, could not help but recognize those ravages as real. And, not comprehending the reason for such a minute, intense and merciless examination, it now was mortified and bewildered, as it saw itself fixed in a frigid grimace that expressed something between revulsion and compassion. But look! The eyes were trying to point out (not, however, as an excuse, not to oppose the well-known reality of those ravages but just like that, almost for their own sake)... they were trying to point out that those swollen bags, for one thing, would certainly not have been there, they could have not been there, or at least not so pronounced, if they had not spent four nights—four sleepless nights—amid violent restlessness and raving. And then the beard, which had grown... But why?

Look, a hooked hand was rising to grasp the flaccid, hairy cheeks.

Why? Why so much hatred for that sickly appearance? Was the poor man suffering? What was he suffering from?

Suddenly a convulsive tremor came from the contracted vitals, and the eyes—those eyes—were filled with tears.

Come now, the hands must quickly look for a handkerchief... in this... no, in the other pocket... Not even there? The keys then... the bunch of keys to open the first drawer of the chest of drawers, where the handkerchiefs were... Quickly!

Oh! There... a handkerchief, yes. The hand was taking one of the many stored there but it took it almost mechanically, groping its way among the other pieces of linen, while the eyes focused on a corner at the back of the drawer... Yes, the small revolver... *With this, yes...* How quietly it remained concealed there, with its smooth white bone handle emerging from its gray felt case...

The other hand rose almost secretly to close the drawer in order to keep the eyes from continuing to stare at that thing over there, small as a toy, which for now was to be left in the drawer, just like it was, quiet and concealed.

The bunch of keys remained dangling from the keyhole.

A gentle, cool breeze from the imminent evening was entering from the window that overlooked the garden. The sudden pity that had occasioned those gushing tears now felt an indescribable coolness. The lungs, oppressed by anguish, swelled with long sighs, while the nose sniffed up those last tears. And the man, with his handkerchief on his eyes, went back to sit on the armchair. He stayed like that for a while. Then he abandoned his hands on his legs, and, yes, the left hand drew near to the right, which was holding the handkerchief. It took an edge and, as if to resume the game, timidly began, with its thumb and index finger, to run over it to the corner.

"We spend our time like this," that hand seemed to say, "but really it would be time to go to dinner, at least to dinner, because today at noon we didn't have lunch... Before going to dinner, however

And the hand, again rising up, but now no longer hooked, again took hold of the cheeks to scratch the stubbly, growing hairs.

"What an awful beard! It really should be shaven so as not to attract everyone's attention when they all entered the restaurant..."

How strange! Even the mind seemed to be joking around for its own sake. It would wander and speak to itself of unrelated alien things. It would follow known images that would appear without at all being evoked. They were airy but precise, outside of consciousness. And it offered suggestions, even though certain it would not be heeded.

All of a sudden, however, it happened as before, because of the tempting mirror. The inimical will, as if lying in wait for every instinctive motion, every suggestion that might tend to counter it, took the man by surprise, took possession of him, to make him turn abruptly against his body.

A shave, yes. Quickly, quickly. Then a bath...

"A bath? What? In the evening? Why?"

Because he had to be clean from head to toe. And he had to have a complete change of clothes: sweater, shorts, socks, shirt... everything. It was necessary that *afterwards* his body *be found* clean. In the meantime, a shave right away!

Contrary to their first wish, the hands now felt that they were being put to the service of the inimical will for an act that, though normal and usual, became an obscure, decisive and almost solemn endeavor.

On the chest of drawers there was a shaving brush, a little can of shaving cream, a razor... But first it was necessary to pour water in the basin and to get the bathrobe... The hands no longer knew precisely what they had to do first. First the bathrobe, yes...

In the little round pivot mirror pulled forward on the marble top of the chest of drawers, the bristly face appeared among the folds of the white bathrobe. Lord, how haggard! It was almost entirely puckered, with its bewildered, grim, unrecognizable eyes. And yes, the hands, frightened by those eyes, were extending their trembling fingers toward the brush. They were opening the lid of the small can of shaving cream, taking out a finger-full, inserting it amid the bristles of the wet brush and then beginning to lather the cheeks, the chin, the throat...

On other occasions, the eyes and ears had enjoyed seeing and hearing the bubbling and hissing of the fresh and very white lather that grew softly in cotton-like spirals on the cheeks and chin. And the fingers had taken delight in the enjoyment of the eyes and ears, and had indulged in the pleasure of making the lather swell in other softer and denser spirals.

But not now. Now they trembled, and the balls of the fingers almost lost their sense of touch. They trembled, fearful of arming themselves with the razor, no longer sure of themselves as before, guided, as they soon would be, by those frightening eyes.

The chest was panting; the heart itself which also suffered and was the cause of everything, now beat in tumult. Only a thin breath of air entered, almost whistling sharply through one of the dilated nostrils. The hands were opening the razor.

Fortunately, the body, leaning against the chest of drawers, suddenly felt a painful pressure in the pit of the stomach. It was the bunch of keys left hanging from the keyhole of the first drawer.

Then the right hand, almost by its own initiative, or rather, obeying an instinctive feeling of repulsion for that most vulgar weapon which was already gripped, placed the razor on the marble top of the chest of drawers and, instead of pulling the bothersome key out of the keyhole, pulled the drawer out a bit, removed the revolver and placed it on the marble top, out of the way.

This was a coming to terms with the inimical will. By placing the revolver on the chest of drawers, the hand was saying to the will,

"Look, this is for you. Didn't you say 'with this? So, let me shave in peace!"

The chest's panting was ceasing, and the hand, no longer trembling, took the brush up briskly and almost with joy since by now the lather had become almost entirely stiff and was cold, there among the bristles.

The danger removed the breathing easier, the fingers, together with the brush, worked joyfully to increase the lather. Then, with the maximum confidence, they picked up the razor again and ran it over the right cheek in neat swaths. And then they ran it over the left and finally, without a hint of hesitation, over the throat, returning, as before, to enjoy the pleasure that the ears took from this thorough scraping.

The eyes, little by little, had lost their grim expression. But now, almost immediately, they grew dim with an enormous fatigue behind which the lost look expressed a pitiful goodness that was almost infantile and distant. They shut automatically, those childlike eyes. Fatigue suddenly overran and weighed down all the limbs. The will, however, had a final sinister glint, and before the body, so suddenly devoid of strength and drooping, dragged itself to the armchair at the foot of the bed, it ordered the hand to pick up the revolver and place it there, right at the foot of the bed, next to the armchair. It was as if to say that it was granting the body a bit of rest, yes indeed, but that, in the meantime, it was not forgetting the pact.

The final glimmer of day, squalid and damp, was dying at the window; shade, then gradually darkness, pitch darkness, entered the bedroom. The rectangular window now became less black, near and very far, since it was punctuated by an infinite swarming of stars.

The body, the whole body was now sleeping with its head resting at the foot of the bed, an arm extended toward the small revolver.

Without noticing the cold night air that entered from the open window, the body slept in that uncomfortable position until the first glimmer of the new day—which was more squalid and damper than the last feeble light of the day gone by—slightly dissipated the darkness in the window, with an indistinct swirling.

But the limbs did not awaken. The first to do so was the heart, gnawed by a torment unknown to the body. It awoke only to feel a frightening void suspended in its gloom and a feeling of raw, horrible bitterness that seemed to emanate from a reality not lived and where it was impossible to live. Yes, it was necessary to take advantage of this instant while the benumbed body was still immersed in the torpor of sleep. Yes, yes, look, the will could plummet on that hand which was still motionless on the bed and make it grasp the revolver... Immediately! Taken out of its case, like this, here, in an instant, in the mouth, yes, here, here... with the eyes shut... like this... Oh, that trigger, how stiff it was! Come on, be brave... Ye-e-e-s, like that.

In the body, which fell heavily to the floor after the rumble, the fingers of the hand released their powerful grasp and, already dead, opened again quite slowly by themselves. And, with that crooked little finger of the left hand in front of all the others, they seemed to be asking, "Why?"

Aunt Michelina

When old Marruca died, his nephew, whom everyone called Marruchino, was almost twenty years old and about to go into the service.

Drafted—*hup, two, three, four!*—poor Marruchino!

Childless in his first marriage, the uncle Marruca had become so fond of the boy that when his wife died, he did not want to give him back to his brother, who was the father. Indeed, precisely because the boy was still at a tender age and needed maternal attention, he had remarried although he was old. He knew that for his part he would never be able to have children. But strong and sturdy like a shade tree that bears no fruit, he had always made it a point to show that, even though he had no offspring, this was not due to a lack of vigor. This is why he chose an exceedingly young woman as his new bride, and he had never regretted his choice.

Aunt Michelina, cool-tempered and mild-mannered, immediately felt at home in that house of newly-rich country-folk where everything had the fragrance of the abundant daily provisions brought in from the distant countryside, and everything retained the solidity of its ancient patriarchal life. She had showed herself satisfied with her husband, even though he was so much older than she, and she was quite affectionate toward the young nephew.

Now, this young nephew—lo and behold—had grown and was twenty years old. And she, who wasn't yet forty, considered herself already old.

Both of them cried a lot when the old man died, she mourning the death of her husband, and the boy, that of his uncle. The good man, full of wisdom as he always was, had provided in his will that his not-so-modest holdings (houses and farmlands) should go to his nephew, and that his wife should have complete use of them during her lifetime, provided, of course, that she did not marry.

Marruchino, whose real name was Simonello, left to serve his country. His eyes were red from weeping, partly because of the obligation he owed his country, partly still because of his uncle's death.

Like a good mother, Aunt Michelina tried to cheer him up. She exhorted him to keep her in his thoughts and to write to her as soon as he needed anything. He should write immediately and she would immediately see to it that his every need was satisfied. Rest assured that she, remaining behind alone—poor thing!—would take care of his room, his small bed, his wardrobe and everything else, just as he had left them.

As soon as Marruchino left, she devoted herself entirely to looking after the fields and the house, just like a man.

Lately, Marruchino had looked after things since his uncle had no longer been able to do so because of his age. He had been taken out of school early not because he lacked intelligence but rather because—in his uncle's opinion—he had too much of it. In feet, there had never been a way of making Marruchino understand that it could be useful to him to know what other men had done from the beginning of time on the face of the earth. Marruchino knew very well what *he* would do. Why get mixed up in the affairs of others? The other parts of the world? Which ones? America? He would never go there. Africa? Asia? The mountains which existed? The rivers, lakes, cities? It sufficed him to know well the small piece of land where God had wanted him to be born!

Could he become more intelligent than that?

The letters he now sent from the regiment were Aunt Michelina's sole comfort even though, because of their content, which cost her no little effort to decipher, it appeared continually clearer to her that in the regiment Marruchino had completely lost that feisty good humor with which he had courageously defended himself in childhood when he rebelled against excessive instruction. He did not say he was saddened because he found military life to be harsh or because he was far from the places and people dear to him. On the contrary! He said, instead, that he wanted to reenlist and never again return to his hometown on account of a certain feeling of desperation that had overtaken his spirit.

Desperation? Desperation over what?

More than once his aunt begged him, pleaded with him, to confide it to her. But Marruchino always answered that he couldn't, that he himself didn't know.

Ah, he was in love, of course... it didn't take much to understand that—some awful love affair gone sour. Terrible boy! She had to send him money, a lot, so that he could get his mind off of it.

With great astonishment Aunt Michelina found that he sent back the money with a furious protest. This was not what he wanted. He only wanted to be understood, understood, understood.

Lost, stunned, Aunt Michelina was still wondering what to make of this when Marruchino suddenly showed up at the house, on furlough.

She was amazed to see him so changed before her that he scarcely looked like himself any longer. He was skinny and all eyes; he seemed to be gnawed inside by a worm that gave him no rest.

"Me? What? What do you want from me? What?..."

The more she lavished her caresses on him, the more he became furious. Finally he ran away like a madman, to spend the final days of his furlough at one of the farms farthest from town.

In seeing him run off like that, and thinking about the way he had looked at her as he tried to avoid her maternal attentions, her caresses, Aunt Michelina found herself suddenly assaulted by a suspicion that horrified her. She collapsed in a chair and remained there for quite some time, pale, with her eyes wide open, to scratch her forehead with her fingernails.

"Is it possible? Is it possible?"

She did not dare send anyone to the farm to inquire about him.

A few days later, a peasant came by to pick up Marruchino's bag and army coat and to announce that the young man was leaving the next day because his furlough had expired.

Aunt Michelina looked at length into the peasant's face, stunned.

He was leaving without even coming to say good-by? So be it. Perhaps it was better that way.

Through that peasant she sent him a goodly sum of money and her "maternal" blessing.

Four days later, her brother-in-law, Marruchino's father, came to Aunt Michelina's home. He hadn't come by since his brother's death, on account of the will.

"Dear Godmother... dear Godmother..."

He called her "Godmother," not "Sister-in-law," because the other woman, his brother's first wife, had stood as godmother to Marruchino at his baptism. It was not a good reason but, having always called his brother "Godfather" because of that baptism, he thought he should also call his second sister-in-law "Godmother."

"Dear Godmother..."

And in his eyes and on his lips he had an ambiguous and embarrassed little smile.

Bald, thin and leathery, he did not at all resemble his brother or his son. A widower for many years, coarse yet clever, filthy and ill-dressed because of his avarice, he spoke without ever looking anyone in the face.

"Our Simonello is raving mad... Hey, dear Godmother, isn't love a terrible, terrible misfortune?"

"Ah, so he's in love?" exclaimed Aunt Michelina. "That poor boy! I begged him, I pleaded with him to tell me what was wrong with him, to tell me, his mother, because I would have done anything to make him happy. You know that, Brother-in-law! I found him here when he was two years old. His mother had died and I raised him as though he were my own."

"Well... well... well," the brother-in-law began to utter, shaking his head, shaking his whole body, as he sat on the chair with that ambiguous little smile constantly in his eyes and on his lips. "That's precisely the problem, dear Godmother! Precisely that!"

"That? Why? What are you saying?"

Instead of replying, her brother-in-law came out with a curious question:

"Have you ever looked at yourself in the mirror, dear Godmother?"

Aunt Michelina suddenly felt assailed again by the horror of her first suspicion. But this time it was mixed with revulsion. She jumped to her feet.

"My son?" she shouted. "Would my son think of such a thing regarding me? You probably put it in his head, you terrible tempting devil! You, you've never put your mind at ease on account of that blasted will. I found out everything; they've told me everything. You've shouted to the four winds that it wasn't right because I could still live thirty or more years, and that your son might even die before I left him the use of the property, and that his uncle left him the property only so he could look at it from afar and that he will have to wait until he's old before he can consider himself the actual owner. Oh, you terrible devil. What are you imagining now? That I would have left my son like that to wait for my death and long for it? As soon as he returned, I, I myself, would have said to him: 'My dear Simonello, choose a good mate for yourself. Bring her here. You'll be the master. I will delight in your happiness and raise your children as I raised you.' That's what I intended to say to him. Well then, you write that to him! If you have someone in mind that he might like, tell me. I myself will suggest her to him! But get out of your son's head the shameful thing you've suggested to him! It's a mortal sin!"

Her brother-in-law, though disconcerted at first, did not give in. He showed himself to be offended by the accusation. He said that he had nothing to do with it, that once all the relatives and friends had found out about the dispositions of the will, they unanimously thought that the thing could be commendably settled like this, and that this was a sign that no one saw anything wrong with it as she did. If there was any difference in age—and indeed there was but not as great as she imagined it to be—this difference almost vanished because she was so extremely well preserved and her health was excellent. Certainly she was one of those ladies who never grow old. And finally, since Aunt Michelina, overwhelmed with shame, began to cry, her brother-in-law took this crying as a sign of submission, and to comfort her and to show her that Marruchino had every reason in the world to fall in love with her, he repeated his advice to her, to look at herself in the mirror.

"Get out of here!" Aunt Michelina screamed, getting up again like a fury. "Get out of here, you devil! I don't want to see you anymore! Neither you nor your son! Out with his bed! Out with whatever is his in this house!

Oh, what a snake, my God! What a snake I raised on my breast! Out, out, out!"

For the sake of prudence, her brother-in-law withdrew.

Aunt Michelina remained there crying for several days straight.

The neighbors came by to comfort her and she opened up her heart to them, still unable to stop her tears.

However, she was amazed when she noticed, at a certain point, that not one of those neighbors either understood or appreciated her feelings. Or, better put, they did indeed appreciate them and took them into account but they also took into account *his* feelings—that is, those of Marruchino—and the unfortunate conditions in which his uncle's will had left him.

Why unfortunate? Why?

Exasperated, Aunt Michelina repeated to the neighbors her intention of finding her nephew a wife as soon as he returned, and of making him the happy master of everything.

The neighbors approved of the plan, oh yes, and praised her a lot for it but they said—only for the sake of discussion, mind you—they said that it was still not the same for the young man.

"And what else then?"

Only this. If she hadn't had that maternal feeling she said she had and instead had been able to share his feeling, for Marruchino it certainly would have been much better. Because, in the way she suggested, he would always remain dependent as a son in a family. He wouldn't notice it, that's true, because of her kindness! But what if some day or other a disagreement should arise, as was easy to foresee between women, that is, between herself and his wife, one against the other, almost as mother-in-law and daughter-in-law?...

Yes, one had to consider this!

Everyone knows how disagreements start but not how they might end up.

Aunt Michelina saw herself alone and felt lonely. Alone and lost.

Well then, if this was the world, if in this world, when confronted with matters of interest, one could no longer understand anything, not even the most sacrosanct feeling, that of maternal love, what did they all think? That she was the real opportunist? That she wanted to remain the owner of everything and keep her nephew subject to her? Is this what they thought? She, an opportunist! Oh, if she really...

It was a flash. She jumped to her feet. She ran to look at herself in the mirror.

Yes, to see, to see if it really was as they said, if her features, her appearance were such as to make her nephew so blind as to no longer think of the sort of love she had loved him with until now, and such that the others could so easily forgive him!

No, she was not ugly. She certainly didn't show her age yet but she was not, no, she *could* not be beautiful to that boy! Already under the blond hair at her temples, she had quite a few hairs that were faded, almost white. Tomorrow they would become white...

No, no! What! It was a disgrace. It was wickedness.

But if to someone else, yes, if at least to an old fellow of her same age she could still be so beautiful and attractive as to be asked in marriage for her beauty alone! Yes, that's it, she would then leave everything to her nephew, to this wicked boy who wanted her, who wanted his mother for her money! She would throw it in his face and would show everyone that she was not standing in his way for that.

So, for several months, Aunt Michelina was seen leaving her home to go to church, and then for a walk, all dressed up despite her mourning. She wore a lace veil and shiny high-heeled shoes, and carried a fen. She was well groomed and had that particular awkwardness of women who do not want to show that they are anxious to be noticed, but which itself is an art for making oneself be noticed.

The fan in her hand quivered nervously under her chin to extinguish the flushes of shame and anger on her face.

"Out for a walk, Aunt Micheli'?" some of the neighbors from their doorways would ask maliciously.

'Yes, out for walk! What can I do for you?" she would answer from the street, bowing in the sun with a spiteful grimace that the shadow behind her repeated clumsily.

But where was she going? She herself did not know. Just out for a walk. As she walked, she looked at the tips of her little shoes because, if she were to lift her eyes, she wouldn't know where to look or at what and, feeling herself turn crimson red, she would have begun to cry, really to cry like a little girl.

Now everybody... as if they understood that she had gone out, not because she had to, but to show herself off, would stop to see her go by. They would exchange glances. Some of them, as a joke, would even call her like this:

"Psst! Psst!" as one does with ladies of the night.

She would walk on redder than ever without turning around. Her heart would pound in her breast until, exhausted and unable to go on, she would thrust herself into some church.

Good God, why was she doing that? A woman seeks a husband to procure a status for herself. Now, who could imagine that she, on the contrary, was seeking a second husband in order to lose the one in which her first husband had left her? They imagined instead that, still beautiful as she was and sick and tired of widowhood, she was seeking someone with whom she could have a good time. They wanted to persuade her that if this was the case, she would indeed find as many men as she wanted and that she could do as she wished without committing the madness of losing the tenancy of her first husband's estate by marrying for the second time. Being free from any obligation of faithfulness, she did not have to give an account of herself to anyone if she went with this or that man.

In hearing such talk, Aunt Michelina was consumed with indignation but could not give vent to that feeling because she realized that the very appearance of her behavior condemned her. Only one man, perhaps, one alone, could understand why she was looking for a husband and receive her and marry her for the same reason. This was her brother-in-law, Marruchino's father, that ugly, withered, filthy, avaricious man who couldn't wait for his son to become the sole owner of his brother's patrimony. This was the only way possible. In this way she could show everybody the sort of pleasure she was seeking.

Resolved, she showed up one day at her brother-in-law's house.

"I know you've been going around telling everybody that I want to go so far as to ruin your son by getting involved with someone else, and to push him to do some dreadful deed as soon as he returns home from the service. Instead I'm looking out for his welfare. As a matter of feet, I want to get married to get out of his way and make him the sole owner. I'm looking for someone to marry me but I can't find anyone. Everyone wants me but nobody wants to marry me because they all think it's crazy that I have to lose what I have in marrying someone else. You're the only one who can't believe I'm trying to ruin him, because you know why I want to get married. Fine, you marry me!"

In hearing that proposal directed at him point-blank, the old man remained there for a while, stunned. Then that certain small ambiguous smile began to form on his lips.

"Well... well... well..."

Finally, with a laborious hodgepodge of words he cleverly gave her to understand that it would be madness—sheer madness, not only for the others but for him too. Yes, indeed, because the important thing was that she, though not wanting to marry his son, not marry outside the family, so that the tenancy would remain in the family.

"But how, you dirty old man?" Aunt Michelina shouted. "By marrying you? Oh, you ugly dog! And the interests of your son that you've been preaching about and defending since last year—is this how they would end up, now that you're entering the picture? Then I'd rather marry a dog than you, you dirty old man! Pooh!"

And Aunt Michelina flew into a rage.

At this point she knew what she had to do.

As soon as Marruchino was discharged and showed up before her, thinner and more troubled than when he had come on furlough, she said to him,

"Listen, you shameless scoundrel, I know why you want to marry me. And this, as I see it, in part excuses you. You want me to get married so that I'll lose everything and you'll be left the owner. All right, for this reason alone I'll marry you... What are you doing? No! Quit it! Don't you dare! Move aside or I'll throw this in your face!"

Marruchino had tried to throw his arms around her neck to kiss her and she had brandished a lamp.

Shaking, her eyes wide open, Aunt Michelina kept on shouting from behind the table.

"If you try that again, you'll be sorry! I'm doing it to leave you completely free to do what you want. Have all the women you want all the pleasures you want on the condition that you never cast your eyes on me again! I'll go to the farm and hide where you went to hide so you wouldn't have my motherly caresses, and I'll stay there forever and you'll never show your face in my presence. Swear it! I want you to swear it!"

Marruchino squirmed at that imposition and pretended to swear only so that he could make her condescend to the marriage, not because he was admitting that she was right in suspecting that he wanted her for her money.

"Watch out!" Aunt Michelina then added. "You've taken an oath. You must realize, young man, that I'm capable of anything, of killing you or killing myself if you don't keep the agreement. If you break the oath, watch out!"

She sent him away and refused to see him again until the day fixed for the wedding.

She went to the church and the town hall, pale, disheveled and dressed in black. She was crying. When the ceremony was over, she left everybody feasting at the banquet table. She got on a mule and set out alone for the distant farm.

But, due a bit to vanity, a bit to the people's jokes, a bit to the lover's role he had assumed, Marruchino decided, after struggling for two days with himself, to go at night to knock on the door of the farmhouse. For hours and hours he battered the door amid a furious barking of all the dogs in the neighborhood in the nocturnal shadows. Finally she came down to let him in.

That very night, after scarcely an hour, he fled, black and blue, with scratches on his face, neck and hands. Returning to town at dawn, he hurried to lock himself in the house. A few hours later they came to arrest him because they had found Aunt Michelina dead at the farm.

The scratches on his neck and face, the scratches and bites on his hands, accused him. He swore by all that's holy that he did not kill her, but that she killed herself because he had wanted from her what every husband has the right to demand from his own wife. He said that, having gotten what he wanted and what he had fought so hard for, he had no reason to commit such a crime. He brought in so many witnesses who were aware of his feelings, his honest intentions and her opposition and threats that he was acquitted.

The neighbors still talk about Aunt Michelina as a madwoman because, good Lord, even if it revolted her to become intimate with a youth whom she loved as her son, to act as his wife —given the fact that this youth had became her husband—did not involve going to war with him. What nonsense!

Nothing

The carriage rumbling in the night through the vast deserted square stops in front of a faintly-lit opaque door of a pharmacy on the corner of Via San Lorenzo. A gentleman wrapped in a fur coat dashes out of the carriage and grabs the handle of the door. He turns it to the right, then to the left but — what the devil!—the door doesn't open.

"Try ringing the doorbell," suggests the coachman.

"Where... how does one ring it?"

"Look, there's a little knob there. Pull it."

The gentleman pulls the knob with furious haste.

"Great night service!"

Under the light of the red lantern, his words vaporize in the cold night air, almost like smoke.

The whistle of a departing train rises mournfully from the nearby station. The coachman takes out his watch, bends over near one of the carriage lights and says,

"Hey, it's almost three o'clock..."

Finally the sleepy pharmacy clerk, his jacket collar pulled up to cover his ears, comes and opens up.

Immediately the gentleman says,

"Is the doctor in?"

The clerk, feeling the cold air on his face and hands, steps back, lifts his arms, clenches his fists and begins to rub his eyes, all the while yawning. He asks,

"At this hour?"

Then, to cut off the customer's protests, he says, "Why yes, for God's sake, yes. It's understandable that you're in a great hurry. Who's disagreeing? But still you should also have pity on someone who has every right to be sleepy at this hour." Removing his hands from his eyes, he first of all beckons him to wait, then to follow him behind the counter in the pharmacy's laboratory.

Meanwhile the coachman, who has stayed outside, climbs down from the box and decides to indulge himself in the pleasure of unbuttoning his trousers and doing openly, there in front of the vast deserted square, crisscrossed by shiny streetcar tracks, what one may not do in the daytime without taking necessary precautions.

It is indeed a pleasure, while someone is struggling with a problem for which he must ask others for relief and help, to attend calmly like that to the satisfaction of a small natural need and to see that everything remains in its place. There, that row of black oak trees bordering the square, the high tin tubes that hold up the streetcar cables, all those glass covers on the streetlights; and here, the customs house near the station.

The pharmacy's laboratory, which has a low ceiling and is full of shelves, is almost in the dark and reeks of medicine. A sooty kerosene lamp burning in front of a sacred image on top of the set of shelves opposite the entrance seems unable to illuminate even itself. The table in the center of the room, which is cluttered with bottles, small jars, scales, mortars and funnels, at first does not allow one to see if the doctor on duty is sleeping on the shabby leather couch under that set of shelves in front of the entrance.

"There he is," says the pharmacy clerk, pointing to a large man who, all hunched and bundled up, is sleeping with difficulty, his face squashed against the back of the couch.

"Call him, for God's sake!"

"That's easier said than done! He's liable to kick me, you know."

"But is he a doctor?"

"'Yes, yes, a doctor. Doctor Mangoni."

"And he kicks?"

"As you can well imagine, waking him up at this hour..."

"I'll call him!"

The gentleman bends over the small couch with determination and shakes the sleeping man.

"Doctor! Doctor!"

Doctor Mangoni bellows into the unkempt, bristly beard that covers his cheeks almost up to his eyes. He then clenches his fists on his chest and lifts his elbows to stretch. Finally he sits down, stooped, his eyes still shut under his drooping eyebrows. One of his pant legs has remained pulled up over the large calf of his leg, revealing his long linen underwear, tied in an old fashioned manner with a small cord on his coarse black cotton sock.

"Please, Doctor... immediately, I beg you," the gentleman says with impatience. "A case of asphyxiation..."

"With coal?" asks the doctor, turning around but without opening his eyes. He lifts his hand melodramatically and tries to force his voice out of his still sleepy throat. He sings a few notes of a *La Gioconda* aria: *Suicide! In these cruu-u-el moments...*

The gentleman makes a gesture of astonishment and indignation. But Doctor Mangoni immediately throws his head back and starts to open one of his eyes.

"Excuse me," he says, "one of your relatives?"

"No, sir! but I beg you, hurry up! I'll explain it to you on the way. I've got a carriage here. If you need to get something..."

"Yes, give me... give me..." Doctor Mangoni begins to say, turning to the pharmacy clerk, as he attempts to get up.

"I'll take care of it. I'll take care of it, Doctor," replies the clerk, turning on the electric light and doing all he can in a happy rush that impresses the night customer.

In an effort to protect his eyes from the sudden light, Doctor Mangoni twists his head like an ox getting ready to butt.

"'Yes, dear boy," he says. "But you've blinded me. Oh, and my helmet? Where is it?"

The helmet is his hat. Yes, he does have it. As far as having one is concerned, he does, and that's for sure. He recalls having put it on the stool next to the small couch, before falling asleep. Where did it go?

He begins to look for it. The customer starts looking for it, too. Then, having entered the pharmacy to warm up, even the coachman lends a hand. Meanwhile, the clerk has all the time he needs to prepare a large package of emergency items.

"A syringe for the shots, Doctor, do you have one?"

"Me?" Doctor Mangoni turns to answer him, with an expression of wonder that provokes an outburst of laughter in the clerk.

"All right, all right. Then, of course, some mustard plasters... Will eight be enough? Caffeine, strychnine... a hypodermic syringe. And oxygen, Doctor? You'll also need a bottle of oxygen, I suppose."

"What I need is my hat! My hat! My hat before anything else!" shouts Doctor Mangoni, between one snort and another. He explains that, apart from anything else, he has become fond of that hat because it is historical. He bought it about eleven years ago on the occasion of the solemn funeral of Sister Maria dell'Udienza. She was the mother superior of the night hospice on Vicolo del Falco, in Trastevere, a place where he often goes to eat some bowls of excellent but cheap soup and to sleep when he's not on duty in the pharmacies.

Finally the hat is found. It's not there in the laboratory but in the other room, under the counter of the pharmacy. A kitten had been playing with it.

The customer quivers with impatience, but another long discussion takes place because Doctor Mangoni, his thoroughly crushed top hat in his hands, wants to show that the kitten, yes, undoubtedly played with it, but he too, the young pharmacy clerk, must also have given it a fine crease by kicking it under the counter. Enough. Doctor Mangoni thrusts his fist deeply and forcefully into the top hat. He doesn't knock the bottom out of it, and miraculously it remains intact. Then he thrusts it on his head at a jaunty angle.

"At your service, esteemed sir!"

"A poor young man," the gentleman begins to say as he mounts the coach and spreads a blanket over the doctor's legs as well as his own.

"Ah, good! Thanks."

"A poor young man highly recommended by one of my brothers who asked me to find him a job. Yes, of course... As if it were the simplest thing in the world. Here you are, no sooner said than done. The same old story. It seems they live in another world, those folks who live in the provinces. They think that all one has to do is come to Rome to find a job. Here you are, no sooner said than done. My very own brother presented me with this fine gift. Yes sir! One of the usual misfits, you know. The son of a farmer who died two years ago in the service of this brother of mine. He comes to Rome. To do what? Nothing. Only to work as a journalist, he says. He shows me his credentials: a high school diploma and a pad of poems. He says, "You've got to find me a position with some newspaper.' Me? It's madness! I immediately set myself in motion to help get him his residence permit at the police headquarters. In the meantime, could I leave him out in the street, at night?

"He was almost naked and was freezing to death, with a thin cotton suit that flapped in the wind and only two or three cents in his pocket, no more than that. I put him up in one of my small apartments here in the San Lorenzo district that I rented to some awful people... But let's not talk about it! Lower-class people who've been subletting two furnished rooms. They haven't paid me the rent for four months. I take advantage of the situation and put him there to sleep. That's fine! Five days pass but there's no way to obtain the residence permit from the police headquarters. The meticulousness of those bureaucrats is like that of birds, you know. They shit everywhere, pardon the expression! To issue that document they first have to get I don't know what papers ready, there in his town and then here at the police headquarters. Enough of that. This evening I was at the theater, at the Nazionale. My tenant's son, terrified, comes to get me at a quarter past midnight. He tells me that the poor devil had locked himself in his room with a lit brazier. Since seven p.m., understand?"

At this point the gentleman bends over slightly to gaze at the doctor sitting in the back of the carriage who, while the gentleman was speaking, gave no sign of life. Fearing that he has Mien asleep again, he repeats more loudly,

"Since seven p.m.!"

"How nicely this little horse trots," then says Doctor Mangoni, stretched out voluptuously in the carriage.

The gentleman is astonished; it's as if he'd been punched on the nose in the dark.

"Excuse me, Doctor, but did you hear what I said?"

"Yes, sir."

"Since seven p.m. Since seven p.m.—that's five hours."

"Yes, exactly."

"But, you know, he's breathing! Slightly, ever so slightly. He's all stiff and..."

"Fantastic! It's been... yes, let me see, three, no, what am I saying?... probably five years, at least, since I've traveled in a carriage. How lovely it is!"

"Pardon me, but I'm talking to you..."

"'Yes, sir, but come now, how can you expect the story of that unfortunate fellow to matter to me?"

"To tell you that it's been five hours..."

"All right! We'll soon see. Do you think you're doing him a big favor?"

"How's that?"

"Why yes, pardon my frankness! If someone is wounded in a scuffle, or a roof tile *fails* on his head, or he suffers some kind of accident... I can understand lending him a helping hand, calling a doctor. But, pardon me, an unfortunate man who quietly, ever so quietly, curls up to die?"

"How's that!" repeats the gentleman, more and more amazed.

And Doctor Mangoni, as calm as can be, says,

"Bear with me. The poor fellow had done the most difficult part. Instead of bread he bought coal. I imagine he probably bolted the door, right? He probably also sealed all the cracks and drugged himself with opium first. Five hours went by; then you go and disturb him at the crucial moment!"

"You're joking!" shouts the gentleman.

"No, no, I'm speaking seriously."

"Oh, good Lord!" the gentleman fires back. "But I'm the one who was disturbed, it seems to me! They came to call me..."

"Yes, I understand, at the theater."

"Was I supposed to let him die? And then there would have been other problems, right? As if he hasn't caused me enough of them already. Such things are just not done in the home of others, pardon me!"

"Ah, yes, yes. In this, you're certainly right," Doctor Mangoni admits with a sigh. "He could have gone to die out of everyone's way, you say. You're right. But a bed is tempting, you know! It's tempting, tempting. It's awful to die on the ground like a dog... Allow a man who doesn't have one, to tell you!"

"Doesn't have what?"

"A bed."

"You?"

Doctor Mangoni hesitates before answering. Then, slowly, with the tone of voice of one who is repeating something already said so many times before, he states,

"I sleep where I can, eat when I can and dress as I can."

And he immediately adds,

"Hey, but don't think for a moment that it troubles me. Just the opposite. I'm a great man, you know, but I'm resigned."

The gentleman's curiosity is roused by this fine sort of doctor with whom he is thrown together by chance. He asks, laughing,

"Resigned? What do you mean by that?"

"I understood early on, dear sir, that it doesn't pay to worry about anything. In feet, the more you try to become great, the more insignificant you become. That's the way it is. Pardon me, but do you have a wife?"

"Me? Yes, sir."

"I believe you sighed when you said, "Yes, sir.' "

"Oh, no, I didn't sigh at all."

"All right then, enough said. If you didn't sigh, let's not talk about it anymore."

And Doctor Mangoni goes back to huddling up in the back of the carriage, thereby giving an outward sign that he no longer finds any need to continue the conversation. The gentleman is irritated.

"Pardon me, but what does my wife have to do with this?"

The coachman, at this point, turns around from the box and asks,

"Well, where is it? We'll be at Campoverano Cemetery any moment now!" "Ugh, right!" exclaims the gentleman. "Turn! Turn! We've passed the house some time ago." "It's a shame to turn back," says Doctor Mangoni, "when we've

almost reached our destination." The
driver turns, cursing.

A dark staircase that seems like a rocky cavern: dismal, damp and smelly.
"Am! Damn it all! Oh God! God! God!"
"What is it? Did you hurt yourself?"
"My foot. Ouch! Ouch! Excuse me, don't you happen to have a match?"
"Damn it! I'm looking for my matchbox but I can't find it."
Finally, a glimmer of light comes from the open door on the landing above the third flight of stairs.

Misfortune, when it enters a house, has this peculiarity: it leaves the door open so that any stranger can go in to pry.

Doctor Mangoni hobbles behind the gentleman as he passes through a small squalid room with a white kerosene lamp on the floor, near the entrance. Then, without asking anyone's permission, the two go through a dark hallway that has three doors; two are closed, the other, at the far end, is open and faintly lit. Still feeling pain from having twisted his foot, he is tempted to hurl the oxygen bottle he finds in his hand, at the gentleman's shoulders but he puts it on the floor. He pauses, leans on a wall with one of his hands and, with the other, raises his foot and squeezes it forcefully at the ankle bone. He makes an effort to move it in every direction, with his face completely wrung.

Meanwhile, in the room at the end of the hallway, who knows why, an argument has broken out between the gentleman and the tenants. Doctor Mangoni lets go of his foot and tries to walk, wanting to know what has happened. Then he sees the gentleman coming straight at him like a storm. The gentleman is shouting,

"'Yes, yes, that was stupid of you! Very stupid of you!"
He has scarcely enough time to avoid a collision. He turns and sees the gentleman stumble against the oxygen bottle.
"Careful! Careful, for heaven's sake!"
Careful? Just the opposite! The gentleman lodges a kick on the bottle. He finds it again in the way. He is again about to fell and, cursing, hurries away, while at the doorway of the room at the end of the hallway a stocky and clumsy old man wearing slippers and a skullcap appears. The old man has a large green woolen scarf around his neck, from which there emerges a plump face, completely swollen and purple, lit up by the tallow candle he holds in his hands.
"Pardon me, but... I say... would it have been better if, waiting for a doctor, we had let him die here?"

Doctor Mangoni thinks that the man is addressing him, so he answers,

"Here I am, I'm the doctor."

But the man raises and stretches out the hand carrying the candle. He observes him and, somewhat dazed, asks,

"You? Who?"

"Weren't you asking for a doctor?"

"A doctor? Not at all! Not at all!" screams a woman whose voice rises up from the adjacent room.

And the wife of that fine old man in slippers and skullcap comes dashing out into the hallway, shaking all over and with a mass of disheveled gray hair, her smoky eyes, bruised and weeping, her misshapen, obscenely painted mouth, quivering convulsively. Raising her head on one side to look, she imperiously adds,

"You can go! You can go! There's no longer any need for you! We had him taken to the general hospital because he was dying!"

Bumping violently against her husband's arm, she says,

"Make him go away!"

Her husband lets out a scream and jumps because when she collided with him, the hot, dripping wax from the candle fell on his fingers.

"Hey, be careful, by God!"

Doctor Mangoni protests, but without much anger, that he is not a thief nor a murderer to be sent away in that manner. He states that if he came there, it's because they came to get him at the pharmacy. He also adds that, so far, the only payment he has received is a twisted leg, for which he asks them to allow him to sit down, at least for a moment.

"Certainly, over here, come, take a seat, make yourself at home, Doctor," the old man hastens to say as he leads him into the room at the end of the hallway; while his wife, her head still raised on one side to see, like an angry chicken, glares at him, struck by that wild beard which reaches right up to his eyes.

Having calmed down, she now says as if to excuse herself, "So now, does one have to endure criticism for having done good?"

"'Yes, criticism." the old man adds. He thrusts the lit candle into the socket of the flat candlestick on the night stand next to the small, empty, unmade bed whose pillows still conserve the impression of the young suicide's head. Quietly he then removes the hardened droplets from his fingers and continues, "Criticism because he says that the young man was not to be taken to the hospital—no, indeed."

"He had turned all black!" shouts the woman, with a start. "Ah, that little face. It seemed sucked from within. And what eyes! And those black lips that showed his teeth just a little, here and there. He was no longer breathing..."

She covers her face with her hands.

"Were we supposed to have let him die without trying to help him?"

asks the old man again, calmly. "But do you know why the man got angry? He says he suspects that the poor boy is a bastard son of his brother..."

"And he dumped him here on us," adds the woman, again jumping to her feet, who knows whether out of anger or excitement. "Here, to have this tragedy take place in my house, a tragedy that won't end just yet because my eldest daughter fell in love with him. Understand? She was like a madwoman when she saw him die. Oh, what a sight! She lifted him up in her arms; I don't know how she did it! She took him away with the help of her brother. They brought him down the stairs, hoping to find a carriage on the street. Maybe they found one. Just look, just look over there how my other daughter is crying."

In entering the adjoining dining room, Doctor Mangoni has already seen a large disheveled blonde girl busily reading, her elbows on the table and her head between her hands. Yes, she is reading and crying but with her bodice unbuttoned and her round, pink, exuberant breasts almost completely exposed under the yellow light of the hanging lamp.

The old father, to whom Doctor Mangoni now turns as if thunderstruck, makes some gestures of great admiration with his hands. Because of his daughter's breasts? No. Because of what his daughter is reading amid so many tears: the young man's poems.

"A poet!" he exclaims. "A poet, that if you were to hear... Oh, what things! What things! I'm an expert because I'm a retired professor of literature. Great things, great things."

And he goes into the next room to get some of the poems. But his daughter angrily keeps them from him for fear that her older sister, returning with her brother from the hospital, won't let her read them anymore because she'll want to keep them jealously for herself, like a treasure of which she alone must be the heir.

"At least some of these that you've already read," insists the father timidly.

But she, bent over the sheets with that large bosom of hers, stamps her foot and screams, "No!" Then she picks them up from the table, again presses them against her bare bosom and brings them into another room.

Then Doctor Mangoni turns to look again at that sad, empty little bed that makes his visit useless. He also looks at the window that, despite the frigid night, has remained open in that lugubrious room so that the stench of coal could be aired out.

The moon lights up the window opening. In the depth of night, there is only the moon. Doctor Mangoni imagines it as he saw it so many times before while he wandered in remote streets at a time when people sleep and no longer see it either cast in its abyss or lost in the summit of the heavens.

The squalor of the room and of the entire house makes him realize that it is one of the many houses of men where two female breasts (like the ones he has just caught sight of under the light of the lamp hanging in the adjoining room) bounce around temptingly to perpetuate the inconclusive misery of life. This induces in him such a cold feeling of discouragement and bitter irritation that he is unable to remain seated.

He gets up to leave, snorting. After all, come now, it's one of the many, many cases that he's used to running into when he's on duty in the pharmacies at night. Perhaps it's a little sadder than the others. Probably that poor boy was a real poet. Who knows? But, in that case, it's better for him that he died.

"Listen," he says to the old man, who has also gotten up to pick up the candle again. "The gentleman who reproached you and came to disturb me in the pharmacy must really be an idiot. Wait, let me explain. Not because he reproached you, but because I asked him if he had a wife, and he answered yes, but without sighing. Understand?"

The old man looks at him, his mouth agape. Evidently he does not understand. His wife understands and jumps up to ask, "So, according to you, whoever says he has a wife is supposed to sigh?"

Doctor Mangoni immediately replies,

"Just like I imagine you sigh, my dear lady, if someone asks you if you have a husband."

He points to the old man, then continues,

"Pardon me for asking, but if that young man had not killed himself, would you have given him your daughter as his wife?"

The woman looks at him askance for a while and then, as if to challenge him, answers,

"Why not?"

"And would all of you have let him live with you in this house?" Doctor Mangoni continues to ask.

And the woman, again:

"Why not?"

"And you," asks Doctor Mangoni again, turning to her old husband, "you who are an expert, a retired professor of literature, would you also have advised him to have those poems of his published?"

Not to be outdone by his wife, the old man, also, answers,

"Why not?"

"And so," concludes Doctor Mangoni, "I'm sorry, but I've got to tell you that you're at least two times more idiotic than that gentleman."

He turns around to leave.

"Can you tell us why?" the furious woman shouts after him.

Doctor Mangoni stops and answers calmly,

"Pardon my frankness, but you'll admit that the poor young man might have been dreaming of glory if he was writing poems. Now think for a moment what that glory would have become for him if he had had those poems of his published: a poor, useless little volume of verses. And what about love, which is the liveliest and holiest thing that it has been granted us to experience on earth? What would it have become for him? Love: a woman. Or worse still: a wife—your daughter."

"Oh! Oh!" the woman says threateningly, almost thrusting her hands in his face. "Careful how you speak about my daughter!"

"I'm not saying anything," Doctor Mangoni hastens to protest. "On the contrary, I view her as being very beautiful and adorned with every possible virtue but, all the same, she's a woman, my dear Signora, who, after a while... Good Lord, we all know very well to what condition she, with her poverty and children, would have been reduced. Now tell me, what about the world, the world where I'm now going to ruin myself with this foot that hurts me so much! The world. Just think, just think, dear Signora, what it would have become for him! A house. This house. Understand?"

And making his hands spring up in curious gestures of nausea and disdain, he leaves, limping and grumbling,

"Books? Women? A house? No! Nothing... nothing... nothing... I'm resigned! Resigned! Nothing."

An Idea

Having left his usual company of friends among the lights and mirrors of the smoke-filled cafe, he finds the night before him: glassy, almost fragile, with bright stars sparkling above the immense deserted square.

To cross it seems impossible to him. The life he has to reenter seems unreachably distant from it, and the entire city looks as if it had been uninhabited for centuries, with its streetlights that continue to stand watch in the mysterious brightness of that icy nocturnal blue. The noise of his footsteps in that seemingly eternal silence also seems impossible to him.

Oh, if by some miracle the life of the city had actually been extinguished! Sitting like a beggar on the curbstone at the corner of the street in front of the square, he would remain like those useless streetlights to gaze upon and suffer the bewildering stillness of all things already now and forever devoid of any meaning.

He finally rouses himself from this spell in order to cross the square.

His body is as light as a feather, and as he walks, there is no noise. Where had the burden that he felt oppressing him a little while ago gone? Now, all around, the city has what seems like the vaporous evanescence of a dream, and his body almost floats about within it, a shadow among shadows.

So then, it's an idea, that constant idea which he cannot at all identify. As soon as he becomes vaguely aware of its presence, he feels oppressed by that burden. As soon as it vanishes, there he is, as empty as a shadow.

But the burden must not be coming from that idea. It comes from the time he wastes in watching others live. He can no longer understand the reasons why they are living or, better put, he tries to understand what else they are looking for if this is life, all of it made up of things one knows, the usual and the necessary, the same every day. We are all under the illusion that, perhaps, once in a while, there can be new things only because events have taken a wider turn, with some unforeseen occurrences at first, an unexpected sensation, so as to seem that another world is opening up. But then either one gets used to them after a while or one suddenly fells again, disappointed, into the usual apathy. He feels such repugnance for the slackness of certain virtues of his—all of them a bit affected—that often, in thinking about them, he would prefer to be a wild animal. What about those women who ruin their feces by turning them into masks! If you should ask them what they're thinking about, you find that they're not thinking about anything. But all you have to do is ask them, for something to cross their minds that they cannot tell you. It's like waking up cats. And the emptiness of all their secret reasoning, always with a foolish smile ready on their lips to the slightest reminder of their dear friends who make fun of you because you're unable to tell them what's wrong with you or what you want. This is the burden. While, perhaps, the idea in itself is the lightest, the simplest and—who knows—perhaps the commonest thing.

He crosses the square. Before entering the narrow street, he stops again. To go lock himself up in his home in this mood frightens him even more than it sickens him. He goes to the right, down the long avenue that leads to the bridge and, from there, to the desolate suburbs beyond the river. Of course, he will turn around and come back as soon as he reaches the bridge. He will not go onto the bridge. Despite himself, he feels a chill at the very thought. The cold is biting. Even the pavement seems livid. As he walks he notices that every single time he passes under one of the electric lights strung high above, in the middle of the avenue, his body's shadow lengthens, growing strangely from each foot, and the more it lengthens, the more it fades until it disappears. His body's shadow, too, is like that idea.

He cannot deceive himself into believing that, the next morning, after he has been restored by a night of sleep, he will get rid of the memory of those moments of obsession, crying out so as not to give them any importance,

"Fatigue!"

He has cried out like that too many times. By now it seems like someone else's exclamation, a formula for certain comforts that it is useless to give yet one gives them. Besides, if it really is fatigue, being that it no longer lasts only moments and neither sleep nor anything else suffices to rid him of it, what relief and what comfort can there still be for him in naming the idea that way? And it's not even disgust over that life of his. No. The feets is that he really doesn't know precisely what that idea is or where it comes from, now so frequently, like a sudden pause that keeps him suspended and absorbed in a lifeless wait.

But what's this? Has he already entered?

His feet have entered the well-known doorway in that avenue by themselves. They've also climbed the first set of stairs that, occasionally, at other times, he has climbed with a vague hope in his heart and from which he has always climbed down, vowing never to climb it again.

A little room and then the writing desk, everything in the dark. Only the large white pages of a ledger opened on top of the desk are lit up. In that darkness one can vaguely discern a green glass lamp shade and on those lit up pages two small pink hands with as many dimples as there are fingers. From the darkness comes a voice without surprise, without reproach, almost blossoming from a slight happy smile.

"Oh, are you here again?"

One has to strain his eyes to see in that darkness, but he manages to see and goes directly to the voice and, as usual, has hands that are all too ready. As usual she takes them and, more than rejecting them, she makes the gesture of returning them to him. She doesn't want them like that. Not even if he still were her fiancé. Oh, he still is? What nerve! He hasn't shown up for the past four months. She hasn't asked for him but she will never ask for him. If he wants to come by, he'll always be welcome. Every evening he will always find her busily working at home after a frill day of work at the bank. She is always there with her ledgers, her numbers and her two pens, yes, two sorts of ink, red figures and black figures, rulers, pencils and her adding machine.

"Aunt!"

It is useless to wake her up, poor aunt. As usual, she is sleeping on the couch, pretending to be knitting. She stubbornly insists on waiting like that, with her glasses on her nose, waiting for her to finish so that they can go to bed at the same time. Her head lolls now on one shoulder, now on the other. Her hands have slipped onto her lap. Her eyeglasses too, in this moment or the next, will slip off her nose.

Those figures? Why ho, what can they mean to her? It's her work, to be done with the greatest care. Then they stay there for the bank. They don't interest her at all. And, having said that, she runs her hands over her shiny, smooth blond hair and smiles at him with bright blue eyes. Her mouth is so fresh and her forehead so serene! Doesn't she ever have any desires?

"No, why should I?"

That is, some momentary ones, whenever possible. She's happy like that.

What if he should marry her?

Why yes! Why not? She would be so very happy.

But he will never marry her. He asks her now only to find out what she will answer.

Well, this is how she answers him: It is sweet to imagine it even without believing it.

Besides, for a woman like herself, it's better not to get married. She wouldn't be able to imagine herself in a different sort of life. This elegant little house, even though it's on the sixth floor, is all nicely decorated with the right colors, and has drapes and carpets. She has the satisfaction of knowing that everything comes from her work: the peacefulness of her aunt, a few pastimes she can enjoy once in a while, the monthlong vacation at the beach or in the hills, some walks, the parties with this or that girl friend. Yes, she has a few. And she smiles. Why shouldn't she? And also some boy-friends, why not? Few women smile with such detached sweetness. She seems distant from everything, distant even from herself, as if not even her body belongs to her and she hasn't the least suspicion concerning the desires she can arouse or the pleasure she might give. In feet, her appeal is so nobly placid and pure that no carnal desire can arise in whoever gazes upon her. Is it possible that she doesn't think about anything? Not even about her future! Will she always live like this, with that reserve of hers, always with the air of withdrawing from everything? There are others. There is life, as long as one steps forward a bit. She doesn't want to. There are the cares of the day, of the things that must be done. Sometimes she reads a few books but she has so little time for reading! Travel books. To the North Pole? No. Why does he say to the North Pole? Another charming burst of laughter, fluid, sincere and bright. Does he really believe she's so cold? Yet, they say that Eskimo women are so warm!

"Me? I don't know. I suffer from the cold a lot in the winter. Put your hands down. Mine are cold, yes."

And this silence, always this silence.
"I sleep soundly. I seldom dream."

On the bridge that evening how bright the stars were!

He looks at the sky so as not to look down at the water in the river. Perhaps this is the very idea he cannot identify. But he doesn't have the courage. He rests his hands on the parapet. He feels as if even here they are being returned to him by the coldness of the stone, just like they were before by the warmth of those other hands. And he remains there, again lifelessly absorbed in thought in that singular way of his. Time has stopped, and among the things which have remained transfixed around him, it seems that there is a formidable secret in the fact that in so much immobility only the river water is moving.

A Challenge

Perhaps Jacob Shwarb wasn't thinking of anything bad. Perhaps only of blowing up the entire world with dynamite. Certainly it would have been terrible to blow up only one person. Blowing up the entire world with dynamite meant nothing at all. But just in case, he thought he'd better keep his forehead hidden under a large ruffled lock of reddish hair.

A large lock. Hands plunged into his trouser pockets. An unemployed worker.

He rebelled when he was admitted to the Israel Zion Hospital in Brooklyn for a serious liver ailment and was shorn. Without his hair, he felt his head had almost vanished. He searched for it with his hands. It no longer seemed his and he got angry.

He wanted to know if in committing this outrage against him they intended to consider him more as a convict serving a life sentence than as a patient.

For the sake of cleanliness?

He couldn't care less about cleanliness.

How about that!

Thank goodness that, though his hair was gone, he still had his thick drooping eyebrows which were constantly furrowed. They helped to nurse in his cloudy eyes, the rancor he felt toward everybody and toward life itself.

For the entire time he stayed in the hospital, Jacob Shwarb couldn't say exactly what color he was, whether he was more yellow or more green due to that liver ailment that gave him endless torments and put him in a mood that one can well imagine.

Terrible liver attacks.

In the summer, for two months, in a ward where day and night all the patients moaned, and if one of them no longer moaned, it was a sign that he was dead. Fidgets and groans. Blankets that were heaped now on one bed, now on another, or were tossed in the air in a gesture of exasperation that immediately brought nurses and night orderlies rushing over at breakneck speed.

Jacob Shwarb knew each of those night orderlies and felt a particular antipathy toward each one of them. Especially toward a certain Joe Kurtz, who sometimes even made him laugh because of the anger he stirred in him. Of course, it was the sort of laughter that dogs come out with when they want to bite.

In feet, this Joe Kurtz had his very own way of being spiteful. He never spoke unless actually forced to. He never did anything. He only smiled with an icy smile that, not satisfied with stretching his mouth with its thin white lips, would also appear in his dim gray eyes. He always kept his head bent over his shoulder, an ivory head without a hair on it, and his fat pale hands hanging over his long white coat as if they were dangling out of his chest.

Perhaps he didn't realize that this perpetual smile of his was utterly incompatible with the continuous moans of the poor patients, because truly one could not imagine that if he realized it, he could continue to smile like that, unless, unknown to the patients, all those moans were somehow comical and pleasant to his ears. They were composed of various tones with different intensities. Some were habitual, others were uttered for the sake of relief or comfort, and all, in brief, composed for him a curious and amusing symphony.

When you're forced to stay awake all night long, you do what you can to conquer sleep.

But then perhaps Joe Kurtz was smiling like that at his own worries. He might have also been in love, although at an advanced age. Perhaps he withdrew from all those moans into a blessed silence that belonged only to his wellborn soul.

Now, one night, when the ward was unusually calm and he alone, Jacob Shwarb, suffered to such an extent that he couldn't find relief a single moment in his bed—a bed which for the past two months had witnessed all his torments—this orderly, Joe Kurtz, happened to be on duty.

When all the lights are turned off except for the orderly's, which was shielded by a green shade on the small table against the wall at the far end, a great deal of moonshine enters from all the large windows of the ward and especially from the largest, which was open in the middle of the opposite wall.

Controlling his pains as much as he could, Jacob Shwarb observes, from his bed, Joe Kurtz seated at the little table, with his ivory face illuminated by a lamp. And, however much he hates humanity, he wonders how anyone can smile like that. He wonders how anyone who keeps watch in a hospital ward can remain so impassive when he sees a patient suffering as he is with that feverish torment increasing from moment to moment almost to the point of making him go crazy, crazy, crazy. All of a sudden, who knows why, the idea inexplicably occurs to him of seeing whether Joe Kurtz will remain like that if he, Jacob Shwarb, should now leave his bed and go throw himself out that large open window at the end of the ward.

It isn't quite clear to him yet whether this idea had suddenly come from his exasperating suffering, which by now is unbearable and appears cruelly unjust to him in that night of calm that reigns throughout the ward, or from the annoyance that Joe Kurtz is causing him.

Until the moment he leaves his bed, he doesn't quite know whether he really intends to go throw himself out the window or rather to test Joe Kurtz' indifference, to challenge his smiling placidity, for the desperate need to vent his frustration on him—on him who of course has the duty of rushing over to restrain him if he should see him leave his bed without first obtaining permission.

The fact is that, under the eyes of Joe Kurtz, Jacob Shwarb tosses his blankets in the air and springs to his feet as if he were actually challenging him. But Joe Kurtz not only doesn't move from the little table, he doesn't even discompose himself.

It is very hot in August. He might think that the patient wants to go and get a breath of air at the window.

Everybody knows that he, Joe Kurtz, is very generous and indulgent toward patients who break certain useless rules of the doctors.

Perhaps, upon close examination, one might discover in that smile that he would shut an eye, even if he imagined that the patient's intention is really that of throwing himself out the window.

If the poor patient suffers to such a degree that he can't bear it, does he, Joe Kurtz, have the right to stop him? He has, if anything, only the duty to do so because the patient is under his supervision. But since he can continue to suppose that the patient has left his bed only for a breath of fresh air, his conscience is at ease, you see. It can justify his lack of action and the patient can then do what he wishes. If he wants to take his life, let him go ahead and do so. It's his business.

Meanwhile Jacob Shwarb expects to be restrained before arriving at the large window at the end of the ward. He is just about to arrive there, when he turns, trembling with anger, to look at Joe Kurtz. He sees him still sitting impassibly at his little table and, all of a sudden, he feels as if he is disarmed. He can no longer move forward or go back.

Joe Kurtz continues to smile at him not to spite him but to make him realize that he fiilly understands that a patient can have many needs requiring him to leave his bed for a moment. All he has to do is ask him for permission, even with a slight gesture. Now, he can certainly interpret Shwarb's stopping to look at him, as a patient's request for his consent. He nods his head several times to tell him that it's all right and signals to him with his hand to go ahead, go ahead...

For Jacob Shwarb this is the height of derision, the most insolent response to his challenge. Roaring, he raises his fists, grits his teeth, runs to the large window and plunges down.

He doesn't die. He breaks both legs, an arm and two ribs. He also seriously injures his head. Taken in and treated, he not only recovers from all his injuries through one of those miracles that certain violent nervous traumas cause, he even recovers from his liver ailment. He should thank God that, though falling so precipitously out of the window like that, and despite all his injuries, he has escaped the death that perhaps was reserved for him if he had remained to wait for it amid the torments of the hospital. But, no sir, as soon as he recovers, he consults an attorney and sues the Israel Zion Hospital for twenty thousand dollars in damages due to the injuries he suffered in the fell. He has no other means by which to take vengeance on Joe Kurtz. The attorney assures him that the hospital will pay him and that Joe Kurtz will certainly be dismissed. In feet, if he happened to throw himself out of the window, the fault lies in the hospital's negligence and lack of supervision.

The judge asks him, "Did someone perhaps grab you and force you to throw yourself out the window? Your act was voluntary." Jacob Shwarb looks at his attorney, then answers,

"No, sir. I was certain that they would stop me."

"Who, the night orderly?"

"Yes, sir. It was his duty. Instead, he didn't move. I waited for him to move. I gave him all the time in the world, and so much so that before throwing myself down, I turned to look at him."

"And what did he do?"

"Him? Nothing. He smiled at me as always and signaled to me with his hand as if to say, 'Go ahead, go ahead.'"

In feet Joe Kurtz, even there in front of the judge, smiles. The judge becomes angry and asks him if what Jacob Shwarb says is true.

"'Yes, Your Honor," answers Joe Kurtz, "but that was because I thought he wanted to get a breath of air."

The judge pounds his fist on the table.

"Oh, is that what you thought?"

And he orders the Israel Zion Hospital to pay Jacob Shwarb twenty thousand dollars in damages.

CHRONOLOGY

according to the date of composition

1896	Sun and Shade	*(Sole e ombra)*
1900	Sunrise	*(La levata del sole)*
1900	The Black Shawl	*(Scialle nero)*
1901	This Makes Two!	*(Edue!)*
1904	Into the Sketch	*(Nel segno)*
1905	In Silence	*(In silenzio)*
1910	The Trip	*(Il viaggio)*
1910	The Stuffed Bird	*(L'uccello impagliato)*
1911	The Lonely Man	*(L'uomo solo)*
1912	The Trap	*(La trappola)*
1912	The Imbecile	*(L'imbecille)*
1912	The Fish Trap	*(Il coppo)*
1913	By Himself	*(Da se)*
1913	The Long Dress	*(La veste lunga)*
1913	Candelora	*(Candelora)*
1914	While the Heart Suffered	*(Mentre il cuore soffriva)*
1914	Aunt Michelina	*(Zia Michelina)*
1922	Nothing	*(Niente)*
1934	An Idea	*(Un'idea)*
1935	A Challenge	*(Una sfida)*

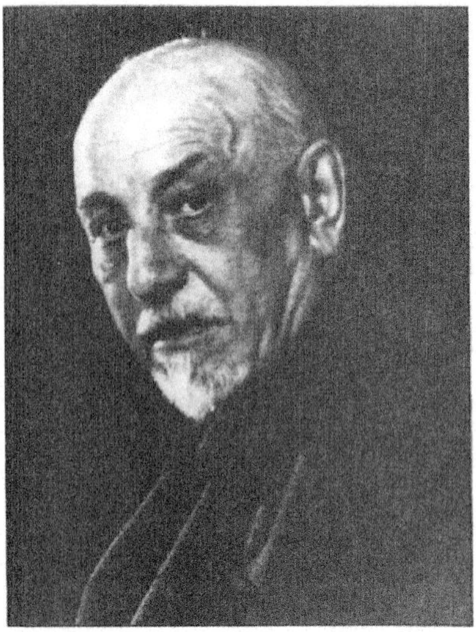

ABOUT THE AUTHOR AND THE TRANSLATOR

Luigi Pirandello, the son of a sulphur merchant, was born in 1867 near Agrigento, Sicily. After studying at the universities of Palermo and Rome, he then attended the University of Bonn, Germany, where in 1891 he was awarded a doctorate in Romance Philology.

Upon his return to Italy, Pirandello settled in Rome and married Antonietta Portulano, the daughter of his father's wealthy business partner, who soon bore him three children. This arranged marriage gave him great financial freedom, allowing him to develop his writing skills. During these years he also taught stylistics at a women's college in the Italian capital and obtained the chair of Italian language at this same institution, a position he was to keep until shortly after World War I.

On the advice of Luigi Capuana, the distinguished Sicilian novelist and short story writer, Pirandello, who had already published an early volume of poems, *Mai giocondo* (Joyful 111) [1889], and other poetical works, began to devote himself to prose writing, for which he soon demonstrated remarkable talent.

In 1903 a cave-in shut down the sulphur mine in which his wife's and his father's capital was invested. This disaster, which brought Pirandello to the brink of bankruptcy and suicide, and mentally unbalanced his wife, prompted the young author to redouble his literary efforts and to request payment for his works. In quick succession he wrote scores of short stories; he also wrote several novels, the most famous being *Il fu Mattia Pascal* (The Late Mattia Pascal) [1904], which deals, among other things, with a double "suicide" (the attempted annihilation of the protagonist's official "self" and the eventual destruction of his assumed identity). His most important essay of this period was *L'umorismo* (Humor) [1908], which contains his innovative poetics.

Many of the short stories, he wrote then and continued to write throughout his troubled life, were collectively entitled *Novelle per un anno* (Short Stories for a Year). He had hoped to publish 365 tales but managed to write only about 245, a number of which served as the basis for his plays.

Pirandello became an active playwright rather late in life. He was almost fifty when he enjoyed his first stage success with *Cosìt è (se vi pare)* (It is So [If You Think So]) [1917]. He gained international acclaim with *Sei personaggi in cerca d'autore* (Six Characters in Search of an Author) [1921]. Other memorable plays include *Enrico IV*(Henry IV) [1922], *Ciascuno a suo modo* (Each in His Own Way)

[1924] and *Trovarsi* (To Find Oneself) [1932]. His theater as a whole bears the title, *Maschere nude* (Naked Masks).

In 1925 he founded an art theater in Rome and with his company played the major capitals of Western Europe, later visiting Argentina, Brazil and the United States.

Pirandello also became involved in cinema. He published several articles about the "seventh art," wrote original film treatments and met with producers and directors, many of whom expressed a keen interest in filming his artistic creations. Significantly, the first Italian talking picture, *La Canzone dell'amore* (The Song of Love) [1930], by Gennaro Righelli, was based on one of Pirandello's short stories, *In silenzio* (In Silence) [1905].

In 1934 he traveled to Stockholm to receive the coveted Nobel Prize for literature and in 1936 he died, a sudden illness ending what he once called his "involuntary sojourn on Earth."

* * *

Giovanni R. Bussino, the translator of the present work, is a native Californian. He completed his undergraduate education at Loyola University of Los Angeles and, after studying at the Università degli Studi di Firenze (Italy), he served in the U.S. Army. He received an M.A. and a Ph.D. in Italian from the University of California at Berkeley and has taught at the University of Wisconsin (Madison), York University (Toronto) and San Diego State University. Besides a volume of translations, *Tales of Madness* (by Luigi Pirandello), his publications include a monograph, *Alle fonti di Pirandello,* and numerous articles and reviews which have appeared in scholarly journals such *as Forum Italicum, Filmkritik, Modern Philology, Italica,* the *Canadian Journal of Italian Studies, Italian Quarterly, The Yearbook of the British Pirandello Society* and *Rivista di Studi Pirandelliani.* Currently Bussino is a contributing editor of *PSA,* the official publication of the Pirandello society of America.

The enthusiastic reception of Bussino's earlier translations, *Tales of Madness* has prompted the publication of *Tales of Suicide,* an ideal sequel to that volume. This original collection of Pirandellian stories, which focuses on the intriguing theme of self-destruction, will undoubtedly cast new light on the author's elusive and multifaceted art.

Pirandello's suicidal characters live in a world of horse drawn carriages, kerosene lamps, dowries and wet nurses, but by and large their stories appear remarkably contemporary as numerous cases of self-inflicted death are reported daily in the media (some uncannily similar), and each year over twenty-six thousand people die by their own hand in the United States alone.

Printed in Great Britain
by Amazon